THE RAVENSTONE CHRONICLE

J. Harper Haines

Epicenter Press Inc.
Alaska Book Adventures™

Kenmore, WA

Published by Epicenter Press

Epicenter Press
6524 NE 181st St. Suite 2
Kenmore, WA 98028.
www.Epicenterpress.com
www.Coffeetownpress.com
www.Camelpress.com

For more information go to: www.Epicenterpress.com

This is a work of fiction. Names, characters, places, brands, media, and incidents are the product of the author's imagination or are used fictitiously.

The Ravenstone Chronicle
Copyright © 2022 by J. Harper Haines

Author photo by Lawrence Haines

ISBN: 9781684920228 (trade paper)
ISBN: 9781684920235 (ebook)

Printed in the United States of America

Ravenstone Comments

""Ravenstone" is not just an exciting whodunit mystery novel. It's a look into an Alaskan society that few outsiders ever get to see. The author's intimate knowledge of the culture and morays of the central Alaskan Athabascan natives allows her – no, compels her – to tell us a story that delights the senses and teaches us some lessons at the same time. The Ravenstone is more than just an inanimate object that has value to prospective buyers; it is an integral part of the culture of these peoples. A culture that we can peek at through the pen of this acclaimed author."

Gene Brown
Author of *Asano No Katana (Sword of Asano), Backstory: The Making of a Novel, The Impoverished Mind: Selected Short Stories, An Alaskan Childhood: Growing Up in Pre-Statehood Anchorage, Alaska, Alaska To Asia: Life as a Military Musician, Asia To Adulthood: Life With Nina – A Tribute*

The Ravenstone Chronicle is a page turner with intriguing plots of murder, deception, corruption and greed. The insight into the life, culture and customs of a small northern Athabascan Indian Village are compared with other cities and areas of Alaska, distinguishing between their unique cultural differences. The writing is moving and inspirational, with an added flair of romance.

Jane Harper, author of *Uuequally Divided*

Great book Jan. I enjoyed reading it. Perhaps the most important thing I can take away from *The Ravenstone Chronicle* is how the Native people are still connected to the beliefs of our ancestors. '
"Now we can work, he said, after creating a very smoky room from the burning sage. Then he started chanting and beating the drum."

Loretta Outwater Cox
Author of *The Winter Walk*

Sink into this enthralling mystery surrounding an ancient and powerful Athabascan relic. When Cara Fielding and aunt Lucy Montalk discover the disfigured body of their murdered relative, they are compelled to join the search for the missing amulet. They understand how reticent Native people are around the police. Meanwhile, the brutal Alaskan weather kills as readily as the thieves who desire the priceless Ravenstone, rumored to be dangerous in malicious hands. But dangerous to whom? And what powers does the artifact possess? Captivating characters and a landscape that simultaneously entices and menaces lure the reader into a page-turning novel of suspense.

Deborah Turrell Atkinson, author of *the Storm Kayama suspense series* and *Feathers in the Soul: A Guide for Families Struggling with a Child's Addiction*

To Larry Haines for his patient understanding.

Acknowledgements

My thanks to Lael Morgan, Gene Brown,
Joe Pendergrass and Andrea Simpson.

Prologue

Goldspring Alaska, 1917

Sam was seven years old when his Athabascan uncle, Redshirt, first showed him the Ravenstone. A feather design had been carved on both sides of a flat piece of black whale Bayleen. It was about four inches long. The dark red eyes looked like garnets and Sam thought they were from Wrangell near Juneau where a lot of garnets were found on the beach.

"The Ravenstone is powerful, more powerful than President Wilson." Redshirt said, his worn teeth marring his otherwise handsome face. Redshirt was Sam's great uncle. He was also Goldspring's *deeyninh,* a shaman.

Everyone in the village of Goldspring knew about President Wilson since the United States had joined fighting in the World War that year.

"The Ravenstone summons the spirits," Redshirt added, his old man's voice was gravelly and low and Sam leaned toward him. "If this person wants to be healed, it will happen."

They were sitting on a log in front of Redshirt's cabin. In the distance, the sunset glowed purple and gold. It was accompanied by distant haunting calls from migrating geese.

"I can help him," Redshirt said, his voice lower. "But I can't change what is decreed. Today you watch. One day the Ravenstone will help you call the spirits."

Redshirt sighed and they got to their feet and walked through the snow-covered leaves to the cabin. The Deeyninh was still limping from a fall suffered while fishing in the Yukon river. At over eighty years of age, his vision was fading and that led to all sorts of accidents.

With Sam guiding him, Redshirt stepped inside the cabin where it was slightly warmer thanks to wood burning in the fire pit. Redshirt's daughter was browning moose meat over the fire's spit. Sam's nose twitched at the aroma of the meat as he watched the smoke unfurl.

Redshirt pulled a stool closer to the fire. As he sat, he watched Sam and sympathized with the boy at having to learn so much in the short time they had together. For Redshirt sensed the shortage of time, but for the boy tomorrow was forever distant.

After they had eaten, Redshirt lay down on the nearby cot covered with assorted fur skins and snoozed. Sam, however, felt oddly alert. Usually after eating a heavy meal as they'd just had, he would be drowsy. But not now. Now he was wide awake and thinking.

He knew Redshirt would summon the spirits of animals and birds whose power fit the need. Sometimes, it was an eagle, sometimes a coyote. Today, the man seeking the Deeyninh's help had lost his livelihood and his wife. Sam wondered which of these creatures the Deeyninh would summon.

After Redshirt woke up and had some tea, he took a deep breath and with the Ravenstone in his right hand, raised his elbows. With his hands in front of his throat, he began to chant in old Koyukon, his Athabascan dialect. After a moment, Sam felt a subtle shift in the air.

The cabin slowly filled with smoke and he saw Redshirt's daughter open the door then lift a corner of a moose hide that covered the window. It was a hole in the wall but had no glass. Fresh, cold air flowed in and the smoke began to thin. Redshirt took a deep breath and began to chant.

His chanting was hypnotic and Sam grew drowsy. After several minutes, he thought he saw a wolf in the haze. It was large and gray, and had a feral gaze. The image faded and a battle-scarred grizzly sow with a cub appeared in the mist. After what seemed a long while, she and her cub ambled away.

With Sam's eyes still closed, a wolverine appeared. It stood in front of an open door. The boy knew the wolverine was one of the most vicious animals in the forest. This one, however, was peaceful and appeared to be chewing something green.

Overhead, he was startled by a raven's raucous caw and opened his eyes in time to look through the window and see it swoop across the sky. As his vision cleared, he saw Redshirt sitting cross-legged in front of him, beating a flat drum.

That night when Sam told Redshirt what he had seen, his great uncle nodded. "The wolf and the bear kill to eat and protect themselves and their mates. They can help this man destroy what is harming him. It could be his own fear or another person." Redshirt paused and took a breath. "The wolverine is clever and a powerful fighter. You saw the wolverine chewing something green?" Sam nodded.

"Green restores power and health," Redshirt said. "It also brings children. This man will find a livelihood and a new wife. He will regain his vitality and have a family."

"The raven flying over these spirits means the wolf, the bear, and the wolverine will aid this man." He broke off and stared into the distance.

After a long silence, Sam said, "How does the raven know which spirits to bring?"

Redshirt smiled. "The raven calls those who can help this man who was near death, with no wife or job or children."

Sam was still puzzled. He plowed on. "And when the raven flies overhead, and you see him, does that mean it is done?" Redshirt nodded and relaxed. Sam was catching on.

"Remember, the raven is the beginning and the end of everything."

Chapter 1

Fairbanks

1998 Four Days before Thanksgiving

Cara's grip tightened on the phone. "No, it's not a problem, it sounds like everyone's having plumbing problems." Frustrated, she stared at her stopped-up kitchen faucet then resolutely looked through the window at the never-ending falling snow. Now she'd have to figure out where to go, a hotel? And what about Mister, her cat? She hoped her neighbor was home to look after him for a day or two. Crap.

"Okay, I'll call you as soon as I've checked my schedule. Guess it's to be expected. Everyone's pipes are freezing in this weather."

Cara Fielding was in her fourth year at the University of Alaska Fairbanks where she taught journalism. Moving to Fairbanks allowed her to be closer to her Athabascan aunt, Lucy Montalk who lived just north of Fairbanks in the village of Goldspring.

An hour later, Cara stepped into the clinic for an appointment with her cardiologist. As she shook the snow from her coat she caught a whiff of air freshener and something vaguely medicinal. The walls of the waiting room were painted a soothing light blue. A half dozen upholstered chairs were arranged near low tables strewn with magazines

None of the others in the waiting room appeared younger than fifty.

A middle-aged man, using a cane was called and was replaced by a family of four. Resigning herself to wait, Cara picked up a three-month-old issue of TIME Magazine. She remembered her father saving the magazine covers and copying them when he painted portraits. When he ran out of canvases, he used scraps of lumber and plywood and Masonite, one of which wound up at the bottom of their silverware drawer in Anchorage. Whenever she opened that drawer, the Shaw of Iran's fierce dark eyes beneath dark brows glared up at her.

Twenty minutes later, Cara was seated in a small room with her knees touching the exam table. Doctor Adams frowned at Cara's test results on the computer screen.

She took a breath and was about to say something when he sent a prescription on the computer to the pharmacy. "I want you to try something new."

"What is it?" She smiled, determined to be polite.

"It's a statin and may not have the same severity of side effects."

He clicked the computer keys, then pushed back his chair and got to his feet. Cara felt her stubborn streak crawl out. The heck with this guinea pig stuff.

"I don't think so," She said as she got to her feet. His hand on the doorknob, Doctor Adams hesitated. He looked tired. He had tried her on so many statin drugs she had lost count.

He smiled faintly. "I guess when you gotta go, you gotta go." She almost laughed.

By three o'clock that afternoon and finished with her Introduction to Journalism class, Cara was leaving the Bunnell Building when Dora, the Department Chair's secretary, flagged her down. "Cara, you have a minute? Dr. Wick would like to see you."

Dora wore a cheerful pumpkin-colored twinset. If Cara weren't so bummed out about her frozen pipes and her cardiologist's diagnosis, she would have complimented Dora.

Dr. Wick was a white-haired woman whose unsmiling blue eyes concealed a sympathetic nature. She waved Cara to a chair and peered at her over half glasses. "Not good news, I'm afraid, Cara." She adjusted her navy blazer and sat back in her chair.

"You know enrollment is down and the university is having to cut expenses." Cara knew this. There had been a faculty meeting last week.

"We've had to cut a number of classes." Professor Wick turned to her computer screen, her chair creaking. "This affects one of yours. Umm, here it is, 'Techniques for Interviewing Alaska Native Elders.'" Cara's heart sank. She had fought for two years to get it on the curriculum. As a Native and a journalist, she knew how important this topic was to serious journalism students.

"But you'll still have 'Writing for the Media' and 'Beginning Journalism.'"

As an adjunct, Cara had a contract with the university for each class she taught. This semester she had three classes. When next semester began in January, she would have two, at least until the end of the semester. After that, who knew? But now it meant a third of her teaching income would evaporate next semester.

After leaving Dr. Wick's office, Cara made her slippery way down the ice-covered steps to the parking lot when she thought of Northern Lights Insurance. In the past she had worked part-time for NLI as an insurance claims investigator. Last spring, in a flurry of cost cutting, NLI had dismissed several part-time and full-time employees. Recently, however, she had heard claims were up and they were hiring temporary help. She had a hunch NLI was rehiring at minimum wages and without benefits. She sighed. As much as it aggravated her, she'd check it out. She had bills to pay.

As she drove home, she couldn't believe the way the day had gone: First her cardiologist *when you gotta go, you gotta go.* And now her shrinking job. She looked ahead at the road, slick with black ice. Think positive she told herself, gripping the steering wheel. *Be thankful!*

Thank heavens she had already had her Toyota serviced and bought new snow tires.

Driving slowly and watching for out-of-control vehicles, Cara switched her thoughts to next week and Thanksgiving. Well hallelujah, there was some good news. In a few days, she would be in Goldspring with Lucy, her favorite aunt. If she ever needed to get away and spend some peaceful time with her favorite relative it was now.

As she pulled in and parked by her back door, it occurred to her that she had no more classes until after Thanksgiving. Today was Tuesday. She could head to Goldspring today. She wouldn't have to worry about getting a hotel room. All she had to do was board Mister with her neighbor, Marilyn who, as far as Cara knew, wasn't going anywhere over the holiday.

Chapter 2

Goldspring
Thanksgiving

When Herb stepped out of Fleming's Market, the snow was falling in thick heavy flakes, deepening the winter's silence. He loaded his Subaru with groceries and drove slowly out of the parking lot toward the Post Office to pick up his mail. Then he headed for home on a road that was slick with ice.

Loaded down with groceries and mail, mostly colorful Christmas catalogues and store flyers, he stomped the snow from his boots on the front step and opened his door to an unfamiliar sound; a ringing. It was the telephone he just had installed last week. He set the groceries on the table and reached for the receiver, surprised to hear his uncle, Sam.

"I want you and Julie to come here for Thanksgiving tomorrow." Sam's voice was harsh and raspy. "We eat around three o'clock." There was a pause. "It's important."

Herb was surprised, although not by his uncle's abrupt manner. That was normal. His surprise was because he and his daughter, Julie, usually spent Christmas with Sam and his family, at Christmas, not Thanksgiving.

"Sure," Herb said. "We can come over tomorrow." Herb was a school custodian and had been looking forward to a few days off to secure his storm windows that were rattling in the November winds. His uncle, however, was ninety-eight years old, an elder and a *deeyninh*. And he was dying.

"Why did Sam want us to come for Thanksgiving?" The Subaru suddenly lurched across the icy ruts and Julie grabbed the safety handle above the passenger door.

"Are we still going there for Christmas?" she said, catching her breath.

"I'm not sure why he wants us to come now, but Sam said it was important." He looked over at her and shrugged. "We'll find out when we get there."

His daughter wore a red ski parka and a matching wool cap with a white rabbit fur pompom. The colors were cheerful and Herb in his heavy army surplus jacket, felt better just looking at her.

Herb had quit smoking over a year ago year, but the sour odor of cigarettes clung to the vehicle's interior. He rolled his window down an inch. A green paper air freshener in the shape of a spruce tree, overwhelmed by its task, swung defiantly from the rear view mirror. Herb was tempted to yank it down, but his daughter had put it there, so he left it.

A loud grinding from the Subaru's anti-lock brakes distracted him and the brake pedal trembled under his foot as they began their descent into the valley below Sam's house. Julie sighed and looked through the window at the snow-covered hills and dark spindly trees. In the gray overcast, two moose munched bark from a tree. A young bull stretched to reach the upper branches.

The road was slick and Herb was forced to crawl along in second gear. Finally, with a sigh of relief, he pulled up in front of Sam's house. Sam shared the small yellow house, clad in shiplap siding, with his widowed daughter and her two children. As Herb shifted into park and pulled the hand brake, he noticed the paint was peeling. Next summer he'd have to get back here and strip it to give it another coat.

The temperature outside had risen to fifteen above and the air was balmy. Herb focused on the back of his daughter's head as he trudged up the steps. She was as tall as he was, he noticed, not sure he liked seeing her grow up so fast.

Julie reached the top step and, grinning, suddenly stamped

her feet, breaking the icy surface. Herb smiled, remembering his daughter in elementary school when she loved to hear the ice crack.

The front door was almost frozen shut and made a loud creek as Sam yanked it open. "What took you so long?" he said peevishly. He was leaning on a cane and Herb thought he looked more bent than he had a few weeks ago. Not expecting an answer, Sam ushered them inside. Herb's nose twitched as the aromas of moose roast, vegetables, and pumpkin pie wafted from the kitchen. His stomach growled.

The furnace was blasting heat and Herb and Julie began shedding scarves, hats, gloves, and parkas, piling them on a wood bench by the door. The table between the kitchen and living room had been lengthened with planks and was now covered with a faded red checked tablecloth. Herb had helped deliver the table a few years ago from a thrift store where Connie had bought it for $25. One leg was shorter than the others and he saw a Leon Uris paperback wedged beneath it. He looked closer. *Exodus*. Seemed to work he thought.

The kitchen was to the left and Julie went in to help Connie. Through the open kitchen door Herb caught sight of a young Native man in a blue Sweater. He wore tortoise shell glasses and was leaning against the sink, talking to Connie's two children.

"That's Connie's friend, Phil," Sam said, making his way to the sofa, his left hand gripping his cane. "He's a graduate student at the university and asks a lot of questions." Sam chuckled. "Well, that's what they teach in school, to ask questions, right?"

Sam's wool plaid shirt was thin from years of washings, and his silver hair was tied back behind his ears with a length of yarn.

Herb couldn't remember seeing his uncle's neck before. It looked thin and vulnerable.

Two unmatched chairs faced a battered green Army footlocker.

Beyond it a sofa, with a crocheted afghan across the back, sagged at one end. On the right, a television set was perched on a bookcase that also held a few Koyukon Athabascan carvings, Koyukon being one of the tribes within the vast Athabascan culture.

Herb settled into one of the chairs and shifted his weight when he felt a loose spring poke his thigh. Sam hooked his cane over the sofa's armrest and pulled a tissue from his pocket, then spat into it.

"The reason I wanted you to come..." He paused and with effort he unbent his arthritic fingers and held out his palm. Herb's glasses were still fogged up from coming inside from the cold, but he saw something dark and flat in Sam's hand. It was about five inches long, maybe three inches across and less than an inch thick. Sam's wrinkled fingers rolled it over.

Squinting, Herb now saw a flat piece of black whale Bayleen with a design that resembled feathers carved on one side. A tuft of black and silver fur poked through a hole in what Herb recognized as a raven's beak. Deep red garnets marked the eyes.

In spite of himself, Herb felt a frisson of fear. This was old. It was shamanic. Nervously, he shifted in his wobbly chair.

"This is from sometime in the 1800's, could be earlier," Sam said, his voice raspy. "It was part of a large mask that's now in UAF's museum." He cleared his throat. "The mask is worth about a half a million dollars. And that's without this." He held the Ravenstone closer for Herb to see. Herb was stunned. What was his uncle doing with something so valuable?

"Why isn't it with the mask?"

Sam paused. "A long time ago, Big William...a powerful *deeyninh* in Nenana." He peered at Herb. "You heard of him?" Herb nodded. He had been raised Episcopalian, but thanks to Aunt Lucy who was always talking about Indian history, he had heard of the famous Athabascan *deeyninh*. From the corner of his eye, he saw Connie's friend Phil pull a few mismatched chairs to the table.

Sam waved the artifact at Herb, catching his attention. "The mask was designed so this Ravenstone, its centerpiece, could be removed and used in ceremonies." He caught Herb's puzzled look and added, "like for spirit travel and soul cleansing." He coughed.

"There's a design carved in the mask, behind where the Ravenstone fits, so when it's not with the mask, it doesn't look like anything's missing. Only those who know about the Ravenstone would know it belongs there. And there are damned few still alive who know about it." Sam smiled, humorlessly. Herb wondered why his uncle was telling him this? Herb was no *deeyninh*.

"Back around 1910," Sam continued, "Big William still had the mask and took out the Ravenstone to use in a ceremony. While he had it, the mask was stolen. About fifteen years ago, one of our tribal members saw the mask in a museum in New York." Sam peered at Herb with milky eyes. "You know about repatriation?" Herb nodded.

"Yes. With artifacts," Herb said, floundering. "It means they should be returned to where they were created, their place of origin."

"Something like that," Sam said. "It took time to prove it was Koyukon Athabascan and not Navajo or Apache or from Canada, from one of those other Athabascan tribes."

Sam stopped and took a deep breath. Herb sensed his uncle's exhaustion. "Anyway," Sam began again, "after it was returned, historians and anthropologists at the University in Fairbanks convinced the tribal council the mask would be best preserved and displayed in their museum. So that's where the mask went."

Sam was disgruntled. For years he'd thought the mask should be kept in Goldspring, but there was no secured museum in town. Or secure anything for that matter. "So this," he waved the Ravenstone, "was passed down to medicine healers. No one else knew about it." He looked at the artifact, his fingers gently stroking it. Watching him, Herb decided the next time he was in Fairbanks he'd visit the museum.

"So I guess, you want it to go to the museum?" Herb chose his words carefully, avoiding the thought of his uncle's inevitable death.

The old *deeyninh* snorted. "Well, those museum people certainly *want* it. But it shouldn't be locked in a glass case." He leaned forward.

"It should be passed on! It belongs with the *dena,* the people!" Herb was startled by Sam's vehemence.

After a moment, Sam sank back on the sofa and lifted his feet, one at a time and rested them on the battered footlocker. In the gray light the lines on his face deepened.

"But now," he continued, "because of its commercial value, art collectors and sellers are suddenly interested. The problem is that there's no one I can pass it on to. Young people are leaving the villages and moving to cities like Fairbanks and Anchorage for education and trade schools and jobs. One man with much promise left Goldspring and is now a baker in Anchorage." Sam took a sip of his tea, which had grown cold.

He grimaced and put it back on the footlocker where it wobbled unsteadily.

"Even Ron wants to build a training center in Goldspring." Ron was Goldspring's Village Public Safety Officer, or VPSO. "The trouble is, there are others...wannabes, people taking drugs, drinking. If this," he waved the amulet again. "If it falls into the wrong hands...it could be turned, it could be *negat deelt aa.*" He saw Herb's blank face.

"Dangerous, ominous," Sam added, Sam wished Herb knew more of his Koyukon language. After a long moment, Herb said "You mean its power could be turned and made treacherous?"

Sam paused as he thought about how to explain it. "Ceremonial objects respond to the healer. Think of a strong sled dog who can run like the wind and lead a team, but on an unfamiliar trail it needs the musher to tell him where to go."

Sam coughed and stopped to catch his breath. "The Ravenstone is like that. If it fell in the wrong hands..." Sam was getting tired and Herb could feel his uncle's exhaustion.

"But no one knows you have it, right?"

Sam glared around the room. "It's that damned article in the newspaper and the research guy at the university."

"Article?" Herb questioned. How did Herb's taciturn uncle get in the newspaper? Maybe food would help. His brain wasn't operating on all cylinders. Looking at the appetizer tray Connie had earlier set near him, he broke off a piece of pilot bread and dipped it in the bowl of salmon pate.

"Phil..." Sam waved his cane toward the kitchen from which

the rich aromas of a moose roast and yams drifted. "Connie's friend is Tlingit," Sam continued. "He already knew about the mask and the Ravenstone, so I told him a little more." Sam looked apologetically at Herb. "Phil's around here a lot and I got used to him," he added, apologetically. "Then he talked to this professor and got him all interested and this Doctor Skarfeld came out here."

"A doctor came here, to Goldspring?" Herb was astonished.

He had not gone beyond the eighth grade, and stood in awe of professors and doctors. And to think that an old rock, *okay, an ancient Athabascan artifact*, would draw such prestigious attention staggered his mind.

"Yes!" Sam gave Herb an impatient look. "He came and talked about its historical value to Athabascan heritage and culture. On and on. This guy is part Haida. Those Southeastern Indians love to talk and one thing led to another. Anyway, ignorant asshole that I am, I let him take it to study."

Sam snorted and reached for another tissue and dabbed at his mouth. "I still don't know why! The medicine makes me forgetful and I must have been drinking.

Anyway, the *Fairbanks Goldstar* wrote about traditional healing and Native art in the Sunday paper. It had photographs. Me and the Ravenstone. I look ancient and the Ravenstone looks like an ink blot."

Sam smiled with satisfaction. "But pretty soon everyone knew I had this *valuable artifact*. We even had two break-ins. Here, in this house!" Sam thumped the floor with his cane. At that moment, Connie appeared carrying fresh tea.

In her early thirties, Connie was short and plump with a pretty face. Her shoulder-length black hair was growing out of a kinky perm, which Herb was glad to see go—the fried hair look he called it.

A burst of laughter drifted from the kitchen – his daughter, Julie with Connie's two children and her friend. Sounded like Julie was over being mad at having her Thanksgiving disrupted. Herb was relieved. He picked up his chipped mug and sipped the cranberry-flavored tea.

Connie returned to the kitchen and Sam began unfolding a small butter colored chamois bag. With a reverence that reminded Herb of the priest with a crucifix at Herb's church, Sam slipped the Ravenstone inside the bag. He leaned forward and held it toward Herb. "I want you take it." A bit of pilot bread caught in Herb's throat and his eyes watered. "Take it!" Sam insisted. "Find a place to hide it." He peered at his nephew's reddened face.

"I'm not a *deeyninh*!" Herb said, coughing. He had lived in Goldspring all his life, but he was not a believer in medicine power. Like other villagers, he wore a medicine bundle. He also attended the local Episcopal Church and stood in line for flu shots. He made dental appointments and had his eyes checked. It was the Native way to do what was practical. When some white guy wearing glasses could spot the moose you couldn't even see, well, you damn well got glasses. Survival depended on it.

He took a breath. "How did you get it back from this Doctor Scarface whatshisname? That couldn't have been easy."

Sam sighed. "Nope, I had to do some fast talking and you're right, you aren't a *deeyninh*." He gave his nephew a speculative look. "But you can sense things. You can recognize when someone has the gift. I want you to look after it." Herb tried to think of a response.

"Have you thought about a safe deposit box?" That sounded lame, but when he looked at his uncle again, Sam was leaning back on the sofa, his eyes closed.

Herb slowly unfolded the pouch, wondering what he had gotten into. A trifle irritated, he looked at Sam again. The old *deeyninh* was snoring. His expression was relaxed, even relieved, as if he'd just handed off a worry, the old bugger.

For a fleeting moment Herb was tempted to leave the Ravenstone here, hide it in this house with its yellow light from the forty-watt light bulbs, or maybe stash it in the cache out back.

But no and his shoulders sank. He knew Sam would know. More to the point, Herb knew he couldn't live with himself if he didn't honor the old fart's wishes. He scratched his chin. So where could he hide it? He glanced at his jacket and his boots and muskrat hat by the front door. Nothing came to mind. Oh hell, what was he fussing over? All he had to do was get it home. There were plenty of hiding places there.

The Subaru bounced over the icy ruts in the road and Julie grabbed the safety handle above the door. Daylight had faded and in the deepening gloom she glimpsed a family of moose munch from a cluster of cottonwood trees. Herb had just finished telling her about Sam's request.

"So where will you hide it?" she said when she could talk without having her teeth snap shut on her tongue. Herb shifted into second gear as they turned toward home.

"You know that big birch in back? The one with the big hole?"

"Where the limb broke off last winter? That one?"

Herb nodded. "That might work." He slowed to turn off the road into their drive.

"What the heck?" He stomped on the brakes and the Subaru skewed sideways. A yellow light shone in their kitchen window and an unfamiliar snowmobile was parked by the front door. "Were you expecting anyone?"

"No." Julie hesitated, staring at the snowmobile. "Unless it's Geof." Geof was a family friend who worked on the pipeline on the North Slope. "Maybe he came home for Thanksgiving."

"Since when does he have a red snowmobile?"

She shrugged. "If he does, it's new."

Herb flicked off his headlights and stared at the house. He thought he recognized the red Kawasaki. It looked like the Gordon's, but hadn't they gone to Hawaii for the holidays? He lowered the earflaps of his hat and climbed out. "I'm going to check this out. Wait here." Julie blinked in surprise.

"I'm cold and I need to pee," she said, pushing open her door.

Herb looked grim. "You wait here, I won't be long."

He pulled on his gloves and gently shut the door. Keeping to the dark shadows of the spruce, he began wading through the deep snow toward the back of his house. No one inside was looking out the bathroom window. Herb stretched to his full height and took a quick look inside.

The door leading to the kitchen was open. Through it, he saw two strange men. They looked to be in their twenties. The kitchen, what he could see of it, was a mess with food spilled on the floor and tipped over chairs. His heart hammering, Herb slid from the house and tried to think. There was so much snow they'd see his tracks so there was no use heading for that birch in back.

Taking off his hat, he turned it inside out and studied it. Finding a loose thread, he pulled at it with his teeth. Then he pulled the Ravenstone from his pocket and slipped it between the lining and fur, working it toward the back of the hat with his fingers. Finally, with a deep breath, he walked around the house to the front door.

Chapter 3

Goldspring

The Day After Thanksgiving

Lucy peered inside the refrigerator and took out a platter of turkey. She glanced at her niece who was pouring a cup of coffee. "Julie and Herb weren't home yesterday so I don't imagine they cooked. Why don't we take over some turkey and ..." Lucy stuck her head back in the refrigerator, "Some of this stuffing and definitely pie." Earlier, Cara had eyed the turkey and pie, thinking *breakfast!*

Since she had arrived at Aunt Lucy's Cara had done nothing but eat and sleep. That and visit with her seventy-two-year-old aunt who, despite her dicey heart and the silver threading her hair, looked not a day over fifty.

Julie and Herb lived half a mile from Lucy and were distant relatives as well as Lucy's nearest neighbors. When Cara was younger, visiting relatives had bored her, but after the last few tumultuous days, the simple, familiar errand felt soothing and welcome. Getting outdoors and into all that fresh air sounded wonderful.

"Where did Herb and Julie go yesterday?" Cara said, pulling on her boots. She took a final sip of her coffee and set the empty cup in the sink.

"Herb said they were spending Thanksgiving with his uncle, Sam." Lucy buttoned her coat and pulled on her lynx hat. The fur shimmered in the kitchen's light. Seeing Cara's blank look, Lucy clarified, "Sam Tallwell."

Cara recognized the Tallwell name as belonging to distant relatives, of which she had many. "The medicine man, isn't he a *deeyninh*?"

Lucy's smile faded. "Yes, he's well known in these parts. It's a shame really." Her voice trailed off.

"What's a shame?"

"He's in the last stage of cancer."

Not knowing what to say, Cara was silent. As for the Ashenbergs, she knew them well. Herb's wife left Goldspring for the nightlife in Fairbanks about seven years ago, leaving Herb to raise their daughter, Julie. Cara had steered Julie, now seventeen, to college prep courses in high school and helped her apply for admission to the University of Alaska in Fairbanks.

When Cara and Lucy left the house, they carried half of a pumpkin pie, half of a mincemeat pie, a large baggie of turkey, and a container of oyster stuffing. "You sure this is enough?" Cara said, drily. "You didn't leave something in the refrigerator?" Her aunt was a generous cook and loved feeding people. She eyed her niece and grinned.

"Don't worry, there'll be plenty left for you to take back."

The thermometer had reached a balmy 29 degrees and, as they walked, a patch of blue sky appeared through a gap in the clouds. "If this weather keeps up, pussy willows will start blooming," Lucy said, taking a deep breath. Their boots crunched through the ankle-deep snow, breaking the winter silence.

Invigorated after an uninterrupted nine hours sleep, Cara felt her shoulders relax. The stress of the past few days seemed a distant memory.

Overhead, a flock of cawing ravens appeared, like black triangles against the pale sky. A magpie flew low, a flash of black, white, and vivid blue against the white winter landscape.

Cara wondered what she and Lucy looked like from the air: two women, heads bobbing as they walked; and Goldspring, a small town, population six hundred, one grocery store, a bank, a clinic, a gas station, a café, a drugstore with a lunch counter, and a tiny public library. And, of course, scattered houses and cabins: each on an acre to several acres of land.

Up ahead, she saw the Ashenberg's house and was about to say something when Lucy suddenly stopped.

Alarmed, Cara looked back at her. "What?"

"Over there!" Lucy pointed to the driveway. "What's that?"

Cara adjusted her glasses, which had fogged up and peered myopically into the near whiteout. At first, she saw nothing. Then, several yards ahead, near the bushes she saw a long, dark lumpy shape in the snow. "Stay here," Cara said, moving closer. She saw what looked like shoulders and a head. They were white with frost. Behind her, she heard Lucy's boots crunch in the snow.

Herb's arms were spread and blood spattered the snow. His hat was gone and his black hair had fallen over his face. Trembling, Cara bent down and lifted his hair. Herb's sightless eyes stared at nothing.

Oh God, she thought as she fell to her knees.

His body lay lopsided against a snow berm. Hesitating, she reached over and lifted the edge of his long jacket. White cotton threads torn from his long underwear clung to the raw stump of his thigh.

Cara felt her bile rise. Her nails dug through her gloves into her palms and she took a deep breath. "It's Herb." Her voice cracked.

The wrapped food slid from Lucy's hands into the snow. "We've got to call Ron," she whispered. Ron Whitfield was Goldspring's VPSO. "Where's Julie?"

Cara looked toward Herb's Subaru. It appeared empty, the passenger door still open. Then she looked at his house. "Julie!" she yelled. "JULIE" Her call shattered the quiet and sent half a dozen ravens skyward, cawing in the gray light

With trepidation, Cara got to her feet and headed toward the front door. "Be careful." Lucy called behind her.

The door scraped the floor when Cara shoved it open. Her heart hammering, she called, "Julie!"

Inside, unpainted sheetrock covered most of the studs and insulation. She knew from past visits that Herb and Julie kept the one-bedroom home tidy. In a small house, Herb said, you had to put stuff away or there'd be no room for people.

Now, her boots crackled over broken glass and dishes. Kitchen cabinets doors were open and food was dumped on the floor. A broken chair lay on its side, a large peanut butter jar rolled next to it, the lid gone. Braided rag rugs, once carefully arranged over the unpainted plywood floor had been kicked into rumpled heaps. She looked around and saw the telephone hanging, torn from the wall.

A metallic smell of blood hung like an invisible mist in the cold, dank air. Beneath it, Cara detected the odor of cigarettes and what was it? Dope? Ahead of her hung a faded lilac colored sheet. It partitioned Julie's sleeping space from the rest of the house. The teenager had stenciled flowers on it in an impressionistic style. Choking back the bile in her throat, Cara stepped through the broken debris. Trembling, she pulled back the sheet.

Julie lay on her side, her legs pulled up. Her cotton shirt was torn open, revealing a plain cotton bra with one breast exposed. Biting her lip, Cara drew closer. Pulling off her gloves, she rested fingers against the teenager's throat. There was a faint pulse.

"Julie, can you hear me?" She reached for a blanket that had been tossed on the floor and tucked it around the girl. "Julie?"

"Is she here?" Lucy was standing outside on the lower step.

"Yes, she's unconscious, but she's breathing," Not for the first time did Cara miss her cellphone, lost somewhere in the University's parking lot.

Lucy grabbed the stair rail and pulled herself up the icy steps. "Call Ron," she said, her voice cracking.

Cara pulled at the cord that dangled from the wall. "The phone's been ripped out and mine hasn't been replaced yet. We'll have to call from your house."

"I see that," Lucy said, irritably. "Go home and call him. NOW! I'll stay with her." Lucy leaned over Julie, covering the girl with a comforter she picked up from the floor.

Oh lord, Cara thought. What if Lucy had a heart attack? What if the killers were still around? "I don't want to leave you."

"Cara, I'm a tough old bird, and I'm not leaving Julie and Herb." Lucy's fur hat was askew and her deep red coat was covered with snow.

"You'll be faster without me. Now GO!"

Shit, shit Cara thought as she took off at a half trot, planting her feet as best she could on the slippery road. This was no time to fall on her ass.

Chapter 4

Goldspring

Village Public Safety Officer

Ron's hand tightened on the phone. "You're kidding!" No one had been killed in Goldspring since the 1890's Gold Rush.

"Listen to me!" Cara was practically babbling. "We found Herb Ashenberg's body. His leg is gone…"

"Gone?"

"Yeah, cut off!" Catching her breath, Cara leaned against the counter and knocked a dish to the floor. "Julie is in the house. She's unconscious and she's been hurt! Herb's phone is ripped out and I've lost mine. I ran back to Lucy's to call you. I need you to GET OVER HERE! NOW!" Outside, the dark boughs of the spruce drooped under the heavy snow and Cara shut her eyes.

"I'll bring Ramona," Ron said referring to the village nurse. "We'll be there in ten minutes." Cara dropped the receiver and grabbed her gloves. As she ran, her labored breathing roared in her head. All earlier promises of sunshine were gone. Even the magpies and ravens had disappeared.

Cara was waiting near Herb's body when Ron and Ramona arrived. "Lucy's with Julie inside." Cara said. The nurse, an Athabascan woman who lived in Goldspring, headed toward the house, stepping carefully over the slippery ice.

"When did you and Lucy get here?" Ron said, crouching near Herb's body.

"Thirty or forty minutes ago." Cara was freezing and she stamped her feet and swung her arms. She dabbed at her nose with a soggy tissue. Her eyes were red and tears she was unaware of had crusted on her cheeks.

"What's all this?" he said, looking at the foil-wrapped food scattered in the snow.

Cara choked and turned away. "Thanksgiving leftovers. Lucy knew they hadn't cooked…" Grimly, Ron got to his feet and he and Cara headed toward the house.

Inside, the sheet that walled off Julie's bed was pulled back.

"She's still unconscious," the nurse said, looking up as they entered. "She needs to get to Fairbanks Memorial hospital as soon as possible."

Cara glimpsed the girl's naked heel poking out from beneath the comforter. She covered the exposed foot and stepped back into the kitchen, crunching over broken glass and debris on the floor.

Craving a cigarette, which she had given up months ago, she glanced toward Herb's bedroom. Didn't he smoke? Before she could check, Lucy brushed past her and headed outside. Startled, Cara watched through the window as Lucy dropped to her knees near Herb's body and begin to chant in a soft guttural, Koyukon.

Cara had been raised in the largely white towns of Fairbanks and Anchorage. She didn't speak Athabascan, but she recognized Indian prayer. Lucy was blessing Herb on his way and calling on his ancestors to welcome him.

As Cara listened to the singsong lilt, she felt her skin prickle. The indecipherable words felt like something more. Like a summoning. No longer aware of her icy feet and hands, Cara stared blindly at the snow as she strained to listen.

"Ramona will take Julie to our clinic, then we'll see about getting her to Fairbanks Memorial" Ron said, stepping around Cara. She followed him outside as he headed toward his truck.

"I'll drop you and Lucy off at her house and come back." The last thing Ron wanted was for Goldspring's favorite elder to keel over.

Lucy was still kneeling by the body. Hearing them, she looked up as she got to her feet. "No, we'll walk," she said. She was pale, but she was as determined as the schoolteacher she'd once been. Cara gave Ron a slight nod. "Walking" or what Lucy called her constitutionals was like medicine for her.

With a sigh, Ron nodded. He and Ramona returned to her SUV for the stretcher and the blankets they'd need to transport Julie.

He looked up at the fading light. "If the troopers aren't here in half an hour, it'll be too dark and we should move the body so you better call Tom." Tom was Ron's part time assistant and invaluable in times like this.

Cara looked at Lucy. Her aunt seemed to have aged twenty years in the past hour. "Let's go," Cara said. "It's getting colder and you shouldn't be out here."

"Wait," Ron said. He bent down and picked up the foil-wrapped food. "You better take this, it will attract animals."

Feeling suddenly exhausted, Cara stuffed the scattered containers into their tote bags, then she and Lucy headed back down the road. Their earlier eagerness seemed like a year ago.

Chapter 5

Goldspring

Searching Herb's House

Other than Lucy Montalk, the Ashenberg's nearest neighbors were a mile or so away. What Ron needed to do wasn't legal, but he was desperate. With another glance at the empty road, he dropped to his knees and began checking Herb's pockets. He found a packet of tissues, half a Hershey bar, a matchbook from Shem's Saloon in Fairbanks, an old grocery list, and a worn leather wallet with $28.

Ron replaced it and sat back on his heels, looking at Herb's body. He knew the Ravenstone was too large for Herb's medicine bundle, but he eased a small beaded felt bag from Herb's neck and upended it in his palm. Out fell a tiny bear carved from walrus ivory, a bit of sage, an uncut agate, and what looked like a lynx claw. No Ravenstone.

Refilling the pouch and tucking it back under Herb's wool shirt, Ron paused, thinking. Then he noticed the heavy boot on Herb's remaining foot. The laces had been sloppily retied. Puzzled, Ron unlaced the boot and pulled it off, then shook it upside down. Empty. Apologizing to Herb's spirit for having further disturbed him, Ron gently replaced the boot on the solitary foot. Disturbing the body was just not done.

Did the killers find the Ravenstone and hack off Herb's other leg in revenge? Or had Herb slid the Ravenstone into the now missing boot? Sickened by the image, Ron shuddered. He looked at Herb's calm face. A rime of frost coated his skin and hair. After a moment, Ron realized something else was missing: Herb's muskrat hat. The fur hat he always wore; the hat Lucy had made for him. Ron looked around, scanning the area and under nearby bushes. The snow was disturbed, but no hat.

The cold was cutting through his parka and he dug a tissue out of his pocket and wiped his nose. Getting to his feet and stretching his legs, he began to unfold the tarp over Herb's body.

Back in the house, the thermostat was turned so low it felt as cold inside as out. He paused at the door and wondered if Carl Clyne had anything to do with this. Oh, surely not. Clyne was an art dealer for heaven sakes. He had already given Ron a finder's fee for telling him about Sam Talwell. Ron had been stunned by the amount the gallery owner had promised for the Ravenstone. The money would go far toward financing building and staffing the training center Ron dreamed of for Goldspring.

At the door, he removed his boots to avoid further disturbing the crime scene. He started with Julie's cubicle and looked through her backpack. In the next twenty minutes, he searched the entire house and even poked at the ceiling and floorboards. He found no hat and no Ravenstone, even though he wasn't sure if the Ravenstone was why Herb had been killed.

Ron was at the door, pulling on his boots when he saw Cara walk up the driveway. "I brought you a moose meat sandwich and some coffee," she said handing him the foil-wrapped sandwich and small thermos. Her eyes fell to his half-fastened boots.

"I um had to use the facilities," Ron said. "I didn't want to mess up any footprints before the troopers got here…"

Cara nodded and turned to leave. "Stop by or call and let us know if they've found anything."

"Have you seen Herb's hat?" Ron called after her. Cara stopped and half turned around.

"No," she said, puzzled. "I haven't. Do you think whoever did this took it?" Ron shook his head.

"If it isn't around here, somewhere, they must have. He hardly ever took it off."

After Cara left, Ron up-righted a chair by the table and ate the sandwich she had brought. His stomach was churning with worry. As much as he wanted the training center built, no one should die for it. As he crumpled the foil left by his devoured sandwich, he heard the troopers' vehicles pull up.

"Ron." Trooper Thomlin gave him a nod and looked at the shape in the snow where frost had crystallized on the tarp. Matthew Thomlin was at least 6'4" and his handsome face seemed older then when Ron had seen him last summer. "Tell me what you know about this?"

The VPSO took a breath. He already knew Matt Thomlin was acquainted with Cara. "Well, Cara was visiting her aunt Lucy." Ron waved his hand in the direction of Lucy's house. "Mrs. Montalk lives about half a mile toward town from here. She and Cara walked over to visit the Ashenbergs this morning and found Herb and Julie, his daughter." Ron glanced at the figure in the snow. "Herb was a relative of Lucy's so this was a big shock."

Ron didn't need to add that it was also a tremendous shock to himself. It was written on his face. VPSOs were often assigned to villages where they had grown up.

Thomlin frowned. "The Ashenbergs are relatives of yours, too?"

Ron nodded. "Distant cousins."

Tomlin looked around. In the snow-laden landscape, no other houses were visible. Kneeling, he pulled the tarp back to examine Ashenberg's body.

For the next forty-five minutes, he and the other trooper lifted fingerprints, took measurements, drew rough sketches of locations and photographed the house; the front driveway, the blood-stained chopping block behind the property and the tracks, sunken beneath freshly fallen snow that lead to a tree in back. They collected samples of blood and other matter to send to the lab in Anchorage.

"Do you think this was done by a serial killer?" Ron was trying to prepare himself for the worst. Matthew Thomlin shook his head.

"No, I think someone targeted these people." He straightened and looked at the house. "There wasn't much food in there," he said. "Nothing to indicate they celebrated Thanksgiving." He began loading his gear. "You have any idea where they were yesterday?"

Ron was chilled through and through and he stuck his gloved hands beneath his armpits. "They had Thanksgiving with Sam Tallwell.

He's Herb's uncle and lives here in Goldspring. Sam is a *Deeyninh*, a medicine man." He looked at the Trooper. "A shaman."

Thomlin nodded. He had been in Alaska long enough to know the terminology. "An ambulance will take the girl to Fairbanks and we need to get the body to the coroner in Anchorage. There's an Alaska Airlines flight leaving for Anchorage at 4:30. I think we can make that." Thomlin glanced at the other trooper who was anchoring the body bag in the vehicle. "I'll have to talk to Mrs. Montalk and her niece, Cara, later."

"I'll go see Sam," Ron said. "He and Connie are going to take this hard."

Thomlin nodded. "Tell them I'll be stopping by to talk to them, probably tomorrow."

When Ron got home, the sky was dark. He wanted to call the art dealer before Herb's death hit the evening news. When he dialed, however, the phone rang, then went to message. With an exasperated sigh, he climbed back in his Bronco and headed for Sam's house.

"I never should have given the Ravenstone to Herb," Sam said, gazing at the floor. He was sitting on the sofa, his bony arms crossing his chest. "It would have been better to turn it over to the museum. But I wanted… I wanted Herb to find someone…" He coughed and spit into a torn paper towel. The cancer was eating him and he looked terrible.

"It's important to the *dena*, the Athabascan people, that our traditions should be remembered and continued." Sam took a labored breath. "If the Ravenstone goes to the museum, it would never be used."

Sam's crippled fingers plucked at the afghan draped across his shoulders. He coughed again and wiped his mouth. The soggy paper towel and handkerchief were done for.

"Herb didn't want it," Sam added. "He was worried, but I made him take it!"

Ron's skin prickled. If the art dealer had the Ravenstone, it would most likely be sold to a collector. It would never be used in an Athabascan ceremony. But still, he thought, what was more important; the trade school or these old fashioned, dying beliefs? He sighed.

Connie pressed a mug of steaming tea in her father's hands and he tried to settle back on the sofa. "So where is it?" he said, looking at the ceiling. "Where is the Ravenstone?"

As Ron drove home, he realized he had another worry. If the troopers linked the missing Ravenstone to Herb's death, as they eventually would, the timing would spoil everything Ron hoped to achieve for his beloved town.

Chapter 6

Goldspring

Saturday after Thanksgiving

The next morning, Cara saw a flock of ravens flying over the Ashenberg's house. They were cawing and the air was crisp with the temperature in the mid-twenties. Cara wondered if her aunt was safe in Goldspring? For that matter, was anyone safe in the village?

"I don't want to leave you by yourself and I can always find someone to take my classes," Cara said, wondering who. Lucy shook her head. "No, no you have a job and you can't stay here forever." She gripped her book on meditation by Joel Goldsmith. It was called *Leaving Your Nets* and Cara remembered having read the metaphysical book years ago. Lucy pointed to the phone. "Call Ethel, she can keep me company."

Ethel Mayo had been Lucy's friend for over sixty years. The woman's take-charge manner used to irritate Cara, but over the years, she had gotten used to Lucy's friend who seemed to love Aunt Lucy as much as Cara did.

"I'll be right over," Ethel said. "Don't worry, Cara. This is terrible. We can't let anything bad happen to Lucy!"

While waiting for Ethel to arrive, Lucy took a nitroglycerin tablet for her heart and settled on an old chaise lounge facing the television set. The room was what she jokingly called her office. A nearby window facing the back of her property let in the afternoon daylight. Major, Lucy's big orange tomcat, leaped up and began kneading the crocheted afghan on her lap, a deep purr rumbling in his broad chest.

In the kitchen, Cara opened the cupboard and took down a fat ceramic teapot, ivory colored with pink roses. Cara's mother had also favored flowers. They decorated everything, from dishes to bed linen to towels.

The kettle whistled and Cara was filling the teapot with boiling water and cranberry tea when Ethel's maroon colored Subaru pulled up outside. With a quick look at her dozing aunt, Cara grabbed her jacket and went outside.

Ethel's puffy quilted coat was a popular style, known for its warmth, but Cara thought it made people who wore them look like beds.

Cara gave the older woman a quick hug, their breath floating in the air like white vapor.

"This is terrible…what a shame." Ethel pulled out a tissue and wiped her nose. She had known Herb Ashenberg for forty years, and Julie since her birth. "And we know how dicey Lucy's heart is." Ethel glanced toward the house and waved at Lucy who had awakened and was watching them through the window. Cara nodded and looked away, unable to reply.

"I can't lose her," Cara whispered.

"I know," Ethel murmured, her arm around Cara, as they made their way inside.

No one was hungry, but Ethel heated a container of moose stew she had found in the refrigerator. At her insistence, Cara and Lucy took their places at the table.

"What did Ron say again?" Lucy's face showed strain and her skin looked like dark parchment. She sipped the tea, the cup rattling in her trembling hand. Her other hand gripped Cara's arm as if they were on a lifeboat.

"He didn't say much," Cara said. "The Troopers should be over there now. You know Ron doesn't handle homicides."

Lucy nodded. She had been the widow of a VPSO for the past fifteen years. She knew what they could and couldn't do.

Chapter 7

Fairbanks

Sunday after Thanksgiving

Blue and green aurora leapt jaggedly across the black sky when Cara pulled into her driveway. The twenty below temperature made the air dry and biting, but not heart stopping cold.

Dropping her overnight bag at the foot of her bed, she shed her boots and faded purple ski parka. She took a quick look at her kitchen sink and turned on the water. Hallelujah, she had water!

Wind gusts rattled the windows and her homemade curtains trembled in the gloomy light. They looked ridiculous, but they covered the depressing blackout shades that were so necessary in the long days of summer. As she unpacked her bag and listened to the wind whistle and whip outside, Cara recalled the myths she'd heard as a child. Whispering winds, spirits rushing by, her grandmother used to call them. But tonight, these winds weren't whispering. They were raging.

She dumped her heavy socks in a drawer as she thought. Who had killed Herb and why? Was it for something he knew or something he had? And why was his body mutilated?

Shedding her clothes, she stepped into the shower and emptied the last of the shampoo into her hair. As the water rushed over her an image flashed of Julie's limp figure, so small on the bed. Then Herb, dumped in the snow like refuse, his leg a bloody stump. Sliding down the wall of shower stall, Cara let the water beat down on her as she sobbed.

Later, in her flannel sleep shirt and old fur-lined moccasins, she wandered downstairs into the kitchen. The cupboard contained soup, beans and spices. In the refrigerator she found cheese, some shriveled vegetables, and a carton of eggs. She sliced off a chunk of a pale Havarti and took it upstairs to her bedroom with a glass of merlot.

Hours later and still unable to sleep Cara switched on the lamp. The light suffused her bedroom in a warm glow of rich wood and soft rose from her quilt and curtains. She glanced at the small clock next to her bed. Three a.m. Her eyes wandered to the phone and she pulled on her robe, a thick black and white number that made her feel like an Orca.

Ian McIntyre was a detective in the Fairbanks police department. He was also an insomniac and one of Cara's distant cousins. Wondering if he was awake, Cara dialed his number. "Yeah?" Ian's voice was gritty. He may not be able to sleep, but his voice was tired. A saxophone wailed in the background and she could almost feel the music thumping over the phone.

"Hey…" Her voice cracked unexpectedly and her lips turned wooden. Tears welled up. Oh damn. She couldn't sleep, and now she was too choked up talk.

"Cara? You back from Goldspring?"

With effort, she said, "I got in last night."

"Good trip? Aunt Lucy OK?" Ian's voice faded as he turned away to lower the volume.

Clearing her throat, Cara took a breath. "Something happened while I was there…" Then she stopped.

"Forcing her voice into a lighter register, she said, "This isn't the time. I'll catch you tomorrow."

"Nah, I'm awake, let me get a chair," he said and his phone clattered to the counter. Gratefully, Cara blew her nose on a tissue and reached for the last few sips of merlot. The wine had warmed her and she was sweating. She loosened her robe and pulled off her socks. Last year's Christmas socks were red and so were her hot feet.

"OK, I'm back." Ian's chair legs scraped the floor. "Shoot."

Cara shifted the phone to her other ear and anchored it with her shoulder. "Aunt Lucy and I went over to see the Ashenbergs. We found Herb in front of his cabin by Big Montalk Creek…he was dead." She spoke fast, trying to get as much said before she lost control.

"Jesus." Ian said, momentarily speechless. He had gotten to know Herb after his wife ran off and was later killed by a white man in a Fairbanks brawl. "What happened? Heart attack?"

"No!" she took a deep breath. "No, he was murdered. His right leg was cut." *Calm down, calm down.* "It was cut OFF," she said in a rush before she choked up. "There was little blood on the snow and no sign of bears or any other predators. His daughter, Julie was inside and she was hurt but she was alive. I didn't have my phone and had to run back to Lucy's to call Ron." Cara wiped her eyes with the soggy tissue and took a deep breath. "He called the Troopers."

Ian was silent and Cara sank back against the headboard relieved to have gotten this much out. "This is unusual for Goldspring." Ian's deep voice was slow and thoughtful. Cara knew his cop-think was kicking in. His disciplined detachment over the tragedies he had seen used to bother her. But over time, she realized it was his training that made him a better investigator.

After a moment he said, "Who did Ron reach at the troopers? Matt Thomlin?"

"I think that's who he talked to." Through the phone she could hear a mournful Jimmy Reed. *Drinking music,* a friend of Cara's had called Reed's easy rhythm. Gripping the phone, she leaned into the sound and closed her eyes. *If only that's all there was: melody, rhythm, and music.*

Ian's voice jarred her back "Sounds a little like the homicides in Juneau and Anchorage." He exhaled. "The medical examiner's office will determine how he died, but that type of mutilation, removing a limb, sounds familiar. Was it found?"

"You'd have to ask Ron or the Troopers. When did those homicides happen, six or seven years ago?" Cara recalled reading about it.

"More like about four," Ian said thoughtfully.

"So why now if it's the same guy? And why Herb?" Her sinuses were stuffed and her voice sounded as if it was coming through a horn. She grabbed the tissue box. It was empty.

"There was another incident, but similar." Ian's voice slowed as he thought back. "It was a few years before the Anchorage homicides."

"If it is the same guy, what's he been doing all this time?" Cara assumed the killer or killers were men, although she knew some women had the stomach for it.

"Good question. He may have been in jail or out of state." Ian sounded tired and Cara's guilt for calling him reemerged.

Outside, hail began pelting the windows and the wind had risen with a wail. Chilled again, she groped the bed for her socks with a free hand.

"I'll see what I can find out, although the troopers may already have a handle on this. Matt Thomlin's gonna want to talk to you," he added before hanging up.

Now the name kicked in. Cara had met the trooper at Ian's promotion party a year ago. Thomlin was unusually tall and very fit and decidedly masculine. Cara remembered his soft Southern accent. And his eyes. His voice and features reminded her of Clint Eastwood.

Ian's promotion party had been at the community hall where a few of Cara's paintings hung as part of an art show. She remembered the Trooper looking at her work. He was with the art instructor at the University and they were talking about the recession between the mountains and the cache in the foreground and how the artist had handled it. She later heard that Thomlin was interested in painting and was either divorced or widowed. In any event, he was single.

She set the phone back on the nightstand and leaned against the headboard. Talking to Ian was a relief. He knew the investigators and, would, she hoped, let her know what was happening. She looked at her empty wine glass. Nope. No more wine. She'd better get some sleep.

Hours later, the ringing phone penetrated a dream: something about a raven. Stiff from leaning against the headboard where she'd dozed off, she squinted at the clock as she reached for the phone.

It was Trooper Thomlin. He wanted to see her this morning.

Chapter 8

Fairbanks Monday

Four Days Past Thanksgiving

After three cups of coffee and dithering over what to wear, Cara managed to get dressed. Glancing in the mirror at her skirt and tall black boots she was disgusted at how formal she looked. He's seen you before, she thought. You don't need to impress him.

To reach the State Troopers office, Cara took Airport Way and turned on Peger Road. Still muttering to herself, she pulled into the State Troopers' parking lot where engine block heater outlets protruded like dwarfed parking meters. It was a thirty below, but she wouldn't be gone that long so her car should start without being plugged in. Grabbing her bag, she duck-walked across the slippery lot before climbing over a soot-speckled snow berm.

The air inside the Troopers' building was warm and very dry. Static electricity snapped at her fingers when she touched the door latch to the waiting area. A receptionist, with puffy blond hair, sat beneath fluorescent lights. She was so pale she looked bloodless. Her nametag read Joy. She looked up from a stack of paperwork and smiled, her lipstick smudging her teeth.

"Trooper Thomlin is expecting me," Cara said, stuffing her gloves in her bag. She pulled off her knit cap and shook her shoulder length hair loose, grateful she had just had it trimmed. She had never liked the hippie look. It always seemed frowsy, at least on women past the teenage years, although she knew many who would disagree.

Joy waved a hand toward the hall, flashing rings on several fingers. "Room one ten." Her voice was breathy and Cara noticed her nail lacquer matched her lipstick. She smiled. Joy was a welcome contrast to the weather.

Matthew Thomlin was facing the window behind his desk, a phone clamped to his ear. He turned and waved her inside. "Have a seat." He still reminded her of Clint Eastwood. Or maybe Paul Newman. Any woman could over-react. Then he was back on the phone.

"Yeah, Jack, I know. We'll get to that as soon as we get the lab results." His voice was soothing and she felt her shoulders relax. This wasn't her show. All she had to do was tell him what she and Lucy had found. Why be nervous?

Cara removed her navy coat, a recent sale purchase from Anchorage, which, unlike Fairbanks still had a Nordstrom. She took a chair facing his desk. The chair was an oak Captain's Chair with a curved back. It didn't look standard issue. Neither did Trooper Thomlin's desk chair. It was leather from what she could see of it. She had a hunch he'd bought them himself.

Matt Thomlin was in his early forties and had a commanding presence even before he stood to his full height of over six feet four inches. As an entire package, he was intimidating. His southern accent lent him a deceptive gentleness. She also sensed the charge of chemistry she'd felt when first seeing him at Ian's promotion party. Well that was then and now is now. She uncrossed her boot-clad legs and with her back straight, knees together, planted her feet firmly on the floor.

Thomlin hung up the phone and put on a pair of glasses. They didn't hurt his appearance at all and she looked away. With his elbows on the paper filled desk, he said, "I understand from Ron Whitfield, you and your aunt had an interesting day yesterday." His faint drawl softened his unsmiling gaze, but his pale eyes were unnerving.

Cara took a deep breath. Looking behind him through his window, she described how she and Lucy had found Herb. As she spoke, she again saw Herb's sad, mutilated body in the snow and

Julie, nearly lifeless inside the trashed house. It was all she could do to finish.

Thomlin was jotting on a yellow legal pad as she spoke. When his pen ran out of ink, he threw it in the waste can and grabbed another from the University of Washington mug on his desk. "I called your aunt before you arrived," he said, reaching for a small notebook. He flipped the pages. "She remembered giving directions to a fellow who was looking for the Ashenbergs."

Cara was surprised. "She didn't tell me...."

Thomlin nodded. "Shock can make people forget things." He looked back at his notes. "She said she didn't recognize him. He was Native, and she thought he might have been Tlingit or Haida...." Thomlin settled back, his chair creaking. "Can you think of anyone who had a problem with the Ashenbergs?" Cara was staring through the window blinds and didn't hear him. "Cara?"

She blinked and tried to focus on the trooper. Shaking her head, she said, "Herb was well-liked. I can't, I can't..." She let out a sigh. "No," she said finally. "Julie was eight when mother left..." Cara choked and looked away.

Thomlin rolled his chair to a metal cabinet and pulled out a file. Flipping it open, he glanced through it. "Her mother was killed in 1991 in Fairbanks..."

Cara nodded. "Herb and Julie were devastated. Have you found anything that might indicate a motive?" Thomlin looked at her. Most civilians would ask *why* someone was killed. The word motive wasn't part of usual conversation. Television, he thought, glancing at his notes. There it was, Cara Fielding taught three classes of journalism at UAF, including broadcast, radio and television.

"Nope. I called the family where they spent Thanksgiving." He glanced at his notes again. "Sam Tallwell and his daughter, Connie. According to them, Herb and Julie left together that afternoon."

"There was so little blood around Herb's body," Cara said. "I guess he must have been moved?"

Thomlin gave an internal sigh and nodded. "There'd been a

light snowfall, but we found indications..." He didn't add that there was blood all over around the chopping block near the cache in back.

She shifted her gaze to the window and tried to imagine what Herb saw in his last moments. Thomlin's office didn't have much of a view: the parking lot, a snow-covered trees and rooftops, and the ubiquitous gray sky.

"Do you think there was more than one killer?" Cara knew Thomlin wouldn't tell her much. She was a civilian and there was that 'need to know' nonsense she was always hearing on *Law and Order*.

"This is off the record," he said, looking at her. "We're already getting crank calls, so nothing I'm about to say is to be repeated." She nodded.

"But judging from the tracks, there were three perpetrators."

Three! Cara looked at the floor and crossed her arms. She had to stay poised or he'd shut down. "How did he die?" Her voice was husky.

Thomlin sighed. He knew Ashenberg had been strangled, but he only added, "We'll know when we get the ME's report."

He was answering more questions than he was asking. He leaned forward and rested his elbows on a myriad of paperwork. There was more he wanted to ask, like was she married or involved with anyone or did she have children, none of which had anything to do with Ashenberg's death.

She didn't see the sympathy in the Trooper's eyes as she turned to put on her coat. At the door, she stopped. "Was he killed before his leg...?"

Thomlin nodded. "It looks that way."

"And Julie, how is she?"

"She hadn't been molested and, before you ask, the nurses at the hospital say she is getting better, and they are allowing visitors." He realized he had forgotten to ask her what she knew about Sam Tallwell's artifact, the raven something that Sam mentioned. But that could wait.

When Cara stepped outside, the freezing air shocked the images of Herb and Julie from her head. Once inside her car, she sat shivering while the engine warmed. Had Herb known the killers? Did he know he was about to die? Or that he would lose a leg?

It occurred to her that if the killers were Native, the Troopers might not learn much in Goldspring, a largely Native village. Even though racism had lessened over the years, feelings were still sensitive and Cara knew the Native people weren't comfortable with law enforcement.

Would she have any better luck talking to them? True, she was half white, but everyone in Goldspring knew she was Lucy Montalk's niece.

That could get her into any house in the village, as well as many Native homes in Fairbanks.

Mulling it over, Cara shifted into drive and pulled out of the lot.

Chapter 9

University of Alaska-Fairbanks

Monday

It was four o'clock when Cara finished her Journalism 301 class. She was pleased with how it had gone. At least nine of her dozen students had completed their interviews with their practice witnesses, some of whom were guilty and others innocent, and were now writing up their summations. Next semester they would delve into the research techniques used in the cold cases she had supplied from thirty-year old police department files.

She was ravenous when she arrived home, but first, she had to call Lucy and ask her about the man Thomlin mentioned. Ethel picked up the phone.

"Lucy's napping. The past few days have worn her out and I'd just as soon let her sleep."

"Okay, but did she say anything about a man looking for the Ashenbergs? Trooper Thomlin said she mentioned a Native guy who wanted to know where Herb lived."

"She remembered after you left." Ethel's voice had lowered and Cara suspected Lucy was dozing on that old chaise lounge near the phone. "She said she didn't recognize him and thought he was from Juneau or Ketchikan. Now she's worried that she may have told the killer where to find Herb and Julie. She's blaming herself."

After they hung up, Cara sat for a moment, thinking about a Native man Lucy had never seen before and was therefore not from Goldspring and maybe not even from Fairbanks. If he was the killer, that might explain the mutilations, but those don't usually connect with the cultural background of Athabascans.

Thomlin said there were three perpetrators. Could they have been on heroin or meth or cocaine? What else but drugs or pure evil could lead to this? Still thinking, she shed her coat and boots and stared unseeing at her kitchen counter, frowning.

The small kitchen, painted a lemon yellow, today felt gloomy. Her stomach growled again and she opened a cupboard near the oven saw a can of tomato soup, and *oh good*, a small can of mushrooms.

When the soup and mushrooms reached a soft rolling boil, she poured it into a large mug and topped it with a dollop of plain yogurt, her substitute for sour cream. As she stirred the steaming soup and waited for it to cool, she remembered that Ian had asked her to call after she met with Thomlin. She reached for the phone.

"Can't get together with you today, but how 'bout lunch tomorrow, say at Shem's?" Ian had a voice best described as mellow and it resonated over the phone. He sang with a local jazz group and Cara had attended a few of their gigs. The women in the audience had amused her.

A hunka burnin love Cara recalled one blond saying, her eyes stapled on Ian. Cara grinned at the memory.

"What's tomorrow," she said, "Tuesday. Sure, Shem's sounds good." Cara wanted to talk about her worries over Lucy and the possible danger to others in Goldspring. But tomorrow would do. She needed to fill the larder, anyway and pick up her dry cleaning before it was donated to the Salvation Army or wherever abandoned cleaning went.

By the time she left the house, the sky's faint promise of sun had faded. At the grocery store, she managed to get in and out without running into anyone she'd rather not tell about her Thanksgiving. She even managed to pick up her cleaning on the way home, cringing at the price. She wouldn't be doing much more of that when her hours at the university were cut.

The temperature, according to the radio announcer, was thirty below. Gauzy ice fog replaced the overcast and the roads were slicker'n snot, as her father used to say. On Johansen Expressway, she slowed to a crawl as she crept by two major fender-benders. At nearly every intersection vehicles, unable to stop, had slid into one another. It made her all the more grateful for every cent she had spent winterizing her car. Now, she realized with her teaching income reduced, she'd have to seriously hustle if a job at NLI didn't pan out. Grim times.

In her kitchen, Cara unloaded the groceries then headed for the shower. As she stood under the water, letting the heat work its magic on her tense shoulders, she remembered something both Thomlin and Aunt Lucy had said: the Ashenbergs had spent Thanksgiving with Herb's uncle, Sam Tallwell.

She turned off the water and reached for her bath towel. She knew Thomlin would interview Sam, but how much would the Trooper learn from the Deeyninh? Most Natives knew more than they said, especially when questioned by a tall, white someone in a uniform.

Pulling on her jeans, tee-shirt, socks, slippers and a sweater, she went back to the kitchen and heated water for tea. Then, she ordered her cellphone, which she had been meaning to do. Finally, hoping her aunt wasn't still napping, she dialed Aunt Lucy in Goldspring.

Chapter 10

Juneau

Saturday

Cigarette smoke spiraled through the living room of the small wood frame house on Douglas Island. Frank, the oldest of the three men, was bone-thin and red-haired with a pockmarked skin. He also had asthma and didn't smoke, at least not cigarettes. But he was so angry he didn't notice Pat, his younger brother, as he nervously lit a fresh cigarette from a burning butt.

"So what do ya think?" Frank said, his face flushed. "Where the fuck is it?"

Pat had stretched out on the beer-stained sofa, his left foot tapping on the floor. No rhythm, just nerves. Frank's question was rhetorical and Brian and Pat knew it.

Brian was Haida and, although he had dark eyes and black hair, he was unrelated to the two brothers who were Tlingit. Haida and Tlingit were the prominent tribes in Southeastern Alaska. He now slouched in an abandoned office chair on wheels that someone had found on the street.

The house was full of mismatched, shabby shit like his chair. It teetered as he rolled between the coffee table and a floor lamp with a grimy white shade. Warily, he watched Frank pace. Frank was coming down off a high and it was never good. He was a loose cannon at the best of times, and what had happened in Goldspring didn't help.

Frank hawked and spit on the tired carpet. The house belonged to a guy who talked about burning it down for the insurance.

"

Frank had offered to do it for a price, but so far nothing had been settled. Still pacing, Frank smacked the back of Brian's chair, nearly rolling him into the battered coffee table speckled with cigarette burns. "Talk to me!"

Brian rolled away from the coffee table and forced his voice into a lower register. He'd read somewhere that deep voices commanded authority.

"You were there, you know we tore that house and shed apart. Searched everything. Even looked through his cache outside." He shrugged. "Found nothing, zip."

"That Ashenberg guy, you idiots weren't supposed to kill him!" Frank's voice rose. "You coulda used the girl. That's how you coulda got him to tell you where it was! What the hell happened with that?

Brian looked at Pat who looked away. Frank was in the bathroom when that was happening, claiming he had an upset stomach. Well, sure, Brian thought. What they'd done to that man and his daughter wasn't a Disney movie.

"Assholes" Frank glared at his brother.

Pat narrowed his eyes, as if pondering the mysteries of the universe. At twenty-one, he was eight years younger than Frank. They shared the same Tlingit mother, but Pat's father was a mild-mannered, philandering preacher from Alabama. Frank's dad, on the other hand, was doing life in San Quentin for murder. The brothers were thin for their six-foot height, but Frank's skinniness was largely the result of a coke habit, whereas Pat smoked dope and ate everything in sight. Like the pizza he had just devoured, tomato paste still on his chin. Everything on it, hold the anchovies. They always ordered two extra-large, one for Frank and Brian and one for Pat. Brian thought the kid had a tapeworm.

Unlike the brothers, Brian, from Ketchikan, was built closer to the ground. He gained weight easily, especially in the winter when he wasn't working his ass off commercial fishing. Except now, he thought bitterly. If this job went south and he didn't get paid, the bank would take his boat. And without the boat and his income, there went his house, sorry place though it might be. Not to mention the fifty he gave his mother every week. The domino effect just kept going.

Pat cleared his throat. "Trouble is, that omelet thing is *little*. It could be anywhere." He paused. "And the girl—you heard her—she was screaming and carrying on and she was strong!"

Frank looked at him tiredly. "Without that piece of rock, which by the way is an amulet, AM YOU LET, we don't get paid!"

As it did when he was stressed, Brian's ulcer was beginning to burn. He rolled his flimsy chair toward the window. Gray sleet blew diagonally, smacking the glass and building piles of dirty slush that heaped the edges of the driveway.

The ice-encrusted thermometer screwed precariously outside the window, read twenty-two above. Southeastern Alaska winters in Juneau were milder than winters further north in Fairbanks and Goldspring. But the humidity, aggravated by a nervous wind from the northwest, cut through clothing and the tired insulation of old houses, bringing with it the promise of all manner of winter ailments.

Brian watched as a tall dark spruce by the road was blown almost flat to the ground. Further out in the Gastineau channel that separated Douglas from Juneau, he glimpsed churning, steel-colored waves. Must be ten or twelve feet, he thought. It didn't take a weather forecaster to know the storm was growing. He wouldn't want to be on that snow machine today, he thought, grateful he and Pat had dumped it. The kid had been such a harebrained driver; it was a wonder they'd made it to the Ashenberg's house in one piece. Frank, of course, in the SUV, was oblivious to his brother horsing around.

Brian reached for a pack of cigarettes and tore off the cellophane. Doing something with his hands helped him think. Even now, fiddling with the cigarette pack, something occurred to him. "Do you know what this Raven thing looks like? I mean *exactly* what it looks like?"

Frank turned from Pat and looked at Brian. Judging from his eyes and tight mouth, Frank's temper was close to blast-off. Brian squinted at a distant point on the wall to avoid looking at the redhead. "I mean," Brian added, speeding up his delivery, "is there a photograph or drawing of it somewhere? Couldn't we get a copy made?"

Frank flapped his bony arms in irritation. "Right, and Carl Clyne wouldn't know? We just hand over some old rock with hairs glued on and he'll pay us? Old stuff is his specialty, man!"

On the sofa, Pat chewed the last of the now-cold pizza and frowned. "Martin's good at making stuff look old. He sells it to the tourists."

Frank raised his eyebrows. Any suggestion coming from his brother was a surprise. But now that Frank thought about it, he had seen some of Martin's work. He called them 'genuine copies'.

"Some museum guy wrote about it," Frank said, his forehead wrinkling in thought. "And there was a photograph in the Fairbanks newspaper." He snorted. "But it was an ink splotch. You couldn't see any details."

For a moment, Frank looked almost happy. Then he frowned. "If we do that, we got to include Martin in the deal since you jerk-offs couldn't find it!" Frank's anger faded and he smiled at his cronies. This did unlovely things to his pitted face and Pat looked away. Brian closed his eyes, letting his head drop back against the yard sale office chair.

Later, passing a joint around, Frank said, fishing for praise. "That was a good touch, huh?" Herb's mutilation had been Frank's idea after he'd seen the body. "Copycat those murders from, when was it?"

Brian ignored him. The dope wasn't working. He should be mellow, kicking back. Pat surprised him by responding with almost prim indignation. "Yeah great! Blood and bones all over, what a mess! That's a hell of a lot of work you know."

Dope and whiskey sometimes did that to Pat, made him mouthy. He didn't usually criticize his older brother, but Pat was as pissed off as Brian had been by the time-consuming work of sawing off that leg. The guy was dead, why bother him more? Brian told himself it was a moose as they hacked away. Even that made him sick.

He let his mind drift, an idle foot rolling his decrepit chair back and forth. He could do a lot with twenty thou. Fix his house, catch up on the mortgage and maybe take a trip. They just had to come up with that raven thing. Course Martin would want a lot of money. That was Martin. He knew the value of things. He'd know if Frank and Brian and Pat wanted something, it meant big bucks. At least bigger than usual. And Brian and Pat would have to pay him out of their cut, cause the way Frank would see it, it was their fault they hadn't found the real Ravenstone.

Tomorrow they'd be heading back to Fairbanks and Goldspring. He hoped to God, they could find this bird rock-thing. If not, at the very least find out what it looked like.

Chapter 11

Fairbanks

Sunday

The three men had met Glori at an Anchorage lounge a few months earlier when they had flown there for a gig. Pat was on drums and Brian and Frank on guitars. After hearing their complaints about how hard it was to find work between performances, the redheaded singer introduced them to Carl Clyne, an art dealer with galleries in Anchorage and Seattle.

"He always has odd jobs," she said. "And he pays in cash." For guys who lived day-to-day when gigs were few and fishing season was over, cash was akin to three cherries on a slot machine.

Clyne had read about the Ravenstone and was sure it was still in Goldspring. He wanted the three men to return and this time find it.

They arrived in Fairbanks on Saturday morning and rented a car and an SUV. By prearrangement, they drove off to meet Glori at Shem's Saloon out near the University. Clyne had said "time was of the essence" so their plan was to split up the next day. Frank and Pat would haul ass to Goldspring, taking the Explorer and do another search for the artifact. Maybe that medicine guy hadn't given it to his nephew. Maybe he still had it.

Right, and maybe spring would come in December, Brian thought.

Meanwhile, if they couldn't find it, Brian, who with his serious expression, could more believably pass for a student, would take the car and head for the library at UAF and the Fairbanks newspaper's archives to find photographs of the Ravenstone.

If this failed and they had to go to Plan B, there was always Martin in Juneau who was skilled at copying Native art. This was not to be discussed with anyone else, especially Glori who was sure to tell Clyne.

Glori had told them Carl was her uncle. Brian didn't buy it. They looked about as alike as a hippopotamus and a cheetah. Plus, Glori looked expensive and the dealer had money. Brian figured such combinations made for certain kinds of "uncles" and "nieces." He suspected the dealer was paying her to keep an eye on them. If so, she had her hands full with Pat, a doper and Frank, a cokehead if there ever was one.

Then there was another problem. Pat was deaf in one ear and his voice rose in normal conversation. It was worse when he was drinking. Three sheets to the wind and he could be heard in Winnipeg.

Brian sighed. Like the kid was right now. In the smoke filled, dimly lit saloon, Pat was laboring to impress Glori. Never had so gorgeous a woman given him the time of day. For her part, Glori was looking at Pat like he was Brad Pitt. Brian snorted and fingered his nearly empty glass. Pat had a snowball's chance in hell with Glori. For one thing, from the vibe Brian had gotten, he had a hunch she preferred pussy.

He lit another cigarette and looked around the smoky Saloon. A big guy had blown in a few minutes ago and now he and a woman at the bar were moving to a table. Brian figured she was part Athabascan. In college, he was surprised to learn there were at least seven major Alaska Native groups, each with distinctive features. Fairbanks was largely Athabascan, so this was a safe guess.

He studied the solid-looking guy with her. More Athabascan there with darker skin, and more Asian features. He paused and took a longer look. Oh shit. Was this the cop who'd arrested Pat last year? The one who warned Pat that if and when he got out of jail, he'd better leave town, "or next time it'll be worse?"

Pat's voice rose. "…Cause we couldn't find it…" Next to him, Glori tapped Pat's hand. The gesture seemed to calm him.

"Loose ships sink…whatever." Frank glared at his brother. He had just returned from the bathroom and swiped at the dab of white on his nose as he settled next to Brian at one of the half dozen tables scattered at that end of the room. Frank glanced around, his pupils like pinpoints. Brian, leaning back in his chair, saw Frank zero in on the man and woman. Brian dropped his chair forward with a thump.

"Isn't that the cop who arrested Pat last time we were here?" Brian's voice was low.

"Whacked those two!" Pat's happy voice rose behind them.

Frank grabbed Pat's shirt, jerking him off the chair. "Shut the fuck up!" His spittle sprayed Pat's face. "There's a cop over there, douche bag!" He shoved Pat back on the chair. Stunned, Pat sat weaving and Glori put a firm hand on his knee. Her expression, Brian thought, seemed both maternal and resigned.

He took a nervous glance around the room. Two older guys sitting at the bar hadn't budged. In fact, they hadn't moved for so long, he wondered if they were dummies. Or cops. On the other side of the long mahogany bar, the bartender continued wiping glassware with his white towel.

Brian settled back, his heartbeat slowing as he glanced around the room. Behind him, the large stone fireplace roared, sending out sparks as the dry wood caught fire. The heat felt good and he pushed his chair closer. Near the door, he noticed a large mirror. It hung at an angle in the left front corner of the saloon. The old glass was rippled and set in a heavy old ornamental frame. After a moment, Brian realized he could see the faces of the man and woman by the door.

Chapter 12

Fairbanks

Sunday After Thanksgiving

Cara arrived at Shem's Saloon ten minutes before Ian. Leaving her parka at a table near the door, she glanced around. The place seemed empty at first. As her eyes adjusted in the dim light, she saw three men seated by the huge stone fireplace in the back of the saloon. Then she noticed a redheaded woman. While the men wore sweatshirts and denims, the red head was a surprise. She wore a pale gray pantsuit and had an expertly styled haircut. This wasn't someone Shem's saw much of if ever. By comparison, the guys looked hardcore.

Cara headed toward the mahogany bar and the menu scribbled on the mirror behind it. "Hey Jake," she said. The bartender was one of her former students, a tall, skinny kid with the start of a beard.

"Hiya teach." Jake slid a glass of water toward her. He gave her a wicked smile and his canines, which were slightly long, gave him the look of a genial vampire. Cara grinned and leaned forward to peruse the menu. She decided on the spicy grilled chicken on rye with slaw.

Five stools down, two men with the look of regulars were hunched, talking, over their beers. The jukebox was playing an old favorite, the Stones' "Satisfaction". The only other sounds were the rising and falling voices of the group by the fireplace. Curious, Cara took another look. Two of the men looked to be in their twenties or early thirties and were probably part Native. The third

51

was definitely a Native. When he glanced at her, she turned back to the bar.

The door banged open and Ian blew in with a snow-covered flurry of freezing air. He saw her at the bar and dropped his parka on a chair near where she had left hers. "Hope you ordered," he said, walking over. Without looking at the menu, he ordered Shem's thick burger and fries. One of the best things about Shem's was the speed of the kitchen.

Moments later, Cara picked up her grilled chicken on rye and Ian, his burger, and they moved to the table. The tension level from the back of the bar had risen and Cara felt her neck prickle as she and Ian pulled out their chairs. She took a sip of water and saw Ian looking at a large mirror hanging in the far corner.

Following his gaze, she was startled to see a reflection of the guys by the fireplace. She also heard snatches of their conversation.

"*We.…spring. We… those two!*"

"*Shut the fuck up!*"

Ian frowned, listening. Cara took a bite of her sandwich, trying to hear the voices as they faded in and out of earshot. After a few moments, Ian swallowed the last of his burger and caught her eye. "You 'bout done?" She wasn't, but nodded and wrapped the rest of her sandwich in a napkin and stuffed it in her bag. As she pulled on her parka, she glanced again at the mirror and was startled to see the Native guy. He was watching them.

"What was that about?" She said, following Ian outside. They headed toward the lot. "Did you hear them?" Ian looked disgusted.

"They're not local. They're Southeastern, maybe Juneau. I arrested the younger one several months back." His voice hardened. "But what are they doing here? And what was Glori doing with them?"

"That woman, you know her?" Cara pulled her hood over her head. The fur ruff was warm and welcome. Ian's stride lengthened and Cara had to trot to keep up with him. Behind them Cara heard voices and looked back. Beneath Shem's flashing neon sign, she saw two of the men had followed and were standing outside Shem's doorway. "Uh, Ian…" Something exploded near her head.

"Get down!" Ian yelled, yanking her to the ground. Cara's face was shoved into the snow and she heard a hissing sound. Turning her head, she a truck's tire near her shoulder slowly flatten.

"Let's go." Ian scrambled to his feet. Hunched over, they zigzagged around parked vehicles to the trees on the far side of the lot. Behind them, Cara heard muffled voices.

"I hope they're too drunk to follow us." Her breath was ragged as she struggled to keep up with Ian.

Her glasses had frosted over and she stuck them in her pocket. Behind her, she heard a car door slam then the crackle of tires on frozen gravel.

"Get off the road!" Ian shouted, pulling her over a snow berm left by road crews. Cara heard a second shot and Ian lurched against her. With a surge of fear, she yanked him down the embankment. It was steeper than it looked and they fell, sliding down the hill, bumping into trees, willows and brush. She lost her grip on his jacket as she tried to catch hold of the nearest bushes. Her parka caught on a snow-covered willow, slowing her descent. In a semi-controlled fashion, she bumped down the slope on her butt, barely aware of the snow bunching up under her parka. Near the edge of the slough, she stopped and tried to sit. Hearing a moan, she peered through the darkness saw Ian lying a few yards away.

"You OK?"

"Asshole winged me."

Cara pushed through the knee-deep snow toward him. "Where?"

"My shoulder." He tried to sit. "My phone, it's in my pocket." He turned so she could reach his right pocket. Cara found his .38, but no phone. Then she tried the inside pocket of his jacket.

"Not here."

"Musta dropped it." Out of breath, he sank back.

Cara looked around. *Shitshitshit.* In the afternoon darkness and without her glasses, she'd never find his phone. She squinted at him, barely making out his expression. "Can you stand?"

He nodded, impatiently. "Yeah." As she pulled him to his feet, he let out a muted yelp. Panting, they stood for a moment getting their bearings. Ian was seven inches taller than Cara and their lopsided gait kept throwing them off balance. There was little vegetation near the frozen slough, which made it easier to navigate, but Cara knew their tracks were clear to anyone following them. From the road she heard voices and a car door slam. Gritting her teeth, she pressed forward, Ian's heavy arm weighing her down. "There's a bridge up ahead somewhere." Cara stopped and leaned forward to catch her breath. "And beyond that a gas station. It should have a phone." Her throat was raw from the cold and the sheer exertion left a cold sweat running down her back. Behind them she heard a yell then another voice. It was closer.

"They must've found our trail." Ian rasped.

Overhead, green aurora leaped against the black sky. There was barely enough shadowy light to follow the winding slough.

After what felt like a year, her legs heavy as cement, Cara saw the vague shape of a bridge. *Oh thank God.* But as they neared it, her hopes plunged. The bridge was at least a dozen feet above where they stood. Worse, the slope up to the road was covered in what looked thigh deep snow. She looked at Ian. The shoulder of his pale gray parka was dark with blood. "Can you make it?"

Breathing hard, Ian's mouth tightened. "Let's do it."

Chapter 13

Sunday

Shem's Saloon

"Where the hell'd they go?" Frank got out of the car and slammed the door. He waved the flashlight ahead, scanning the roadside. "I know I winged one of 'em,"

Pat crawled out of the back seat and stood shakily on the passenger side. He held a half empty bottle of J&B he had found on the sedan's floor.

Brian was standing near the shoulder, looking at the trampled snow on the berm. "Looks like this is where they went over." No way did he want to go down the steep embankment.

Other than the car's headlights, it was too dark to see more than two feet in front of them. They had one flashlight and one gun. "We have a snowball's chance in hell of finding them," Brian muttered.

Frank shook his head. "We gotta go after 'em, they heard us. You, anyway." He glared at his brother, who was leaning against the car, his eyes blinking. "Bragging how we got the *omelet…* Christ—coulda heard you all the way to Haines!" Frank spat in the snow.

"Come on." He stepped over the berm and began side-slipping down the bank. He waved the flashlight, its narrow yellow beam showing about four feet ahead. "Colder'n hell down here!" He yelled back, "Come on, I've found blood!"

"Crap," Brian muttered and began to side-step down.

Behind them, Pat stood, leaning against the car. After a

moment, he slid to the ground and closed his eyes—just for a minute, he told himself. Then he'd go help his brother and Brian. Full of scotch and images of Glori on a beach, wearing nothing but her charm, he rested his head against the car.

After struggling through the snow and finding only sporadic tracks, Brian and Frank headed back to the road. Climbing back was harder and they slid back a step for every two they took. Brian was panting and his legs were trembling when they reached the road. "What's that? Is that Shem's?" Frank was staring at something to his left. They were a good distance from where they'd left the car. "Whatchya bet, Pat's gone back there?" he said, heading for the saloon.

Too worn out to talk, Brian slogged along behind him. When they entered the saloon, it was nearly empty. Even the two guys hunkered down at the bar were gone.

The bartender had just walked through the swinging door from the kitchen when he spotted them and ducked behind the bar. He had just called the Fairbanks Police and now hoped to hell that Miss Fielding and the cop she was with were okay.

"Maybe Pat's in back taking a leak," Frank said, heading toward the bathroom. A moment later, he returned, shaking his head. "He's not there." He paused and looked around, "Where's Glori?"

"She's got a show." Brian's teeth chattered. His face was so cold he could hardly move his lips. "Remember? She sings with some group when she's in town." Where was the bartender, for heaven sakes? He'd kill for a cup of hot coffee.

"The cops are going to be all over this place. We should get out of here," Frank said, ever nervous.

They climbed into the SUV. Aside from two other vehicles, including a truck with a flat tire thanks to Frank's shooting, their Explorer was alone in the parking lot. "We gotta go back and get the car," Frank said, sliding across the frozen seat. "Fuckin A, freezing my nuts off, couldn't pay me to live here."

"Let's find Glori, I bet he came back here and went with her," Brian said as he climbed into the drivers' seat and pulled out of the lot.

Frank shook his head. "First, we gotta get the car, my name's on the paperwork in the glove compartment. Besides, Pat might of passed out in the back."

The gas station attendant, whose nametag read Nick, was a heavy-set kid with bad teeth and large pale-gray eyes. When he saw the two people enter the gas station, his fingers crept to the gun beneath the cash register. Under the harsh yellow lights, Ian's weakened condition and the blood on his jacket were obvious. The kid did a double take when he saw the woman, then he relaxed. She taught at the University where he took classes.

"We need to use your phone." Cara was trembling and she leaned against the counter. Next to her, Ian slid to the floor and came to rest against a display of winter tires.

"Call the station, they'll send someone," Ian said, his scratchy voice now a whisper. The kid leaned over the counter to look at him and Ian waved his badge.

"Sure, sure!" Nick shoved the phone across the battered Formica counter, but Cara's fingers were like ice cubes and she dropped the phone. With Ian calling out the number, Nick dialed.

Brian steered around a pothole and looked up in time to see a flash in his rearview mirror. Three cop cars were approaching. "Shit," he muttered. Frank turned to look through the back window. The red lights reflected off his pitted face. Brian turned off his headlights and speeded up.

"You're going too fast, we'll miss it," Frank said, turning forward. "There it is, goddamn it. slow down!" But even at twenty-five miles an hour they were moving too fast for the slick curve. Grappling with the wheel, Brian tried to steer out of the skid, but the big SUV slammed into the side of their parked Ford.

"Jesus!" Frank squawked as they came to a crunching halt. He jerked at the door, but it was wedged against the sedan. In the rearview mirror, Brian saw more flashing red lights through the trees. He pulled ahead a few feet, tension clenching his gut as the SUV scraped the car.

Frank jerked on his door again, then fell out. Catching his breath, he climbed inside the car, jammed the key in the ignition and stomped on the gas. It didn't move. He tried again, but the tires spun and whined uselessly. "Shit!"

"Let me try." Brian stumbled out of the SUV and got behind the wheel, he gave it a little gas and rocked the car. Gaining traction, he inched it back on the road. In the rearview mirror, he saw one of the cop cars had left Shem's and was headed toward them.

"We're outta here." Frank yelled, already in the SUV and moving.

On the road behind them, a bottle of J&B Scotch lay half buried in the snow. Off to the side, partly concealed by a berm, lay the comatose Pat where the car had pushed him over the edge of the road.

Chapter 14

Fairbanks

Monday

"Abody was found out near Shem's, near where you and I went over the embankment."

Cara had just arrived and was sitting across from Ian in his office. Her eyebrows went up. "A body? This is one of the guys who shot at us?"

Ian nodded. "Looks like hypothermia aided by booze got him, but he had help rolling off the road. There were tracks and they matched the tread of the Ford we found at the airport. It was damaged."

"Was there any ID?" Cara shifted in her seat. She was still feeling the effects of their tumble down the hill. With his wounded shoulder, Ian was in worse shape, but he had a padded cushion on his chair. She had no sympathy.

Ian nodded. "Yeah, we found his wallet. It was Pat Holmsman, Frank Barnetti's half-brother. I think Frank's the guy who shot me. There was an empty J&B bottle nearby. Pat might have passed out, but I can't figure why they left him."

"Unless it was deliberate and they pushed him over the edge." Cara paused. "Or maybe they didn't see him."

Ian looked at her. "Could be. Oh, and we found a beaded bracelet and a beaded hairclip. They were in Pat's pocket. I think they were Julie's. Could you take a look at them?"

"Sure. If I don't recognize them, Aunt Lucy might." Cara realized she hadn't thought to look and see if anything was missing when she and Lucy found Herb and Julie.

"Okay, more news…" He leaned forward. "Remember the redhead, Glori?"

"You're kidding, she's with the FBI?" Cara groaned and leaned back to stare at the ceiling. "Does that mean they're taking over Herb's murder?" Now it would never be solved, she thought, remembering how the FBI took over cases and then nothing was reported. Nothing

Ian shook his head. "Not that we hear much, but they are working with the Troopers." He gave Cara a sardonic smile. "Other than these hair clips, there's no indication that these guys are responsible for Herb and Julie. But there's a possible connection to another Native art theft case. The art dealer lives in Seattle; he's got a shop there and in Anchorage."

After a moment, Cara said, "You think he was after the Ravenstone?" A surge of rage flashed through her. Ian saw her expression and leaned forward.

"Hold on there, Cara. These aren't college kids. This group kills and doesn't think twice about it. You saw what they did to Herb."

Cara shifted uncomfortably in her chair. Pain from her falls and exhaustion after trying to run through thigh high snow was making her crabby. She looked through the window behind Ian.

Ian frowned. "Listen, you could screw up their case. Not to mention getting you hurt or dead."

Cara got up and pulled on her jacket, her mouth tightening, "I don't give a flying fuck about some art dealer! The FBI would make a deal with the killers just to get this guy,"

"No, no," Ian got to his feet and began pacing. "Art theft does not take precedence over murder. The Fed want this guy in other states as well. And he could be responsible for Herb's death."

He paused. "Listen, it would be worse if you learned something and didn't tell anyone. Just don't go off half-cocked on your own."

"Copy that," she muttered as the door shut behind her.

Ian slowly let his arms drop unaware he'd raised them. *Christamighty.*

Chapter 15

Fairbanks
Monday Afternoon

"Connie is a widow with two children and, as you know, her father is a *deeyninh*," Lucy said when Cara called the next morning. "They're taking Herb's death pretty hard. Thank the lord, Julie is getting better, even if she still doesn't remember much." No, my angina isn't troubling me, and no, Ron hadn't said anything more."

Cara set the phone down then moments later, she dialed Connie.

"Dad gets tired pretty easily." Connie's voice sounded stuffy as if she had a cold or had been crying. "But we are here now if you want to come."

The morning had dawned gray with a threat of snow. The temperature hovered at twenty-nine below and the Toyota started reluctantly. Cara prayed it wasn't an omen and her heater would work.

Twenty minutes later, she pulled up behind a long line of cars. As she slowly moved forward, she discovered a traffic accident had closed two lanes of the Steese highway. Fire trucks and an ambulance filled the lanes. Lights flashed through the fog. A Consolidated Van Lines big rig and a blue Volvo wagon were fused into a wrinkled mess with the Volvo getting the worst of it. A dejected looking Native family stood shivering by the side of the road. Broken glass and torn metal glistened dully against the frozen slush. Hoping no one had been injured, Cara inched to another halt as oncoming traffic took over the just opened single lane.

After several minutes, a cop, his breath swirling white clouds, began motioning the stalled traffic around the wreckage. The Toyota's heater was making more noise than heat and Cara's feet felt icy as she shifted into gear.

An hour later, she pulled up in front of the Tallman's yellow house.

Aunt Lucy had said Connie was thirty-seven, two years older than Cara so she was unprepared for the frazzled, plump woman at the door who looked at least fifty.

"Dad will be out in a minute," Connie said, motioning Cara inside before disappearing behind a swinging kitchen door. As it shut, Cara glimpsed an aging yellow refrigerator and a stove with a large black pot on top. She caught a whiff of stew.

After her chilly drive, the house felt overheated and stifling. A moose rack was mounted by the door and a hat dangled from one prong. Cara peeled off her scarf and hat and hooked them over the rack. She dropped her parka and bag near the door on a red fake leather chair that looked like it would collapse if you breathed hard. The chair faced a battered footlocker covered with magazines and a sagging sofa. A flattened, indented cushion lay on one end of the footlocker and Cara imaging Sam at that end of the sofa, his feet resting on the cushion. She gingerly lowered herself to the red chair. It wobbled as she had feared.

Connie reappeared from the kitchen and sank onto a dining chair.

"Some days were harder than others for Dad," Connie said, moving with deliberation as if her back hurt. There were dark circles beneath her eyes. As first cousins, she and Herb shared the same dark, deep-set eyes. Otherwise, Herb, who was six years older, had been lanky, his face gaunt at times, while Connie was plump.

"The kids are at the church, rehearsing for a play. Usually, it's rowdy here." She glanced around the room. It reeked of illness and sorrow. Cara had a feeling the youthful energy of Connie's children must, at times, be welcome. The vinyl chair teetered as she tried to get comfortable and she froze in place.

"I wanted to get some sense of Herb and Julie's last day," Cara began. She stopped when a thin, elderly man entered the room. His brown eyes were filmy and his hair was heavily streaked with silver. He wore a plaid shirt and baggy jeans that probably had once fit, but were now at least three sizes too large.

"Dad, this is Cara," Connie said. "Lucy's niece."

Looking at Sam, Cara could well believe he had cancer. Lucy said that Sam followed the old ways and refused the "bag of tricks," or what he called white man's medicine. Cara assumed that meant chemo, and radiation. She wondered if the "old ways" allowed something for the pain. If he was taking anything, it didn't seem to be working. She remembered something else Lucy had said. "Sam believes our time is short, it is our spirits that are diseased and need healing."

Weak as he was, Sam's dark eyed gaze reminded Cara of a sharp-eyed raven. She had a feeling that little escaped him.

Sam settled exactly where Cara had imagined, on the sofa, the foot cushion within an easy distance on the trunk. At one time he would have lifted his legs and reached it. As if reading Cara's mind, Connie walked over and lifted her father's feet, placing them in the pillow. He seemed both embarrassed and resigned. Cara looked away.

"You and Lucy found Herb and his daughter." Sam's voice was stronger than Cara expected. Knowing he had already heard much of this from Ron, she began describing her visit with Lucy to the Ashenberg's and how they had found them. When she finished they sat for several moments in silence.

Heat radiated from the wood-burning stove and sweat crawled down her back. She pulled off her cardigan and dropped it on her bag on the floor. A sheen of perspiration shone on Connie's face, but Sam, his long underwear visible beneath his open collar, seemed comfortable.

"That Trooper was here." Sam coughed, revealing stained teeth. "We couldn't help him much, though." His eyes smiled.

"Hmm," Cara murmured, in an agreeable Native response. After a moment she said, "Were Herb and Julie here all day on Thanksgiving?" This wasn't what she wanted to know, but she wanted to get the ball rolling and focused on the bright afghan to his left.

Connie surprised her by answering. "They left around 3:30 or 4." Cara nodded. "Did Herb seem upset or worried about anything?" In her peripheral vision, she noticed Connie shake her head, no.

Cara plowed on. "Did Herb mention anyone being mad at him … or that he'd had an argument with anyone." She tried to frame her words as wandering thoughts or ruminations rather than questions. She studied the coffee table as if it held the secrets to the universe. This was like an oral exam in slow motion.

Sam coughed, a hacking sound, and wiped his mouth with a tissue.

"The people who killed him weren't from here!" Agitated, he spat the words and Cara could feel effort it took for him to not cough.

"He had something I gave him. That's why he was killed." Sam's face turned red and Connie looked nervous.

"You don't know that for sure, Dad," she said. "How could anyone know about it anyway? You gave it to him just that afternoon."

"Gave him what?" Cara said, before catching herself. *Interrupting, just like a white person.* She felt a flash of sympathy for Matt Thomlin before remembering he never interrupted anyone.

Sam looked away, his shoulders sagging. "*Eetaa?*" Connie said, addressing her father in Koyukon.

"The Ravenstone." Sam's gaze drifted around the room. "It belonged to Red Shirt." He looked at Cara to see if she understood the significance.

Whoa. Cara sat back. Her chair creaked and sank a little. She had heard Red Shirt was the most powerful *deeyninh* in Koyukon history. Some believed he and the powerful Chief Larion, Cara's ancestor, were one and the same. But little had been written or recorded so it was all word of mouth.

"You've had it a long time?" Cara said, circling the more direct and confrontational sounding *how did you get it*? Aware that her shoulders had lifted, as they did when she was tense, she forced them down and sat back, doing her best to appear relaxed.

After a moment, Sam nodded. "Red Shirt gave it to me." He cleared his throat again. "I was a little shit back then. He told me to make sure it didn't get in the wrong hands." Sam paused to catch his breath and Cara thought she could hear his chest rattle. Besides cancer, Lucy told her he had a heart condition, which explained his difficulty breathing.

"So you gave it to Herb…?" *And not to a deeyninh*?

Sam waved a hand, irritably. "I wanted him to keep it safe. To hide it…it's *ts'hoot'e* for a non-Native to have the Ravenstone." Now that Sam had started talking, Cara couldn't believe she'd forgotten her tape recorder. She was a journalist for heaven sakes. But she wasn't about to break the tenuous mood by digging through her bag for a note pad. Sam pulled his feet off the footlocker and leaned forward.

"The Ravenstone is sacred," he continued, unaware of her dilemma. "Dangerous if the wrong person gets hold of it." His expression darkened. "That's why Herb was killed—some peoples want the Ravenstone." He rubbed his face and rested his bony elbows on his equally bony knees.

Cara gave him a quick glance. "Did many people know about it?" When he didn't answer, she looked at Connie who shrugged.

"I didn't even know he had it until the article in the newspaper." She gave her father a fleeting look of exasperation.

Article? "Umm," Cara nodded. "Ah, what does it look like?" Cara sat back cautiously, praying her chair wouldn't collapse.

"It's small and flat," Sam began. "It has fur through the beak and garnets for the eyes…"

"You can hardly see it's supposed to be a raven, it's so old and the design is almost worn off," Connie added.

Cara felt a chill. It dawned on her that the Ravenstone had

historical as well as monetary value to collectors and Alaska Natives. This raised the question how much would a museum or private party pay for it?

"How was it used?" she asked. Sam assumed a bland expression that she recognized. Native elders hid behind this look when asked something they had no intention of answering. She sighed and raised her eyebrows at Connie who shook her head.

Cara added, "I don't think Trooper Thomlin or Ron found the Ravenstone. If Herb hid it, I hope he put it someplace safe."

"He didn't want to take it." Sam waved his hand as he spoke. "He was afraid." The old *deeyninh* looked at her in confusion. "It belongs to the *Dena*, it wouldn't bring bad luck to us. …"

As Cara left the overheated house, she realized Sam had said something crucial. Herb hadn't had the Ravenstone long enough to have it turn against him. And that shouldn't have happened anyway since Herb was Koyukon.

Chapter 16

Goldspring
Tuesday

The door scraped over the frost-heaved threshold and freezing air blew inside as Cara left the house. Connie pulled her father's empty mug from his gnarled hand. "You can't blame yourself," she said, taking the mug to the kitchen.

"That girl," he called after Connie. "She's determined…she'll find out what happened." Sam pulled himself to his feet and shuffled into the bedroom he shared with his grandson. Even before Herb's death, Sam's heart had pained him more than his disease-filled stomach. Was that why he hadn't seen the danger coming? In his earlier days he would have at least *sensed* something; he would have been more careful with the Ravenstone. But he had been having dreams: ravens flying low, cawing, the sky above turning black.

Sam loosened his slippers and sank back on his bed. His breathing was shallow. After being diagnosed at the hospital in Fairbanks, and again at the Alaska Native Service Hospital in Anchorage, he had refused treatment. Enough was enough. He knew his time was near.

That's one thing the whites got right. How did it go? *A time to live, a time to die, a time to sow, a time to reap.* Something like that. Dying would be a relief. No more feeling rotten, with pain killing his energy, his spirit. Besides, he wanted to see his wife again, his ancestors. Even Red Shirt. Sam chuckled. What an imagination you have, his mother used to tell him, *Aatsagaaha*, she'd say, shaking her head at his foolishness.

The past few days had exhausted Connie, yet she was having trouble sleeping. Now she stretched out on the sofa her father had abandoned and pulled the afghan over her legs. She thought of her mother, Beth, who had died when Connie was twelve.

"Trust your father," Beth had said when she'd had that fatal bout of flu. "He'll know what's best. "You won't always like what he says," she added, making an effort to smile, "but his advice is good."

Her mother had been right, of course. When Connie wasn't too stubborn to listen, Sam had helped her through her first pregnancy after her boyfriend disappeared. He had helped her buy a used Honda that was dependable instead of the little sports car she loved but was too lightweight for icy roads.

Chapter 17

Anchorage

Tuesday

The last time Carl Clyne had seen his oncologist, he was told he had six months left, maybe less. As much as Clyne hated to, he had to get his affairs in order and that included finding out who had been behind his daughter's death a year ago

A few days later he called Glori in Juneau, and told her to get Frank and Brian back to Anchorage. It was too bad about Pat's death, but at least now there were fewer mouths to babble about his business.

Near midnight, Brian and Frank were parked in a brown Chevy, just off the old Seward Highway, a few miles from downtown Anchorage. "Why do we need to wait so long?" Frank was in the passenger seat, smoking. An empty pack of Chesterfields lay crumpled at his feet. "We coulda done the job and been in bed by now."

Brian lit a cigarette from the burning stub in his hand and turned off the ignition. In the light of a fading moon, only the falling snow, wetly smacking the windshield, was visible. "Guess he wants to make sure everyone's asleep."

The car was full of smoke and Frank coughed. Bracing himself against the freezing air, he opened his window, spat, and rolled it up again. Brian pulled his fur-lined hood over his head and tightened the cord under his chin.

After another ten minutes, they pushed the doors open and stepped into the whipping wind. Struggling to stay upright, Frank leaned inside the trunk for the gas can and rags. The gun in his pocket thudded against the side of the car.

Brian's eyes watered in the freezing wind and he tried to relax. Tensing up only made the cold worse. Earlier, the temperature had warmed up to zero, but then this bastard wind had risen. He stuffed his gloved hands in his pockets and stamped his feet to keep the blood moving.

They had earlier checked out the area and decided on the most direct route to the trailer. For a short distance, they trudged single file along the old Seward highway. Then they turned right and slid down the embankment into thigh deep snow, ice-coated willows, and scrubby brush.

After about twenty feet, they were sweating through their long underwear. "That's it," Brian said pointing to a house trailer near a two-story, tar-papered house in the distance. A light shone in the windows.

"Just the trailer, not that house?" Frank was trying to catch his breath, but it was so cold he was sucking air through his gloved hand. His left foot had slid under a log beneath the snow. He jiggled his foot, but one of his shoepacs, bought used at the Fourth Avenue surplus store, remained stuck.

"Yeah," Brian said. "Just the trailer." From their earlier visit, they knew that half a dozen families lived in the area, each on an acre or more of land. But there was only one trailer. It shared land with a two-story tar-papered house. In the moonlit darkness, spruce, skinny birch and cottonwood loomed like snow covered sentries. About half a mile away, yellow lights shown from a few scattered residences.

Frank managed to free his foot and was wobbling precariously on a loose log. "OK," he said, "let's …"

A tremendous explosion lit the black night and rocked the two men off their feet.

"What the…!" Stunned, Frank fell back into a snowbank. Although shaken, Brian stared at their target. Flames shot upward, some landing on the roof of the nearby tar papered house.

"Holy crap," he said, struggling to his feet in the deep snow. "Let's get out of here!"

Chapter 18

Anchorage

Thursday

Frank and Brian stopped at Peggy's Café near Merrill Field before meeting Carl. Small aircraft droned overhead, taking off and landing as they studied the menu and later munched their burgers, finishing with a selection from Peggy's famous pies. Since Frank hadn't been able to score for a couple of days, both his appetite and temper had increased.

"Sorry about Pat," Brian said. He'd read in the Anchorage Times about the kid's death. "Looks like he froze to death."

"Yeah," Frank replied. "Don't know how to tell mom, she won't be happy, losing her baby boy." Despite his effort at sarcasm, Frank wasn't happy.

It was after two o'clock and daylight was fading when they drove to Carl Clyne's Alaska Art and Antiques store. The heater blew lukewarm air, barely making a dent in the frost inside the windows. Exhaust fumes unfurled like white specters behind their rented car.

"Shit, all that time in Fairbanks, and for what?" Frank said as Brian came to a stop sign. Frank slunk down in the passenger seat, picking his teeth. A lot of guys went to Fairbanks to polish their arson techniques with the agreement that the fire department look the other way. Money changed hands and it was a done deal. At least that was the way it used to be.

Brian wanted to tell Carl immediately about Wade's place, but Frank said Carl was in Seattle and they shouldn't bother him. On the plus side, this gave them time to ask around about the fire.

At first Frank thought they could still take credit for the job—until they learned a kid and dog had died and no one else was in the trailer. Which meant Wade was still alive. Worse, he was being watched by the cops who thought he might have had something to do with the fire.

Brian pulled up behind Carl's shop and parked. He lit a wrinkled Camel and stared through the windshield at the darkening landscape.

"What're we gonna say?" Frank's large ears were pushed out by the mouton earflaps of his cap. With no coke, he was impatient and jumpy. He was also overly-proud of his gun, which Brian hoped to hell he'd never use again, not after that session at Shem's. Frank's full stomach, unaccustomed to food, gurgled and he let loose a ripe fart.

Brian cranked his side window down a few inches, letting the icy air snake inside. Facing the window, he ran his tongue across his teeth, digging out the remains of the peppery burger.

Frank let loose again and Brian practically hooked his nose over the window. "We better tell him what happened," Frank said, shifting in his seat, relaxing in the gassy warmth against his backside. Unbuttoning his jacket, he reached in his breast pocket for another toothpick.

"We'll say someone got to it before we did." His bony fingers twirled the toothpick nervously. "Either that, or it was an accident." He snapped the toothpick, flicking the pieces to the floor. "We won't get paid, we'll just tell the truth." Frank felt oddly virtuous. Telling the truth was so rare it was like going to church. He pulled on his gloves in an unexpected show of decisiveness. "Come on," he said. "Let's get this over with." He shoved his door, kicking it at the bottom where it stuck.

Brian turned off the engine and hoped it wouldn't freeze up before they came out again. The rental had a head bolt heater, but he didn't see a place on the street to plug it in.

"We'll just tell him the truth," Frank repeated, clapping his hands to warm them up, as they headed toward the house. "The trailer blew up before we got there," he added, rehearsing his speech, his breath a fog. "The kid wasn't our fault. Shit, we didn't even know he was there."

Brian didn't remind him the kid's death couldn't have been their fault since they hadn't burned the trailer in the first place. Frank was easily distracted and very temperamental. One thing at a time, otherwise things got messed up. Brian dropped his cigarette in the snow and rubbed it into a black smear with his boot.

He thought about his first job for Carl. A few months ago, Carl had told him to drive some guy up to the Valley. "Just get this guy and hand him over to Ed Stewart. He drives a green pickup; meet him in Palmer at the parking lot next to this big warehouse called The Grange." Brian delivered his increasingly alarmed passenger to Ed, who looked like a farmer and smelled like manure.

Back in Anchorage, Brian asked Carl why take the guy clear to the Valley just to get rid of him? "We don't leave messes where we do business," Carl said, chewing his pipe stem.

This Wade job was turning into a mess, Brian thought. It was just as well that someone else beat Frank and him to it. Hunching his shoulders, Brian glanced around the posh downtown area. He wondered if he'd ever be able to afford the Captain Cook Hotel. The Cook and the downtown Marriott and the Westin or whatever it was called, were the crème de la crème of hotels in Anchorage.

He sighed and returned to his basic worry as he followed Frank into the shop. Carl Clyne wanted the trailer guy gone and neither Brian nor Frank knew why. Brian did know he and his flatulent partner could still find Wade, but assuming Wade was being watched made it harder to get to him.

Maybe Clyne, even with his periodic loss of memory that only Brian seemed to have noticed, had some thoughts about it. Stranger things had happened.

Chapter 19

Anchorage and the Matanuska Valley

Wednesday

Oscar stretched his arms over his head and rotated the kinks out of his neck. Ignoring the scalded smell of Hills Brothers, he refilled his cup from the pot on the stove. Don't pay attention to every little worry, he told himself, still uneasy as he stirred milk into the boiled coffee.

He finished his coffee and put his cup in the sink. He looked outside again, but it was too dark to see the Wright's house or where the Brown's trailer had been. The sky, dark and heavy with un-fallen snow, wasn't helping his mood.

Behind him, Elsie dropped her purse on the table. It was heavy from the .38 that Oscar insisted she carry. *It's better if you have it, I don't want you being alone out there.* He worried about her making that drive to her part-time job at the Grange in Palmer. He had even offered to go with her, but she knew he had a lot to do on the house and she relished her time alone. Then there was the money she earned. He had to admit that in the winter when his work at the Alaska Railroad was slow and his part-time job leasing out big equipment to contractors dried up, what income she brought home was useful.

"Did Wade and Judy reach his relatives?" Oscar said watching her button her coat. Bought at Sally Ann, the coat now sported new, large buttons, all the rage she said when she replaced the original buttons.

Elsie was pulling on her boots and as she straightened, her

face flushed. "He called and told them about Jimmy and the fire." She pulled a red wool cap over her head, and stood for a moment eyeing her husband. Feature by feature, Oscar was gawky, rawboned, even homely in his patched wool shirt and work pants, but people gravitated to his easy smile and something Elsie's sister, Jane, called charisma.

"I'll be home around six, depending on the traffic," she said, reaching for her sack lunch and purse. It was their joke. There was no traffic, at least not what you'd call *traffic*. One could drive for miles and see fewer than half a dozen vehicles. Unpredictable road conditions due to heavy snow, black ice, big rigs cross-wise in the road or in ditches and, of course, moose ambling down the center of the road, were another matter.

Elsie's ancestors believed that naming every worry invited mischievous spirits to make dreaded things happen. Some of her beliefs, however, put a damper on Oscar's normal exuberance. Like the time he'd won a bet on when the ice in Nenana would go out in the spring. He would have talked – okay, *boasted*—about it if not for Elsie's warning: *When something good happens, don't brag about it or it will disappear.*

Of course, bragging, or *sharing the good news,* as Oscar preferred to call it–seemed inevitable. In that case a number of Athabascan words could be used to ward off bad luck. *Hootlani,* uttered juicily with plenty of spit, was a favorite. Oscar had memorized that one.

The sky let loose and snow started falling thick and heavy as Elsie picked her way toward the truck. From a mile up the Seward highway came a mournful chorus of malamutes and huskies. It was feeding time at the Norwood Kennel.

The truck's tires had frozen flat on the bottom and made a hard *flump, flump, flump* as she drove toward the Matanuska Valley, where cabbages grew to the size of wheelbarrows in the summer. The snow had stopped by the time she reached Palmer, one of the two best known towns in the Valley, the other being Wasilla.

She parked behind The Grange's Feed Store where she kept the books and climbed out of the truck, pausing to stretch the kinks from her shoulders. Solitary columns of wood-smoke plumed skyward from chimneys. Soot from distant coal burners sprinkled the snow-covered ground like black pepper. In the distance, the faint shape of the mountains was visible. At 20,320 feet, Denali was the tallest mountain in North America, but the top was seldom seen in the cloud-filled winter.

Despite her wool coat and heavy boots, the air felt icy against her bones as she made her way toward the Grange's door. To her right, a solitary raven chortled and dipped its black wings toward the back of a parked green pickup. A second raven landed with a solid thump on the truck's bed. Must be the remains of a moose under that tarp, Elsie thought. Unlike the ravens, she couldn't smell anything but snow.

She pushed The Grange's heavy door open and was assailed with the familiar odors of old wood, seed, feed, and fertilizer. Today, there was something else and her mouth began to water.

"Hiya Elsie, you're just in time," Harry Grange bellowed. "The wife's baked a pie to celebrate The Grange's tenth anniversary. Get over here before the boys eat it all." Harry's white teeth gleamed beneath the gray bristle of his mustache. His teeth were so perfect Elsie suspected they were false. At fifty, Harry was solidly built and stood several inches over six feet. He had the clear, smooth complexion and thick brown hair of a younger man. His jovial personality concealed a savvy business sense that had kept The Grange running when other businesses had gone under. Elsie shed her coat and tucked her purse inside a drawer.

"Congratulations," she said reaching for a paper plate and dishing up chunks of golden apple oozing from a pale crust.

"To us." Harry gestured to the yard guys, hunched over the counter, forks busy. "We all did it." He included her with a nod as he refilled his mug.

By half past five that afternoon, Harry and crew had left. Elsie was buttoning her coat when the door banged open and Ed Stuart entered with a blast of cold air. His beard was flecked with snow.

"Harry around?" he pulled a handkerchief from his pocket and blew his nose. "My truck broke down."

"He just left." Elsie said, pulling on her gloves. "I think the garage is still open." The garage further up the street stayed open until six o'clock. Ed shook his head. His lips were red and chapped in the nest of his heavy beard.

"I was just there and they're closed…." He sneezed and looked around the empty store. "No one else here, huh?" He sighed and looked at her. "I don't suppose you could give me a lift? I'm just a couple miles over in Wasilla."

Elsie reached for her purse and keys. Oscar was always saying don't pick up strangers, no matter how innocent they look. Still, Alaskans helped one other and it's not like Ed, a customer at the Grange for several years, was a stranger. Would Oscar give Stuart a lift? Of course, silly question.

"Sure," she said, flicking off the lights at the door. She wished she could telephone her husband, but he'd be outside working. Besides, giving Ed a ride wouldn't take long.

Ed pushed open the door and she caught a whiff of his coat —cigarette smoke and machine oil. As she stepped outside, she noticed snow was falling again. In the dim light from the Grange's electric sign, she saw the green truck in the lot. "Is that yours?" she said as they waded through fresh snow to her pickup.

"Yeah, I didn't know where else to leave it." Ed's shoulders were hunched against the cold. His hat flaps hid his face. Elsie wondered what he'd been doing all day that he couldn't get to the garage? When they reached her truck, she climbed in and warmed up the engine, while Ed scraped snow from the windshield.

"Flo, my wife, is getting over the flu," he said, climbing inside and tossing the scraper on the floor as he slammed the door. "I came in to get her prescription refilled and take care of some other business. When I was ready to leave, the truck wouldn't start. It's probably the distributor." He sounded discouraged.

Elsie pulled out of the lot. "You'll have to direct me." A few lights were on at the Palmer hotel. The gas station, she noticed, was closed as he'd said. Leaning forward, Ed peered through the windshield.

"Turn right at the corner." His voice was gravelly, the sound of a smoker. "Then go left at the next intersection." The Chevy's yellow headlights beamed straight ahead, leaving the sides of the road in darkness. There was no other traffic and Elsie kept to the middle of the road. "It's just another couple miles," Ed said, directing her through the second turn. The truck's heater blasted warm air, and the frost in his beard melted and dripped on his canvas coat.

"You have a big place out here?" Elsie kept her tone neutral.

"About ten acres," Ed said. "I've got a few goats, a couple cows. The wife has some chickens. We grow what we need, that's about it." Half hearing him, Elsie relaxed a little. Soon she could turn around and think about what to have for dinner.

Suddenly the steering wheel jerked in an almost convulsive move and the front of the pickup slid off the road. The engine quit and Elsie flipped the ignition off, then on again. Nothing.

"Take your foot off the gas, you'll flood the engine." Ed said opening his door and nearly falling out of the tilted pickup.

She cranked open her window. "There's a board in the back," she yelled.

Ed clumped around to the back pulled out a two-by-six Clyde kept in the back. Minutes later he wedged it beneath the right front tire. In the glare of the headlights, he brushed snow off the grill. At his wave, Elsie turned on the ignition and stepped on the gas. To her relief, the tires caught and Ed motioned her forward. He pushed from the rear while Elsie steered, pumping the gas pedal in short spurts until the pickup lurched back to the road.

Ten minutes later, he directed her to a narrow driveway that led to a single-story farmhouse. "Why don't you come inside, warm up, get some coffee before you head home?"

Hospitality was customary and he probably wanted her to meet his wife. Elsie felt a momentary pang. Trying to sound regretful, she said, "I'm late already and my husband will be worried."

"OK, well, just a minute," Ed said, climbing out of the truck.

"I've got something for Harry you could give him. This will save me a trip."

Puzzled, Elsie watched him head toward his house. *Save him a trip? Didn't he have to go back to the Grange's lot to get his truck?* Lights flickered on in the windows and she tried to think of something else before a flurry of nerves got to her. *What to have for dinner. Let's see, there was some left-over stew, unless Oscar had eaten it for lunch and…* sensing movement on her left, she turned. Ed was looking at her through her side window. He held a rifle.

Chapter 20

Wasilla

Wednesday

"**G**et out!" He yanked her door open. "No more pussyfootin around."

With Ed jabbing her with the rifle, they headed toward the small house. At the door, he reached around Elsie and kicked it open, then they entered a small room. A worn sofa and two chairs were on the right. Straight ahead, Elsie saw a square wooden table and mismatched chairs and beyond that, a single counter with a sink and stove. Off to the left an old white refrigerator hummed.

"Sit over there." He pressed the rifle against her back and shoved her ahead to a chair near the table. The chilly house felt stagnant. In the kitchen, faded yellow linoleum stopped short of the living room, leaving bare plywood skimpily covered by a braided rug. Freezing air snaked through the floor's knotholes, some stuffed with rags.

Elsie felt a sudden flash of rage. *The nerve of this changh!*

He prodded her again with the rifle. Gritting her teeth, she dropped into the chair.

"I'll make some coffee," Ed said, now smiling and revealing small, stained teeth. He set the rifle on a kitchen counter and shrugged off his jacket. His abrupt mood shift startled her and she tried to calm her thudding heart.

Whistling tunelessly, Ed filled a coffee pot with water from a pan on the stove. He doesn't have running water, must be snowmelt, Elsie noted with grim satisfaction.

"Pipes froze," he said, as if reading her mind. The quiet house smelled of burned toast and furnace oil and now, coffee. Faded chintz curtains covered the window over the sink, so possibly a woman lived here. If so, where was she? When the coffee burbled, Ed filled two mugs and carried them to the table.

"You take milk? Sugar?" Not trusting her voice, Elsie shook her head, no. When he turned to get the cookies, she slid her hand into her bag and released the gun's safety. God knows she didn't want to use it, but Oscar was always saying be prepared.

Ed hadn't lived in the country for over ten years without developing a sixth sense. Now, almost thoughtfully, he set the cookies back on the counter and reached for his rifle. Watching him, Elsie panicked. Scrambling to her feet, her chair toppled.

"Hey!" Ed gaped at the .38 wobbling in her hands. Holding the rifle away from his body, he stepped back. The strap of Elsie's bag had caught on one of her coat's large buttons and the bag swung from her hand.

The movement startled her and her fingers tightened. A sound roared. Stunned, Elsie stared at Ed. Had she shot him? He looked at her, his eyes wide. His dirty white undershirt, visible beneath his plaid wool shirt, turned pink. "I didn't … scare you, is all…" Ed slid to the floor, his head thudding against the table leg.

Elsie backed away, her ears ringing. After a moment, she saw the faint rise and fall of his chest. *Oh, thank God, he's alive. I didn't kill him,* Gripping the back of a kitchen chair, she tried to slow her breathing.

After a moment she became aware of something behind her. Turning she saw a woman so thin Elsie could almost see through her. She wore a nightgown but in the dim light, her features were indistinct. Behind her, Elsie saw the door she had passed earlier. It was now open.

"Is he dead?" The woman's voice was faint and her long white fingers were bent with arthritis.

Suddenly shivering, Elsie grabbed her bag from the floor and moved back toward the door. "No, I don't know, I don't think so." The woman shuffled past Elsie toward the kitchen table. Her bony shoulders under her ragged gown grew more visible. She trailed a musty odor.

"Are you Flo?" Even in the poor light, Elsie could see the glittering misery in the woman's ravaged face. "I'm sorry, I'm so sorry," Elsie blurted. *Lord, she had just shot this woman's husband.*

The woman didn't answer. Gripping the table for support, she leaned over and picked up the rifle where Ed had dropped it.

"Now it's my turn," she muttered.

Chapter 21

The front door banged open and wind gusted inside, fluttering the curtains and riffling the week-old newspapers on the sofa. The truck's engine coughed to life eagerly, as if happy to leave this place and Elsie's headlights flashed through the front window across the living room wall. Her lights receded as she backed out of the drive way leaving the kitchen shadowed in sour yellow light from an old ceiling fixture dotted with dead flies.

Flo's arms trembled as the rifle butt slid to the floor. In the sudden quiet, she lifted her head, waiting. The smell of gunpowder hung in the air with the tang of fear and brutal rage. But she had no sense of Ed's presence. Not yet. Not the way she had felt the presence of her two sons after Ed was done with them.

She started breathing again. Thank the Lord that woman was gone. Flo worried she might faint. She would have had to kill her too and Ed's body was enough. *There were too many bodies.*

She looked at her husband, his blood adding to the stains on the yellow linoleum. The once cheerful yellow had worn out to gray after so many scrubbings, so much blood.

When Flo and Ed were first married, she was so relieved to have a home for her sons that she had brushed off any hint of future problems. For a long time, she made excuses to her sister and friends. She lied about her battered face and Ed's unpredictable temper and her constant lack of money.

The last incident when her boys were still alive was almost the worst. Ed had stomped outside, slamming the kitchen door. Flo tried to lift her head. Her left eye was nearly shut and her nose felt crushed as she tried to breathe. She wheezed through her torn mouth that dripped blood down the side of her cheek. "Mom, let's get out of here," Jack said. He was crying and gripping her sleeve. With her right eye she glimpsed his feet. His shoes were worn through. Ed said there was no money for shoes, but she had seen all that cash. Where had it come from? What was he doing with it?

Ted, her older son, was holding his right arm awkwardly and the crotch of his pants was wet. Then she remembered Ed swinging a scrap of lumber at the boy.

"We can't stay here." Ted's voice shook as she struggled to sit up. Tears streaked his dusty cheeks and his voice broke. "Please, Mom." Sunlight danced through the window and across the spattered floor. *Where could we go she wondered?*

A week later, the tractor flipped and killed Ted. Flo knew Ed had rigged it. Then her younger son, Jack died. And even though the doctor and police told her that Jack's death was an accident, she knew something they didn't. Ed was a chemist. He had a science degree from the University of Pennsylvania. And he was careful. Worse, no autopsy was required in what the troopers called accidental deaths.

The authorities thought she was hysterical when she kept screaming about lions and how the male killed the cubs spawned by another male. Ed was like that lion she told them. Her sons we by her first husband and Ed hated not having been the first. He wanted her to have his sons. *His sons.*

She remembered how the Troopers had looked at her, shaking their heads. They had sent for Ed and suggested he take her to a psychiatrist. He did. He found a genial man who pretended to listen then gave her a prescription for pills to calm her nerves. All they did was make her sleep.

Tonight, the one-sided conversation from the kitchen had roused her from bed. In the dim light, Ed was by the stove and the woman was at the table. They didn't see her. The woman was

Native and nicely dressed. The scene felt almost sociable. Until Ed picked up the rifle from the counter. Flo wanted to yell at the woman to run, to get out, but her throat was too dry, she could only make a feeble croak. Then suddenly the woman was out of her chair and Flo heard the gun and saw Ed sink to the floor.

She didn't remember walking across the room or picking up the rifle. She did remember looking down at him, his head tipped to the side, the struggling rise and fall of his chest. She felt the years of fear and rage unraveling in her gut.

"I'm sorry, boys," she whispered. "I should have done this a long time ago."

The next morning, Flo went to the shed behind the house. The night before, she had dragged Ed's body and left it by his worktable with its arrangement of well-cared-for tools. It never failed to amaze her, Ed's workspace was so neatly arranged compared to the messes he left in the house.

Now, she pulled up the loosened floorboards. Beneath the boards and a thin layer of grime was Elaine's slender figure wrapped in an old sheet. Ed had said he didn't mean to hurt Elaine. He just wanted her to stop yelling when he'd grabbed her. But Flo knew better. After his *moments*, which always involved sex, he strutted around, full of himself, like that rooster with the hens out back.

Sweating and increasingly furious with herself for not having had the gumption to get out when her sons were alive, she tried to stomp his body into the crowded grave. Rigor and freezing temperature had stiffened his body, but she persisted. By noon, it was done. Propping her hands on her knees, she leaned forward to catch her breath. Despite the chill, sweat ran down her back and strands of gray-blond hair stuck to her face. The long hair Ed twisted around his fingers when he pushed inside her. The hair she hated.

In her growing rage, she didn't hear the SUV pull up outside. Nor did she see the State Trooper standing in the shed's doorway, staring at her and the hole she was covering with floorboards.

Chapter 22

Anchorage

Friday

"Hey Paul, you gotta minute?" Oscar said when his brother-in-law opened the door. Oscar had to talk to someone and Paul was the most close-mouthed guy around. Plus, he and Jane would want to protect Elsie.

"You bet," Paul said, stepping back and closing the door behind Oscar. "Want some coffee?"

"Naw, I'm coffeed out." Oscar said as he sat at the table across from his brother-in-law. He took a breath. "Do you know anyone named Stuart, Ed Stuart, lives in Wasilla?" He leaned forward, elbows on knees and studied his laced-up boots.

"Well, there's Stewart's Photo," Paul said, slowly. "I don't know any other Stewart."

"Naw, not that one," Oscar said, sitting up and stretching his back. His eyes half closed.

Paul studied his brother-in-law and was surprised to see how gray his hair was. Jimmy's death, he thought. His own hair would probably be gray too, if he'd had any hair. But Paul had been bald since he was in his twenties. "What happened?"

Oscar hunched forward again and told Paul everything, from what had happened to Elsie and to his drive to Palmer to talk to Harry, Elsie's boss at The Grange.

"You didn't tell Harry what happened to Elsie and this Ed?

"No, no." Oscar shuddered. "I just said she wasn't feeling too good and would probably be back to work next week." He looked at Paul's mug and said, "Think I'll take that coffee." After Paul had filled a second cup and topped off his own, he sat down and Oscar picked up where he'd left off.

"Harry and I got to talking. I said I'd seen Ed's truck in The Grange's lot and wondered if Ed was thinking about selling his. That's when Harry told me what the troopers had found at Ed's place. Looks like, for a few years, Ed Stuart's been bumping off guys and even a neighbor woman from up the road."

"Do you think he was working for someone? You don't find guys knocking off folks for free."

Oscar shook his head. "Not unless he's crazy."

"What did Oscar want?" Jane had just gotten home from visiting a neighbor and had seen Clyde leave.

"After we eat," he said, filling the kettle for tea. He knew as soon as he told her, she would run over and see Elsie.

Jane saw him glance at their daughter, Kena who was setting the table, and nodded. Kena was curious and sometimes alarmed her parents with how much she understood. After lunch of split pea soup and cold chicken, Paul sent Kena outdoors. Then he told Jane about the shooting.

"Oh no," she moaned, leaning forward. Tears streamed down her face. *Her baby sister had shot a man.* Paul reached over to grasp her hand.

"The police found Stuart's wife trying to bury him in a shed and that's where they found several other bodies… Main thing is, the Troopers don't know Elsie was there and Stuart's wife is, well, she's not talking sense."

"What do you mean 'not talking sense'?" Jane pulled a tissue from under her sleeve and blew her nose.

Paul shook his head. "Apparently, Ed, her husband used her as a punching bag and the Troopers couldn't get anything coherent out of her. Some of her bruises were pretty old."

"Elsie will be fine," Paul added. Jane looked ready to slide to the floor. "Oscar will make sure of that."

"How can he make sure she'll be fine?" Jane cleared her throat and dabbed her eyes. In her family, Jane was the oldest. It had always been her job to take care of her younger sisters and brothers.

He peeled the plastic from a toothpick and rolled it around in his mouth. "You know how stubborn your sister is. Oscar says she's pretty determined to go back to work. He doesn't want her to, but if she does, whatever talk there is, she'll hear it."

Chapter 23

Anchorage

Friday

"Why didn't you tell me what happened?" Jane's eyes were tearing up again and she blew her nose. She had hiked over to Oscar and Elsie's house on the narrow path she and Elsie had beaten into existence with shovels, and laying scrap lumber over the swampy spots of the two acres between their houses.

"You better not have had any beers or you'll fall on your ass," Paul had muttered when he first navigated the roots and haphazardly-placed boards. Now everything was frozen so even if Jane slid off the boards, she wouldn't sink to China as Paul liked to tease.

Elsie leaned back on her lumpy sofa from Sally Ann. It was covered with a bedspread and the fringe dragged on the floor. "Oscar didn't want me to tell anyone until he could find out what happened," she said.

In the dim light, Jane had never seen her younger sister so exhausted. She leaned over to pick up a wad of cat fur from the braided rag rug. It had irritated her ever since she arrived. "How did he go about learning anything with you not there? Wouldn't that have looked suspicious?"

Elsie exhaled and shook her head. "He had some fool story in case anyone asked, that I wasn't feeling good and that he wanted to buy a pickup he'd seen advertised in the newspaper." She shut her eyes and put her head back against the sofa.

Jane sat back, and thought. The kitchen area to her left smelled of roasting meat. A few brown potatoes beginning to sprout lay on the kitchen table near a knife. She sniffed, her mouth salivating. "You get a moose?"

Elsie blinked and nodded. "A friend of Oscar's got two."

"Are you sure you want to go back to work so soon?" Jane said. Her sister's lethargy worried her. Elsie nodded, her mouth firm, but Jane saw her hand tremble as she lifted her cup of coffee.

"Do you remember the medicine man, the one who helped Mom before she died?"

Accustomed to her sister's abrupt shifts, Jane nodded. "Sure. Sam Tallwell, he lives in Goldspring? He's a *deeyninh*."

Elsie's dark eyes bored into her sister's. "I need to see him."

Chapter 24

Anchorage Alaska Railroad

Saturday

The train to Goldspring pulled away from Anchorage's termi-nal, swaying and clanking as it gathered speed. In the passenger car, a faint smell of diesel clung to the upholstered seats even as cold air rushed in through a partly open window.

Kena pressed her face against the glass, watching trees, tarpaper covered sheds, and the occasional moose flash by. Minutes later the whistle blew and they crossed a bridge spanning a canyon. Far below them, black water churned through broken ice.

"Woe be it to you, if you fall through that," Jane said, looking through the window. Kena shivered. She was thrilled to be on the train, going somewhere. Anywhere.

"How is Aunt Lucy doing?" Jane had heard about Herb's death and had visited Julie Ashenberg in the hospital in Anchorage.

"Lucy sounded better when I called. I think she's looking forward to having us spend a couple of nights with her," Elsie said. "We might even see Cara. She's been visiting Lucy almost every other day."

"Is she still seeing that pilot, what's his name?"

Elsie shook her head. "I've forgotten, but Lucy said that seems to be over." Jane raised an eyebrow.

"Cara really liked him."

"She's a lovely girl," Elsie said, her voice drifting.

"Of course," Jane said, fluffing her hair. "She looks just like me."

"Yeah, well, when you were her age, maybe." Elsie gave her forty- five-year old sister a look.

Chapter 24

Goldspring

Thursday Morning

Sam clumped around his small house, his boots unlaced, waiting for Connie to leave for work. She was running late this morning. He glanced at the kitchen clock that was spattered with Crisco. Thank god his grandkids had already left for school.

"I'm going now, Dad," Connie said, pulling a crocheted wool cap over her hair. "Anything special you want for dinner?" Her bag bulged with her lunch, a book to read during her break and her indoor shoes. Watching him, she hovered, trying to be upbeat.

"No, no," Sam waved his hand as he wandered back to his bedroom. He hadn't cared what he'd eaten for so long, he didn't remember when he had last enjoyed a meal. Between the cancer and his heart medications, food tasted like sawdust.

Finally, the door banged shut behind her and Sam felt his shoulders relax. He just had to make the tea and write his letters. He had the ingredients. The tea wouldn't kill him; just relax him. Of course, so would a bottle of Seagram's or vodka. He had considered lacing the tea with whiskey, but he didn't want to get tipsy before leaving this world. Maybe it wouldn't matter, but he wanted to face it head-on, not drunk. Anyway, it was forty-five below and that alone should finish him off when he went outside to lay down in the shed, even if it took a few hours.

The letters for his daughter and Ruby took time to compose. Sam was just finishing them when he heard footsteps, then a knock on the door. Peeking through the window, he saw two well-dressed Native women standing inside his storm porch. Behind them, he saw Lucy's old Mercury Cougar. *I'll be damned.*

He let the curtain fall back. It had been years since he had seen Fanny. He was surprised to recognize her daughters. Crap, what were they doing here now?

With a sigh, he opened the door.

"Hi Sam!" Jane smiled, stomping the snow from her boots. Elsie was standing to Lily's left. She was pale, but she caught his attention. She looked like she had seen death. The women stood awkwardly on either side of a galvanized tub on the front steps. It held the hide of a gray wolf frozen almost solid in tanning solution. Behind them stood a young Native girl with pale eyes and a grave expression.

Sam stepped back and motioned them inside. This had better be quick or they'd screw up his timetable. Yet, he had to admit that seeing them was like seeing Fannie back when they were cocky with youth and sexy as rabbits; before the rub of life had worn them down like that wolf pelt in the tub.

Jane glanced at Elsie as they took off their coats. "We need to talk to you." Well shit, Sam thought, waving them toward the sofa.

Jane's nose twitched. Sam's cabin smelled of moose meat, sauerkraut, stale cigarettes and coffee. Lily noticed the bottle of whiskey on the table. She knew Sam had cancer, so any pain remedy was understandable. He certainly didn't look good. His skin was gray and he was almost skeletal, his face bone-sharp. Hardly any wrinkles, she noted. Good, tough Indian skin. And he still had hair. Of course, there weren't many bald Indians around. Like none. She glanced at Elsie who had also seen the whiskey.

Sam settled on the sofa and studied his guests. Elsie had perched at the opposite end of the sofa with the girl next to her while Jane took the red vinyl chair. After some hesitation, Jane began telling him about the neighbor boy, Jimmy's death. This roused Elsie who was not to be outtalked no matter how bleary she felt. She told him about giving Ed, a white man, a ride then being forced into his house and shooting him and finally, fleeing from his wife who had a rifle.

Dumfounded, Sam stared at them.

What was it his father used to say? *You don't have to answer all the questions. You don't have to solve any problems. What you do is settle the spirits and restore peace. Only then will the answers come.*

He struggled to his feet and retrieved a bundle of sage from a kitchen drawer. After lighting it, he and waved it around the small room until the fragrant smoke thickened. When everyone's eyes began to water, Sam opened the window. "Just enough to let in the air...."

"Now, we can work," he said.

With the smoke swirling around them, Sam began beating a flat drum. Then he started chanting.

Chapter 25

Leaving Goldspring

Sunday

"What did he say when he was speaking Indian, yesterday?" Kena swung her legs as she tried to get comfortable on the train seat made for taller people. Much of what Sam had said was in Koyukon, one of the Athabascan dialects. Kena had already learned some of what Sam had chanted that evening when her mother and Elsie were with Aunt Lucy and most everyone spoke English.

Jane shook her head. "When he was singing he was calling the spirits to help him and help Elsie. Beyond that, I don't know. Mom spoke Indian. She would have known."

"It was so smoky. Was that to call the spirits too?" Kena's hair still smelled like smoke and would until she washed it. Jane shrugged.

"I think it was to add to the ambiance. What do you think Elsie?"

Kena knew she'd have to look up "ambiance" at home. Her mother was always sending her to the dictionary when they spoke.

The train rattled and vibrated as it came to a stop in Fairbanks to pick up and drop off passengers. It started again and Kena watched through the window as the small houses disappeared and there were only trees, mountains, and rivers; and animals foraging for food.

What had he said when he was chanting, she wondered? At least Aunt Elsie was more relaxed today and her skin and eyes were clear.

Jane chewed her lip and looked at her sister. "Did you understand him?" she asked again. The train rounded a corner and Jane and Elsie braced for the turn. Elsie grinned.

"I caught a swear word or two when the fire didn't catch."

Jane laughed. "*Chaunghnaha!*" A Native family across the aisle grinned and nudged one another.

Before leaving Goldspring, Elsie had filled the thermos with tea while Aunt Lucy, as she was known to everyone, wrapped cheese and peanut butter sandwiches and salmon strips in foil. Once on board, Elsie hoisted their bags on the shelf above their seats while Jane helped her daughter, Kena. This was the most energy Elsie had shown since she'd shot Ed Stuart.

"What did Lucy tell you?" Jane said, with a quick glance at Kena. The girl seemed riveted on the rushing water breaking through the river ice below and Jane relaxed.

Elsie thought for a moment. "She said Sam had given Herb something called a Ravenstone and Cara is looking for it"

Jane frowned. "Why Cara? It's a police issue, isn't it?" Jane had always thought Cara was too curious for her own safety. If only Cara would give up journalism, get married, and settle down.

Elsie's head was still foggy from the session with Sam and she had to concentrate. "I think Ron and Ian are helping the Troopers. Cara wants to find out who killed Herb and she thinks the Ravenstone might lead to that."

Jane thought. "Did Ron seem nervous to you?" The Village Public Safety Officer was visiting Lucy when Jane, Elsie and Kena returned from seeing Sam.

"Ron, nervous? No, I don't think so. Why do you ask?" But as Elsie thought about it, Ron did seem to be more on edge. Darn it, so much was going on.

The train whistle blew and minutes later they slowed to a stop where freight was removed. Then they were off again. Overhead, a red hawk flew low, searching the ground. A flock of ravens surrounded it, cawing loudly, chasing it away.

Elsie opened the thermos, releasing the aroma of tea and got out their sandwiches and slices of yellow cake Aunt Lucy had made. Soon she and Jane were chatting about relatives and family gossip.

She divorced him when she found out about him fiddling with those boys and the judge granted her all his property. To a Native woman! That's a first!

Uh huh, but she knew that judge hated her husband.

Even so, a Native woman winning in court! That'll go down in history...

Chapter 25

Fairbanks

Monday

Phil pulled up outside his apartment in Fairbanks and left his Honda running as he sat back and tried to think. At least Connie had stopped talking about marriage so he didn't have to tell her he was Sam's son and therefor her half-brother.

His mother, Eliza was Tlingit and lived in Juneau with her fourth husband and their three daughters. Back in the early sixties when she was enrolled at the University of Alaska in Fairbanks, Eliza met Sam who, she told Phil, had sweet-talked her and gotten her pregnant. She never told Sam, but had simply returned to Juneau and given birth to Phil, her only son.

After he moved to Fairbanks to do postgraduate work in Anthropology, he learned Sam Tallman had a daughter named Connie. A few months later, he met Connie through a mutual acquaintance. She took his attentiveness in stride, which, accustomed to female attention surprised him. He wondered if she already knew he was her half-brother? But he stayed in touch, curious about his father. Through Connie he got acquainted with Sam and learned more about the Ravenstone. Enough for him to talk to his department head, Professor Skarfeld, about it.

A few months lapsed and over drinks at the Elbow Room in Fairbanks, he suggested to Skarfeld and his journalist friend at the Fairbanks Goldstar that the newspaper should do a special in their Sunday edition on Athabascan *baat's* or stone amulets.

Three months later the Goldstar featured the Ravenstone and other historical Alaska Native talismans in their monthly special edition. Unfortunately, one result of this article led to a break-in at Sam's house. That's when Phil decided to try to talk to Sam and let him know he was Eliza's son.

A few days before Thanksgiving, he told Sam that he could make sure the amulet was loaned to the right people at the university. Sam, however, had done his own research and learned that Phil was a graduate student and not a professor as he'd originally presented himself. Wondering what else Phil had lied about, Sam muttered something in Koyukon, his tone and body language not flattering.

After Herb was killed, Phil approached Sam again. Phil figured someone had to know where the Ravenstone was and Sam must at least have a hunch. But the old guy was weary and he again lapsed into Koyukon and literally turned his back on Phil.

This time something snapped inside the anthropologist and to his own horror, he hit the old *deeyninh*, "You no good son of a bitch, you won't even help me, your son!" he screamed at the Deeyninh

Knocked to the floor and caught by surprise, Sam had stared at Phil. After a long moment, he whispered. "You're Eliza's boy?

Sam's head lolled to the side and he seemed to lose consciousness. Panicked, Phil grabbed a mug of coffee from the footlocker and poured it over Sam's face. When there was no response Phil tried to remember the CPR he had been taught. But after twenty minutes, with no reaction from Sam, he stopped. He was shaking and nearly crying.

Chapter 26

Anchorage

Monday Carl and Wade

By six o'clock that afternoon, Wade, whose recurring thoughts of Jimmy and his wife Judy nearly brought him to tears, had a feeling his trysts with Val were coming to an end. For one thing, he had a funny feeling he was being watched. Twice he'd seen the same guy outside on the sidewalk, peering inside the garage. He knew the police had been keeping an eye on him, but this guy was well-dressed and older and didn't look young enough to be a cop.

He wondered if it wasn't time to find another job or even move to another town. Then there was Val, talking about how he was now a free man, which puzzled him since she was married and certainly not free.

He didn't feel free. He couldn't bring himself to talk about it, but he carried a lot of grief over Jimmy. Poor kid didn't deserve to die, especially, not in that sickening blaze. And Judy! He'd give a lot to get her back, he'd begged her not to leave.

"It's not forever," she had said, picking up her suitcase. "I just can't be here now."

He wiped his hands on a clean rag and flipped the OPEN sign to CLOSED. His stomach growled and he thought he'd stop by the Nugget café and get a London Broil. He'd been eating his own cooking since Judy left and had lost over ten pounds. Enough was enough.

Carl sat in his rental car outside Mac's Garage with the engine and heater periodically running. He had called the garage earlier and heard the answering machine give the garage's hours. At nine o'clock that morning, he had watched a redheaded woman enter the garage's office. She looked familiar, but he couldn't place where he'd seen her.

Now, at 5:30, it was black outside, with only a few streetlights and nearby shops still lit. He wished he'd had Frank or Brian to help. He was getting too old for this.

Chapter 27

Goldspring

Friday

"I was driving by Herb's house and saw Ron's SUV," Lucy said. "Course I had to ask him what he was doing, he doesn't tell me everything. He didn't say anything about his new girlfriend. I had to find out about her from Ethel." She took a sip of Earl Gray before continuing. "Anyway, he said he was looking for the Ravenstone."

Cara heard the smile in Lucy's voice. Ah, small towns; no secrets.

After they hung up, Cara called Ron and told him about her visit with Sam and Connie Tallwell. "I just talked to Lucy. She said you were at Herb's house, looking for the Ravenstone?"

"Yeah well, she probably told you I couldn't find it," Ron's heart speeded up again. He had hoped it would be a few weeks— if ever—before anyone connected the Ravenstone to the murders.

"I want to take a look," Cara said, picking at the crumbs of her cinnamon roll. Something dropped behind Ron and he turned to look. Cindy, his latest girlfriend, was loading the tape player. Oh crap, she was mixing his jazz tapes with Linda Ronstadt.

Cara heard a woman's voice in the background and grinned. Ron and his girls: all cute, curvy, and as interchangeable as tee shirts.

"Anyway," Cara continued, "Thomlin said he's through with the Ashenbergs' cabin. It's OK if I want to take another look. With you, of course," she added.

"We looked in the cache, we looked EVERYWHERE." Ron caught himself. "But sure, if you want to take a look just let me know when."

Chapter 28

Fairbanks to Goldspring

Saturday

Cara looked through the plane's weather-scarred window at the rapidly-approaching trees and narrow runway, and braced her legs as the ten-passenger aircraft touched down. It bounced and touched again before rolling toward the one-story terminal painted a drab olive green. The color reminded her of the military and their bases spread throughout Alaska. In the distance she saw Ron's dark blue Bronco pull into the parking lot.

"What made you fly this time? Come into some money?" Ron climbed into the driver's seat and Cara fastened her seat belt, a habit from living in Fairbanks. No one buckled up in Goldspring.

"Don't I wish," she said, patting her pocket in search of her other glove. "The road is too icy and flying is faster." She didn't tell him about the free trip she'd won in a lottery last July at the fair. Nor did she mention that driving the ice-slick stretch from Fairbanks and back for a third time in almost as many days was more than she wanted to deal with. The flight took 30 minutes max and she didn't want to push her car beyond its limits, let alone out of a ditch. She couldn't afford for anything to happen to it now.

Ron pulled out of the lot, his winter tires humming over the snow-caked road. He kept his speed at a minimum. It was too easy to hit a patch of ice and spin off the road or see a moose on the road and be unable to stop.

"What's Thomlin's take on this?" Cara suspected the trooper had said more to Ron. Unable to find her glove, she slid her right hand under her thigh for warmth.

"He's waiting for the Medical Examiner's report and hasn't said much. But I *can* tell you what he found when they were here." Ron glanced over to make sure he had her attention. "They used dental stone powder and water on some tracks in the snow. They weren't Herb's." Ron looked at her again. "They found fresh blood behind the house near the chopping block."

Cara grimaced at the image and turned toward the side window. The ghostly shape of a tree limb, heavy with snow loomed through the heavy fog. Suddenly, the limb plunged to the ground with a sharp crack that sounded like a gunshot.

"Trees exploding," Ron said, wishing he hadn't mentioned the blood and the chopping block.

"What causes that; trees exploding?" Cara asked, eager to change the subject.

"Moisture inside the tree freezes and expands, but the bark is dry and frozen and can't expand. Pretty soon, kerploohey! That's the scientific explanation anyway." Ron wiggled an eyebrow at her and she smiled. He wasn't sure if what he'd said was true, but at least it distracted her.

There was no other traffic and they passed a cow moose and her calf munching bark from a tree limb. Ron steered off the road onto a less bumpy narrow drive, nearly hidden in the fog.

"I wonder where they got the snowmobile? What do you bet they stole it?"

Ron looked at her, startled. "How did you know about that?"

"I saw the tracks. They were everywhere and Herb's was still in the shed." She dug in another pocket for a tissue and found her glove.

"The snow machine belongs to the Gordon's. He reported it missing when they got back from Hawaii. It turned up behind that empty house next door. He thinks some kids took it for a joyride." Ron paused. "The Troopers looked at it. I don't think they found anything." He pulled up and parked in front of the Ashenberg's place.

As she got out of the Bronco, Cara looked toward Aunt Lucy's house, almost hidden in the ice fog. She wished she could talk Lucy into staying with her in Fairbanks.

Inside the house, Julie's pitiful collection of clothing hung neatly behind the pink sheet tied back with a purple bow that had started life on a SEES candy-box. A faded pink and yellow flowered quilt remained on her single bed beneath a shelf holding a boom box and a dozen or so tapes that ranged from the Supremes to the Doors to hip-hop and a few newer artists Cara had never heard of.

On the top of a small chest of drawers, lay a wolf pendent on a chain, a string of purple beads and a beaded hair clip. A wave of grief suddenly hit Cara and she sank down on the bed. Her gaze fell again on the jewelry on top of the chest of drawers. As she sat staring at it, she realized something was missing. Where was Julie's gold locket?

Aunt Lucy had given Julie the locket for her eighth-grade graduation. Then Cara remembered seeing two plain silver rings on Julie's long, slim fingers. Pushing herself off the bed, she looked underneath it and found a lone sock. Then she went to the chest of drawers and began looking through the folded tee shirts, underwear, and sweaters. She pulled out each drawer, then pulled the entire chest from the wall and checked the back. Only dust motes and three bobby pins: no jewelry, no Ravenstone.

She could hear Ron in the living room, pulling books from the case and putting them back. Giving the chest of drawers a final look, she joined him. "I can't find Julie's gold locket or her silver rings."

"I'll tell Thomlin," Ron said. "He can check the pawnshops in Fairbanks. Herb's rifle is still on the wall and it's loaded, so it doesn't look like robbery was a motive."

Cara glanced at the desk. It was a mahogany veneered three-drawer model with an extra-wide drawer at the top. "You checked this?" she said, opening the top drawer.

"Yeah I did, but have at it," Ron said, turning toward Herb's bedroom. As Cara shuffled through papers, she found utility statements and correspondence with relatives who had moved to Georgia. Stationary, legal sized envelopes, and a dusty address book that looked like it hadn't been used in years were in the side drawers. The bottom file drawer held reams of paper for a printer. Cara looked around. "Did the troopers take Julie's laptop and printer?"

Ron was now crouched behind a bookcase he'd pulled away from the wall. "I don't think so, I didn't know she had a computer and printer."

"Aunt Lucy gave her both last Christmas."

"I'll ask Thomlin," Ron opened a manila folder. "Here's something. It's his pay stubs," Ron said, flipping through the contents.

"Why didn't the troopers find it?" Cara peered over Ron's shoulder at the amount, $500.

"Maybe they did and left it – it's not evidence of anything except what he earned."

"That's his net?" Cara said, looking over his arm. "$500 a month is what, $6,000 a year?"

"Not much for two people, especially when one is a teenager." Ron frowned. "What other income would he have had?"

"Aunt Lucy should know if he had another job."

Back outside, they tramped through the snow scouting Herb's five-acre property. Their breath fogged in the freezing air and Cara's breath froze on her glasses. She took them off and turned away from the bloody chopping block when they passed it. The hinges on the shed's door squealed loudly when Ron tugged it open. He gave Cara his flashlight while he climbed the shaky ladder to the cache.

"He got his moose," Ron called down, peering inside. He would see about donating the meat to needy families.

"I thought you'd been here before?" Cara called to him.

"Just with the troopers and they checked this out."

"Well, let's go over to Lucy's and warm up," she said, stamping her feet. Jeeze, she was freezing. "And get something hot to drink."

Back in Lucy's kitchen, Cara peeled off her gloves, her ten-year-old lynx hat, heavy sweater, and fleece vest. This left a red turtleneck over thermal underwear. She had shed her boots and one of three pairs of socks. Feeling ten pounds lighter and almost naked, Cara piled everything except her boots on a nearby chair.

As she always did when stressed, Lucy was hovering over her thirty-five-year-old G.E. range, baking. The small yellow and white kitchen smelled like apples and fresh bread.

Pushing grizzly thoughts of Herb's chopping block out of her mind, Cara steeled herself against the onslaught of baked bread. It was easy to pig out on Lucy's bread, especially when slathered with the blueberry preserves Cara had helped put up last summer.

"Herb helped out at the retirement center, cleaning up and clearing the walkway, stuff like that," Lucy said. "I don't know what or if they paid him, but he could sure pinch pennies. He was determined to get Julie into the university."

"Couldn't she get student aid from Doyon?" Cara referred to the Native Corporation Herb and Julie belonged to.

"I think she qualifies for a scholarship, but Herb never said and I didn't think to ask. Anyway, sit!" she said, waving them to the kitchen table. "Wasn't there an article in the Fairbanks Goldstar about the Ravenstone?"

Cara nodded as she buttered a chunk of steaming bread and added a dollop of jam. "Sam said there was an article in a Sunday edition about a month ago. It included photographs!" She grinned. "He was pleased. He said the Ravenstone looked like a smudge." While Cara was talking, Ron polished off three slices of bread topped with cheddar.

"You ought to talk to Ruby Gordon," Aunt Lucy said, adding tiny marshmallows to her cocoa. "She's ninety if she's a day. Won't tell her age, probably doesn't know it. Anyway, I think she and Sam once had a thing." Lucy's old white cardigan was spotted with batter, but every hair on her head was in place. Cara's eyes watered and she yawned. "Don't fall asleep." Lucy said, holding out of pot of coffee. Cara raised her cup, It still had a little cocoa in it. Lucy knew she liked them mixed and shoved the cocoa tin toward Cara.

"Ruby lives in Goldspring?" Cara didn't recognize the name.

Lucy nodded as she filled Ron's mug. Smelling the fresh coffee, he sat up.

"She's from Galena, but she moved here to be with her granddaughter." Lucy cocked an eye at her niece. "You might know her, Rebecca? She married Joe Hebstrong." Now there was a name Cara recognized. She had dated Joe in high school. A tall, part Athabascan guy. Very good looking. On the order of Montgomery Clift.

"Isn't Ruby a medicine woman?" Ron said, stifling a yawn. He already knew she was, but wanted them to know he was awake.

"Sure, Sam probably thought she'd die before him. Maybe that's why he didn't give her the Ravenstone." Lucy snorted. "You know, I think only men are supposed to use it. I mean if it went from Red Shirt to his nephew, then to Herb… Maybe it's *enjee* for women," she said using the Athabascan word for bad luck. She reached for the phone. "You should talk to Ruby before you leave. I'll see if she's home."

As it turned out, Ruby was home, and Ron and Cara wearily pulled back on their heavy clothes and climbed back into his Explorer.

"Joe Hebstrong built a two-room addition to the house he inherited from his parents," Ron told Cara as they drove. "He and Rebecca had a couple of kids and Ruby was moving in with them. They needed the space." Cara gripped the handle above the door to brace herself as the SUV bounced over the ridged ice and gravel. When they pulled up in front of the house, she saw what Ron meant.

"Wow, five people live there?" She stared at the cabin. It looked no more than 700 square feet, if that. It was smaller than her house in Fairbanks.

"No choice in the matter," Ron said.

Cara paused. "How's Ruby's health?

He sighed. "Joe says she's deaf in one ear and her eyesight's weak, but she's sharp as a tack and loves to talk." Talky women bugged him. He opened his door and got out. "Here goes."

Chapter 29

Goldspring

Ruby opened the door and peered at them before waving them inside. "Wondered how long it would take you to come see me," she said, grinning. She was missing two teeth and unselfconscious about it. The front door opened into the kitchen that felt boiling hot to Cara. She and Ron quickly shed their parkas, hats and gloves and everything else they had just put back on at Lucy's. Cara wondered if Joe was here. She hadn't seen him in years. Their parting had been friendly and she had sometimes wondered what would have happened if she hadn't left for graduate school in Washington.

"He's not here," Ruby said, looking at Cara. "Just me, but I'm all you need for what you want to know." She laughed at Cara's startled expression and flapped her arms. The sleeves of her oversized sweater had been rolled up to her elbows. Now they unrolled down to her knees. Cara glanced at Ron who was grinning.

"What we'd like to know, auntie," he said, "is have you heard of anything called the Ravenstone? It's an old Athabascan ceremonial object that Sam Tallwell may have given to Herb for safekeeping. It disappeared when Herb was..." Ruby impatiently flapped her sleeves at him.

"Course I know about it! He should've come to me, I'da taken care of it, but old Sam couldn't let a woman take it. It's because we broke up and he's not forgiven me." Without her teeth, her laugh was like a cackle.

"When was this?" Cara said, sensing she'd have to fight to get a word in.

"Well, it was before he and Fanny got together, but I had him first and I was fourteen and he was fifteen and I'm 89 now, so you figure it out." She grinned again and Cara smiled. She liked this woman.

As they drove back to the terminal and Cara's flight back to Fairbanks, she and Ron were quiet. "What a day this has been," she said, finally. "You didn't tell me she could read minds!"

Ron smiled as he turned into the terminal's parking lot.

Wiggling his eyebrows, he said, "So you had a thing with Joe, huh?"

Chapter 30

Goldspring

Saturday

Brian peered at the gas gage. It was over half full, more than enough to reach Ashenberg's place and get back to Fairbanks. "We've got gas, so what's the problem?" He stomped on the gas again and got a high-pitched whine. He slipped the gear into neutral, popped the hood and climbed out. It looked all right to him, but what did he know about cars? Boats he knew; cars, he didn't. He jerked his chin toward the small gray house behind a few scraggly trees. "I'll see if they'll let us use their phone." His cellphone had died. He also had to pee. If no one was home, he'd use the backyard.

Hugging himself against the cold, he said, "Why don't you go on up to Ashenberg's place and check around back… he must have stashed it somewhere before we saw him."

"Sure, why not?" Frank said sourly as he got out and slammed the passenger door. He needed a hit and he fingered his wallet in his pocket. He had one small amount of coke left, but was too cold outside; he'd wait until he reached the Ashenberg place. Gritting his teeth, he pulled his hood over his head and began trudging up the road.

Lucy had just put down the phone when she heard a car door slam. She peered through the window and saw a black truck parked in front of her house. Two men got out and she adjusted her glasses, but the driver had turned away and she couldn't see his face. Her heart began to hammer. She pulled back from the window, hoping she had locked the front door. Picking up the phone again, she dialed Ron. "Someone's outside," she said, her voice low.

"What?" Ron reached over to turn down the volume on the radio.

"SOMEONE'S OUTSIDE MY HOUSE!" Catching herself, she lowered her voice. "It looks like one of the guys I saw at Flemings, the one who…"

"Is your door locked?" Ron interrupted. "I'll be right there. Don't answer the door!"

Brian squinted as he looked through a gap in the curtains into a small dark living room. It was stuffed with furniture. Beyond it he saw an opening that looked like it led to a small kitchen. He knocked again, this time with his foot. Silence. *Shit.*

He glanced around and spotted faint footprints in the snow. They marked what appeared to be a walkway that led around the side of the house toward the back. He slithered down the icy steps. Hanging onto the side of the house he made his way to the pathway.

Lucy flattened herself to the wall and crept to the front door. To her relief it was locked. She turned and went into the room off the kitchen, where she kept the television, her books, and desk for writing letters and paying bills. She left the television on, mostly for company.

A commercial was showing two youngish women pretending to be middle-aged and extolling the benefits of a hemorrhoid supplement. She peered through the kitchen's side window.

Her phone rang. "I'm out front," Ron said over his cell phone. "I can see their SUV, but there's no one around." Just then Lucy heard a sound like a thud against the side of the house. She dashed over to the side window and saw an arm flail in the air, then drop below the sill.

"I think he's on the right side of the house," Lucy whispered into the phone.

"My right or your right?"

"Your right!"

She pulled the sheer drapery aside on the larger window in the living room and saw Ron bend over something in the snow. Then she remembered her old bear trap that Herb Ashenberg had left. No one used that side entrance to her house and it had seemed a safe enough place to leave the trap. It belonged to Lucy's late husband and was jammed. Herb offered to fix it come spring. Since October, it had been buried under the snow.

She pulled on her winter jacket and went through the kitchen to the back deck. "What happened?" she said, leaning over the rail as she peered around the corner of the house. She saw a figure lying in the snow. "Is he all right?"

Ron was crouched, scraping snow off the steel trap. "He's out cold. He must have knocked his head on whatever you've got here when he fell." Ron gave Lucy a curious look. "What is this, homemade protection?"

"Oh that," she said, both relieved and disgusted. "That's the old bear trap Hamilton had," she said, mentioning her deceased husband.

She shivered and wished she'd put on her heavier parka. "Herb was going to fix it, although I don't know why. I'm hardly going to use it."

"Looks like you got some use out of it," Ron said. He got out his cellphone and called the infirmary. "Better bring an ambulance," he added before hanging up.

"There were two men, did you see the other one?" Lucy asked when Ron hung up. She looked toward the road. "One of them looked like the man I talked to at the grocery store."

"The one who asked you about Herb?" Ron stuck his phone in his pocket and got out his handcuffs.

She nodded "But I couldn't be sure." She climbed down her back steps and moved closer to Ron.

"It's not this guy, huh?" Ron turned Brian's face slightly to face her. Lucy took a look at him.

"Yes, that looks like him" she said, wrapping her sweater more tightly around her. "Should we bring him inside?"

"Nope. If he broke something, moving him could make it worse. I'll get a thermo blanket from the car. The ambulance will be here in a few minutes." He looked at her. Her lips were blue with cold. "You better go back inside."

Frank was still looking off the side of the road for the Ashenberg's house when he heard a yell in the distance. He turned and saw the VPSO's SUV pull up behind his rental. He slid off the side of the road and squatted behind the bushes. His head, even under his knit cap, was already freezing. He looked through the scrubby willows and tried to make out what was happening.

Several minutes went by with no activity and he was too cold to think. He moved back to the road and began an awkward trot toward the Ashenberg house. His legs were stiff from the cold and he had just reached a smooth spot in the road when his feet slid out from under him and he fell, hitting his head on a chunk of ice-covered gravel.

"Hey, you OK?" Frank opened his eyes and tried to focus on the voice above him. Then he heard a door slam and felt himself being lifted to the irregular back of a pickup. "How you doing?" The voice seemed to be near his feet. The truck was now bouncing over the rough road and Frank was jolted into a semblance of alertness.

"What's going on?" He struggled to sit up. The man was sitting in the back of the truck with him.

"I saw you fall." He reached over Frank and tapped on the window and the truck lurched to a stop. The driver who looked like a teenager climbed out. "My name's Jackson. This is my nephew, Jerry."

Frank started to say something, but as he struggled to sit, a wave of dizziness nearly knocked him over. His head ached like a full blast migraine. Jackson looked at him and tucked Frank's wallet back in his jacket. "You OK?" He peered at Frank

"You slipped and fell back there," Jerry said, sliding back into the driver's seat. "You'll be okay."

"We'll drop you off at the infirmary in Goldspring," Jackson said.

Frank felt like throwing up.

Chapter 31

Fairbanks

Friday

The next morning Cara's Toyota refused to start. Then she noticed the front of the car was leaning to the left. Crap. She got out of her car and checked. A flat tire and it seemed like her battery was dead. *Damn it.* Struggling on the slippery ice, she got to her feet and cautiously made her way back to her house.

"It'll be three, maybe four hours before we can get there." Ed was the manager of the towing service. With a sigh, Cara called Dora at the University. She reached her voice mail. "This is Cara, I've got a flat tire and my car won't start. It might be the battery," she added, remembering that cold weather drained batteries fast in the winter. "The towing service said they couldn't get here for a couple of hours and it's too late to call a cab or grab a bus."

"If you would, please tell my class to start in on their feature story." She took a breath. "I'll see them next week." Having gotten that settled, Cara went upstairs and changed into jeans, a long-sleeved tee shirt, her old velour hoodie, and her consignment shop fleece vest. She sank down on her bed and pulled on a pair of athletic socks and her slippers. Wiggling her toes, she got to her feet and headed back downstairs, wondering what to do with this unexpected break in her schedule.

Still thinking, she made herself another cup of coffee. As she was mulling over whether to call start calling around, looking for work, the phone rang. It startled her and she nearly knocked her mug over reaching for it. It was Ethel.

"Have you heard about Sam Tallwell?" Ethel's voice was shaky.

"No, what happened?" Cara grabbed some paper towels to mop up the coffee.

"It's been a hell of a shock. Could you come up here?"

"Sure," Cara said, alarmed. "But what happened? Is Lucy…"

"Sam is dead," Ethel interrupted. "Ron said it looks like suicide. The Troopers are coming."

Sam, suicide? "Who found him, was there a note?" Cara leaned against the counter to control her shaking. *She had just talked to Sam.*

"I don't know," Ethel said. "Ron didn't say. Lucy is lying down. Can you come?"

"Of course," she said, automatically.

"Oh good," Ethel breathed out a sigh of relief. "I've got to go. I'll tell Lucy you're coming."

Cara peered through her window at her Toyota slouched cockeyed in her driveway. *Oh shit, her flat tires.* She held the phone a moment before replacing it. What could she do? She stared at the counter, at the scattered breadcrumbs she'd missed cleaning up earlier, at the spots from her spilled coffee. She could call Ian. Maybe he could take time off for a visit to Goldspring. If not, he might lend her his Bronco.

"I've got something going on here," Ian said, glancing at his partner who was gathering the paperwork they'd need. "But Thomlin just called. He wants us both in Goldspring, as soon as possible."

In the background, Cara heard Ian's partner yell, "I've got it." Ian looked over as the lieutenant waved the papers for the judge's signature.

"OK, I can pick you up in about twenty minutes," he said, returning to the phone.

Cara ran upstairs to get her heavy parka and tote bag. On the way back down through the kitchen she stopped to call Ed and tell him she'd leave the car key under the floor mat on the driver's side.

Then she left a pile of dry cat food and another scoop of canned food for Mister, who was crouched on the counter, watching her warily. "I'll be back later," she promised as she changed the water in his dish. With an eye on the street, she tugged on her boots then went to her back door to wait.

"Why did Thomlin want both of us there when he talks to Connie?" Cara couldn't imagine what she would contribute to the interview. She shifted in her seat, trying to create some warmth while waiting for the defroster and heater to kick in. She liked Ian's Bronco where she sat higher and had better visibility than in her Toyota. PLUS, it was a four-wheel drive. If she ever got some money, she'd shop around for a used one.

Ian shrugged. "I guess we'll know soon enough." He flipped on his turn signal and moved over a lane to reach the Steese highway. Trooper Thomlin was standing outside the Tallwell house when Ian and Cara drove up. Seeing the trooper again, Cara felt her stomach flip. *Get control of yourself, girl.*

After one look at the beleaguered woman Cara felt her heart twist. Clutching Cara's arm, Connie motioned them all inside. Almost dragging Cara with her, Connie sank down on the sofa before looking at Ian and Thomlin.

"How are you doing?"

Connie looked awful, but she seemed coherent. She looked at Cara and shook her head. "I don't know" she said

If Cara could get Connie, who wasn't even an elder, on video right now, she could probably make a case for keeping her class on "Interviewing Alaska Native Elders" on the curriculum.

Ian and Matt Thomlin offered their sympathies, then Thomlin began. "You told my troopers that Sam was here when you got home?" He was familiar with the rickety red chair from his previous visit and remained standing. "Do you know if he had any visitors?

Connie shrugged. "He may have, but..." She stared at her lap a moment. "I called him before I left school where I teach." She looked from Thomlin to Ian. "Dad didn't answer. Then when I got home about 4:30 he was leaning against back on the sofa and not sitting right." She looked at the corner of the sofa where Sam usually sat, his feet up on the footlocker.

"What do you mean, he wasn't sitting right?"

"He never crossed his legs like that—he couldn't, he told me it wasn't comfortable. His arthritis. He'd just rest his feet on the locker."

"So someone forced his legs like that," Ian said. Connie nodded.

Thomlin had already spoken to the medical examiner. He knew Sam had suffered a blow to his head. He had also learned from Ron that Sam's position on the sofa was not how he usually sat. Whoever had been here had propped Sam, wedged against the corner of the couch, most likely to keep him upright. But why?

"He wasn't breathing?" Cara asked. Connie hesitated

"No, I thought he was breathing because he looked at me, but then," she shook her head, "then there was nothing."

"Did you find a note or anything he might have left?" Thomlin said. Connie shook her head.

"No," she said. "But he didn't kill himself. I know he didn't. He wouldn't."

Connie sat back on the sofa with her lips pressed tight. "Ron and someone else came and took him. I didn't want my kids to see him." She swallowed and looked at Cara. "I'd sent them over to Mrs. Melrose—she lives down the road."

"Did you or your kids handle anything here?" Ian said. Connie shook her head.

"No. I told them he was taking a nap," Connie said looking at Thomlin. "They didn't come in here," she added.

"Wasn't he in some pain?" Ian said, wondering if Sam had somehow helped the end come.

"After he stopped taking the medicine the doctor gave him, the pain was worse." Connie stopped and thought for a moment. "Day before yesterday, two women and a little girl came to see him. They'd taken the train from Anchorage. I think they're related to us." She looked at Cara, who nodded. She knew who they were. Thomlin looked surprised and leaned forward.

Fresh tears slid down Connie's face. "I only saw them drive up in Lucy's car. Her old Mercury. I was leaving for work," she took a deep breath. "But when I got home, he seemed, well, like there was something he needed to do."

"What do you think they wanted?" Thomlin's southern accent seemed to soften the tension in the room and Cara felt Connie's shoulders relax.

Connie shrugged, she didn't know.

"Did he usually use two different cups for his coffee?" Thomlin said, staring at the mug on the trunk.

Connie looked puzzled. Then Cara saw a cup next to the lamp on the end table. There was also a dirty ashtray.

"That was his cup," Connie said pointing to a mug on the footlocker in front of the sofa.

"What about that one?" Thomlin nodded toward the end table.

Connie frowned. "I don't know why that's out here." Without touching it, Cara leaned over and peered into the mug. There was a cigarette butt floating at the bottom. "Did Sam smoke?" Cara looked at an ashtray and the ashes in it. There were so many odors in the house, but she was surprised that she hadn't caught the cigarette smell earlier.

"No, no, he didn't." Connie looked at the ashtray. "I don't know where that came from either, maybe one of the woman …" She paused. The tissue in her hand had wadded into a wet knot.

"There's no lipstick on this butt. Maybe it was left by someone else?" Cara didn't think Lena or Lily smoked either. She found herself glancing at Thomlin who looked at her with a faint smile. Her stomach did a small flip. She cleared her throat and turned back to Connie.

"I'd like to take these mugs if you don't mind," He said and Connie nodded. He pulled a couple of plastic bags from his pocket and scooped up both mugs.

They were outside and Thomlin was putting the bagged evidence in his SUV when he said, "So what's this about a bear?"

Cara stamped her feet to get her circulation moving. "To some Athabascans the bear is bad luck for women. It was thought that when a woman ate bear meat, she could not bear children." She looked at Ian. "Is that the way you heard it?" He nodded.

"That's what Lucy said. If true, it would be great for birth control." Ian grinned.

Cara groaned and leaned against his SUV. "I've also heard that the bear's spirit is a protector for women," She looked at Thomlin and smiled. "So take your pick." The mountains behind them glistened in the increasing daylight and Thomlin put on his dark glasses. Cara looked away. *Lordy, he was gorgeous.*

Ian opened the door to his Bronco. "We're going over to Lucy Montalk's house. Ron should be with her."

Thomlin nodded, pulled on his gloves and climbed into his SUV. "Your aunt thinks the man in her yard is the one she talked to in the market. He was knocked out when he hit his head on her bear trap. Maybe the bear thing is already working." He smiled at Cara, who rolled her eyes.

"So we will get to talk to him?"

Thomlin shook his head. "Not today. The nurse said he's had a concussion; he's on his way to Fairbanks Memorial."

Chapter 32

Goldspring

Monday

"I'm pretty sure that man who fell on my bear trap is the guy I spoke to at the grocery store," Lucy said. She was sitting at the kitchen table with Cara and Ethel. She took a deep breath and pushed a plate of cold toast to the side of the newspaper. Her hair was frazzled and what lipstick she had put on earlier was long gone.

"Good thing it wasn't set," Cara muttered. A set bear trap could do serious damage.

"His name is Brian," Ian said. "He's from Ketchikan and the other guy might be Frank Barnetti." He looked at Thomlin who had also had run-ins with Barnetti.

"The agreement in the glove box was made out to Frank," Thomlin said. "When Lucy saw them at Flemings, they were probably with his younger brother Pat Holmsman, the guy whose body was found off the road near Shem's."

Cara shuddered. She remembered that afternoon well. "What about this other guy, Brian?" Cara looked at Thomlin. "Has he said anything?"

"He was unconscious when they took him to Fairbanks," Thomlin said. "We'll have someone with him when he comes around." He looked at Lucy. "Looks like they had car trouble. Anyway, we're having their vehicle towed to Fairbanks." He had already put in the call for another trooper to conduct house-to-house, looking for Frank. "I'll need to take your bear trap," he told Lucy. "It's evidence…"

"Take it, take it," Lucy said, waving her hands. She never wanted to see it again.

After Ron and Thomlin left, Cara told Ian she would spend the night with Lucy. Ian put his jacket on and headed outside to his SUV, Ethel following.

Lucy's house seemed suddenly empty after everyone had gone. The two women sat for a moment. "Have you heard anything about Julie? She must remember something by now!" Lucy was tired and ready for a nap.

Cara shook her head. "I'll call her when I get home." Restless, she stood up, shoving her chair back. "And I want to talk to Elsie and Jane." Lucy's eyebrows rose. Cara's habit of plunging into things worried Lucy. "I just want to know how Sam was when they saw him…if he was, well, I suppose, depressed."

Lucy gave her a dubious look. "They didn't say much about him when they were here."

Cara looked through the window at the darkening sky. "Why don't we go for a walk and get some air while it's still light outside? I'll call them tomorrow."

Chapter 32

Fairbanks

Tuesday

Cara finished marking the last of her students' papers and stacked them in a pile. She was exhausted. Maybe it was better that she had one less class next semester. She needed a break and a lighter working schedule would offer a change, even if she dreaded the break in her income.

The day before, she had called Northern Lights Insurance and talked to her old boss. After they talked awhile, he suggested she come in on Friday and they'd see what kind of hours she could handle. Cara hoped they could work out something. At least that call had gone more productively than her calls to Julie in the hospital (sorry, but she's sleeping) and Elsie who had hemmed and hawed and said how nice it was to hear from her and, after some excuse had hung up. Cara decided she'd wait a few days before calling Jane.

On the way home from the university, she stopped for groceries. She was putting them away when the phone rang. Her uncle David's voice surprised her. She had never known him well, but after her father's death, they had grown closer and she welcomed his visits.

"I'm in Fairbanks and thought I'd see if you feel like having dinner tonight at Wolf Creek Inn?"

"Sure I'd like that. I could meet you there around six-thirty."

After she hung up, her gaze rested on her Toyota. Since she'd had the battery replaced, it was running fine, thank goodness.

When she arrived, David was standing near the front, talking to the hostess and Cara paused to study him. He wore a dark blue sport coat and gray slacks; he looked good for all his sixty years.

"Hey," he said walking over and giving her a hug. "Good to see you ." He steered her to a corner table where she saw his overnight bag. "I'm catching the eleven o'clock flight to Seattle," he said, when he saw her glance at his bag.

The waiter came with the menus and a wine list. After they'd ordered and their glasses were filled, David cleared his throat. "I don't think you know I've got a daughter." Surprised, Cara shook her head.

"How old is she?"

"She's eighteen and at the University of Washington. Her mother says she wants to study law. ." He paused. "I just found out about her in October."

Cara gave him a look. "And you're sure she's yours?" David smiled. "Direct as always. Yep, Kiley's mine. I had a blood test done."

"So, where does she live?"

"She's with her mother in Seattle when she's not in school.

"In fact, Kiley looks more like me than Karen." Cara sat back and studied him. Handsome uncle David, three times married and no children, now a dad. Who'da thought?

David snapped his fingers. "I just thought of something. Kiley wanted me to ask, do you know Phil, umm, forgot his last name? Anyway, he's part Athabascan and a graduate student here at UAF? I think in anthropology. He says he's Sam Tallman's son. The medicine man that's well known in this area. Anyway, Phil claims he is Sam's son."

Cara blinked. Sam's son? "I know Sam's daughter, but I didn't know about a son" She frowned, then added. "I could ask his daughter, Connie."

In her peripheral vision, she saw someone approaching.

"Hello, Cara." She looked up and her mind went blank.

"Matthew Thomlin," he said as David got to his feet and shook the Trooper's hand. Both men appeared so tall they could have once played basketball.

"Are you here alone?" Cara asked, looking around.

"No." He gestured to his right where Cara saw her cousin, Ian, talking with another man. Ian, catching her eye, smiled.

"Who was that?" David said, after Tomlin had moved on.

"Trooper Thomlin, he's working on a case that Aunt Lucy and I …" She sighed. "I'll back up. Over Thanksgiving, Lucy and I found Herb Ashenberg and his daughter, Julie, at his house. Herb was in his driveway, he'd been murdered."

Cara took a breath and glanced at her uncle. David looked horrified

After a moment, he took her hand and squeezed it. "Cara, this isn't good." He took a deep breath and exhaled. "You're having a heck of a life. And here I am boring you with my tale. For heaven sakes, be careful."

Chapter 33

Fairbanks

Wednesday

"You planning on shooting someone?" Thomlin said, looking at the gun Ian had just finished cleaning. The trooper had stopped by Ian's office to check on progress with the Ravenstone theft.

"There's a few I'd like to shoot," Ian said, thinking of Phil and Brian. He slid the gun back in its holster and put it in his desk drawer.

"So any idea what's going on with Cara and the guy she was with?" Ian grinned. The trooper wasn't beating around the bush.

"David Patric is her uncle on her dad's side," Ian said. "He's a retired pilot and working in Seattle for an outfit that's got offices in Fairbanks and Anchorage."

Before Thomlin could reply, the department's secretary stuck her head into Ian's office. "Ian, there's a call for you on my line and the chief wants to see you."

"Who's the caller?" Ian glanced at Thomlin as he headed for the door, giving Ian a *we'll talk later* nod.

"He wouldn't give his name," the secretary said. "He just said it concerned that shaman's death in Goldspring."

"Put him through" Ian said, but when he picked up the phone the line was dead.

"Carol," Ian yelled. "What happened?"

"He must have hung up."

"If he calls again, come get me. I'll be with the chief."

"Will do."

At Fairbanks Memorial, Brian replaced the phone on its cradle and sank back on the hospital bed. He wasn't sure why he'd called, but he wanted to talk to the cop who'd stopped Pat about a year ago. The one who had thrown the three of them out of Fairbanks.

Brian knew the police had stopped near Shem's where the Tempo was parked. If he talked to the troopers, they wouldn't tell him squat. But that cop knew Brian and might tell him something. Brian and Pat hadn't been close, but Brian admired the kid for standing up to his brother. And he felt bad for leaving Pat behind when Brian and Frank had taken off.

His head felt like it was splitting open; he hadn't been in this much pain since the accident when he'd nearly sunk his boat in a storm off Lynn Canal. Troopers had been questioning him most of the morning and he couldn't remember what he had said. Then he heard voices in the hall and shut his eyes.

"I thought you said he was awake?"

"He was, I just heard him use the phone…"

The nurse checked Brian's pulse and his vital signs. "He's asleep," she said, looking at the troopers. "He's scheduled for an MRI in about twenty minutes."

"Check with the switchboard to see who he called," Thomlin told his younger partner.

"I just did, he called the FPD twice, but he wasn't on the phone for more than a few seconds."

"The FPD? Well, call them, let's see what they know about it."

On the bed, Brian kept his eyes closed. The pain in his head was intense. He needed the nurse. He needed more of that painkiller she'd given him earlier. Morphine, something, anything. And where was Frank? Had he reached Clyne? And what the hell was an MRI?

Chapter 34

Goldspring

Wednesday

Back at the clinic in Goldspring, Frank was watching the nurse in his room through half closed eyes. After his rescuers dropped him off and he produced his wallet, he discovered his driver's license was missing. The two men had also relieved him of his cash and credit cards, plus his minute stash of coke. He figured it happened when he had passed out in the back of their pickup.

Thinking as quickly as his foggy brain would allow, Frank told the infirmary guy he was a member of the Sealaska Corporation in Juneau and his name was Pete Baxter. Baxter was real and a member of Sealaska, in case the clinic guy looked. Frank added that he had been robbed and dumped on the road to Chena Hot Springs.

He was put in a room alone and now he peered through the window at the parking lot. He saw only an old white Ford parked in the open. It was too obvious to steal. He fell back on the bed. *Where was that damned nurse?* But even in his craving coke state, he realized his new identity had saved him from immediate arrest.

Then he thought about Brian. What the hell had happened to Brian? Was he arrested when the VPSO showed up at that house? Brian had hollered like he'd been shot.

In the reception area, near the clinic's entrance, the nurse handed a cardboard container of blood vials to the orderly. They were marked with the numbers of the tests to be done. "You're sure about this?" he said, filling out the paperwork for the courier.

"I've seen a lot of withdrawals, the agitation, the depression and he's jumpy. Plus, he's skin and bones, but now he's eating everything in sight. I'm sure this is another one."

"You sure this is Frank?" Thomlin and Bill Carmedy, another trooper, were sitting in their vehicle on the other side of the infirmary. Through the trees, they could see the infirmary's parking lot. Carmedy nodded.

"He checked in as Pete Baxter, but it's Phillip Franklin Barnetti, alright." Carmedy had seen Barnetti's mug shot. "You still want to let him go?"

"Let's see who he contacts first. We've got Milo on him?" Thomlin said.

"Yep," Carmedy said, glancing at an unmarked Ford on the street near the hospital's parking lot. "He'll be on him like white on rice."

"Barnetti will head for Fairbanks and most likely Anchorage. With no ID or cash, he'll be looking to hitch a ride or lift a car. He may head for the Fairbanks airport. But even with money, he won't get off the ground without a photo ID." Thomlin glanced toward the Ford, but couldn't see the trooper through the darkened windshield.

"I hope Milo's not in uniform?"

Carmedy shook his head. "No, no. He'll go in, chat up the nurse and make sure Barnetti finds out he's heading for Fairbanks." Carmedy's glasses had fogged when they got back in the SUV and he wiped them with well used handkerchief

"You can't wear contact lenses or get that eye surgery?" Thomlin asked, watching. Carmedy shook his head.

"My daughter swallowed one of my contacts last night. She's four," he added, shifting into gear and pulling back on the highway. "And I've got dry eyes, so Lasik surgery is out."

Thomlin didn't know much about children. After his daughter had died, Thomlin and his wife had gone their separate ways and he had no desire for another family. But lately he'd been wondering how Cara felt about kids. He didn't have the impression she was chafing at the bit to add to the population. Still, you never know, he thought, feeling vaguely discouraged. A guy and his lady used to be safe past a certain age. Well, he'd ask her. Or maybe he'd run it by Ian. No, no, he thought. Nope, he'd ask Cara. At least for now, the fewer people who knew of his interest in her the better.

Chapter 35

Anchorage

Wednesday

Carl was turning his shop's sign to CLOSED when he saw the police cruisers pull up in front of the Captain Cook Hotel across the street. A robbery? He hoped Val had left the hotel. There was no need for her to get caught up in whatever was going on. She had insisted on staying in the room and taking a bath. Carl smiled, remembering debating on getting in the tub with her.

He glanced through the window again. More police appeared. It must be a robbery. As he emptied the register for the day, he thought about how she'd come into the store and how they had gone across to the Captain Cook's coffee shop and then wound up in a room overlooking the city.

Carl's *therapy*—as he called his time with Val—had temporarily lessened his enthusiasm for wringing Wade's neck. He switched off the lights and headed for the back door and his rental car in the lot.

Val's husband, Mack drove home and pulled his car behind his garage. His thumping heart began to slow down. It was done. It was over. He had even managed to enter Clyne's store and stash Val's panties in the bottom of a desk drawer. That had been chancy, waiting for Clyne to leave, with the cops just across the street at the Captain Cook. Now, even if the police didn't question Clyne, the evidence was there. He smiled, remembering Val's reaction. She wasn't even surprised to see him.

"I knew you'd be watching," she'd said when he slid into her room at the Cook. Her smile had the confidence of money and all of it in her name. Not anymore. Of course, he'd still have to pay Jack Johnson in Portage for vouching for Mack's whereabouts and providing Mack with an alibi. But according to their lawyer she hadn't updated her will so the rest was all Mac's.

For years he had looked the other way. Val had her lovers. He had his. What surprised him was when she refused to finance his campaign for mayor five months ago, he was dumbfounded.

"I know she *wants* to be First Lady, but doesn't she understand that politics is a long road." He said to Sylvie, his long-time girlfriend. She had made sympathetic sounds and held his hand against her chest. She was Aleut and Tlingit and built like a brick outhouse. And she was patient.

After Val's refusal to help, Mack had hired a private investigator through his lawyer, Krane. "I want to know who she's seeing." Which is how his lawyer learned that Valerie had put a tail on her own husband.

"For somebody who runs a garage, you do get around," Krane told Mack as he turned over his investigator's report. Other than Wade, however, Val seemed to be slowing down. To Mack's surprise, she was nearly faithful. If he hadn't followed her, he'd never have known about Carl Clyne.

• • •

"Is this Valerie linked to the guy the troopers found in Wasilla?" Ian's feet were propped on his desk. It was late afternoon and he had been up since midnight. He put down the Fairbanks and Anchorage newspapers and looked at Thomlin.

"You mean Ed Stuart? What made you think of him?"

Just then, Cara walked in and sank down in Ian's second visitors chair.

Thomlin nodded at her before continuing. "Val checked into the Captain Cook with a man the clerk thought he recognized. "The guy paid for the room with cash and she ordered a bottle of champagne and put it on her Visa." He paused. "Her purse was in the room with her driver's license."

"How did she die?" Ian asked.

"She was found in the bathtub and she'd put up a struggle so this was a homicide."

Ian sucked his teeth as he thought. "Did the Anchorage Police pick up Wade?"

"He was at the garage all day. The other mechanic and a customer can vouch for him."

"And Val's husband, Mack?" Ian said.

"Mack was in Portage. His client confirmed it. Mack said Valerie told him she was going shopping, looking for a gift for a relative. She had a business card in her pocket for Carl Clyne of Alaska Art and Antiques. It's on Fourth Avenue, across from the Captain Cook. The Anchorage Police are checking that out." Thomlin got to his feet and headed for the door."

"So, no ties to Ashenberg's death?" Ian was frustrated.

The Trooper shook his head. "Not yet anyway. We did hear from Julie Ashenberg. According to her, her father said something about hiding this Ravenstone in a tree behind their house." Ian tried to picture the area behind Herb's house. He smiled.

"You know there's a forest back there." Thomlin sighed and nodded. He had already spent several hours back there.

"She said to look for a white birch. A storm last winter ripped off a branch and left a hole. She said that's where her father talked about hiding it. I'm going back there now."

"But you don't think you'll find it?" Cara said. Thomlin took a breath and shook his head.

"We'd have to cut down every tree, but no, I don't think so."

"Did she say anything about these guys, what they looked like, anything like that?" Ian frowned.

"She just said she was in the car, waiting for her father. He told her to stay put." Thomlin slipped on his gloves. "She remembered being pulled out of the vehicle and a Native guy slamming the door. She doesn't remember anything after that."

"Have you told Ron?" Cara said.

"This is on a need-to-know-basis," Thomlin said, shaking his head. I'll tell him Julie is recovering. That's it." He gave her a look. Cara nodded. She'd keep her mouth shut.

As Thomlin pulled onto the Steese Highway and into the lane for Goldspring, he could feel the weight of the past press down on him. After his daughter died and his wife left, his tendency to isolate himself had kept him from close relationships. So when the opportunity to move to Alaska came, it felt right. And it had been. But now he'd met Cara.

Chapter 35

Goldspring

Wednesday

Cara didn't want to put her Toyota through any more long distant driving. Within an hour, she was behind the wheel of a Ford Fiesta. The rental was three years old and painted bright magenta. The previous driver had been a heavy smoker, so she rolled her side window halfway down and turned up the heat.

As she approached Goldspring, she remembered Fleming's Market had installed a deli/bakery. The local lineup of pastries was tempting and she pulled into the parking lot. Peering through the Fleming's broad front window, she saw a line of customers at the deli counter. With ten people ahead of her in line she had time to pick up some cheese and a few grapes.

At the Goldspring clinic, Frank peered through the window blinds as a man climbed into a plain gray station wagon. The guy wasn't in uniform, but Frank was sure he was a trooper. He poked his head out of his doorway and looked for his nurse. When he didn't see her, he quickly got dressed and slipped the salve samples she had left for his hands in his pockets. If she didn't appear for the next five minutes, he ought to be able to make it out a back door he had seen earlier.

Troopers Bill Carmedy and Matt Thomlin were parked down the road, concealed from the clinic by trees that had escaped last summer's forest fire. They couldn't see the rear exit, but knew it was locked and would sound an alarm if opened without a key.

From his vantage point inside the clinic, Frank watched an orderly open the back door and push a cart filled with soiled linen out toward a truck. Concealed by the floor-to-ceiling shelving units near the door, Frank moved closer. When the orderly reentered and headed back to the laundry room, Frank slid outside before the door shut.

The cold hit him like a shovel. His frostbitten hands throbbed and he was already sorry he'd left the clinic. He peered around the edge of the building. Other than a few cars passing by out front, he saw nothing unusual. Sliding his damaged hands into his jacket pockets, he moved through the shadows of the clinic to where he could see down the road. There he saw the blue Suburban the trooper had driven earlier. Looking for a short cut to the main road, he trotted over behind a small group of log houses. Goldspring, he discovered, had no consistent network of streets. Off to his left, he saw the grocery store. Wasn't that where he and Brian and Pat had stopped, like when, a few days ago? Slowing to a walk, he turned toward the market and studied the small parking lot and the road beyond.

Thomlin's phone rang. It was the clinic's nurse. "Pete Baxter or the guy you call Frank, is gone, I looked in his room and checked the other rooms and bathrooms. He's nowhere in the building. I think he may have gone out the back door when we were loading the linen truck."

Thomlin, his mouth grim, looked at Carmedy. "Frank slipped out. Let's find him."

Frank had lost his hat somewhere and his head was freezing. Hell with it. He pulled his collar up covering the back of his head. He'd get a cap at a gas station or that grocery store if they carried them. Then he remembered his empty wallet. He slowed his pace and was moving toward the glass door when a woman pulled up in a god-awful bright red car and parked next to a large van.

He remembered that reddish purple color from when his mother came back from the fabric store with curtain material. "There!" she'd said, admiring the soft light that filtered through the vivid curtains into the living room. Frank and Pat had looked at each other smirking. *Yeah, yeah,* but they'd secretly enjoyed the illusion of sunshine and their mother's giddy happiness.

Frank turned and headed toward a truck that looked promising. Then he saw two large malamutes watching him from the truck bed. *Whoa.* He skittered to a stop and glanced around. In his peripheral vision, he saw a woman get out of that bright Ford and enter the market.

Cara was heading toward Fleming's deli carrying a bag of grapes when she glanced through the plate glass doors. A familiar looking car was leaving the parking lot. Standing on her toes, she peered toward the space where she had parked. *Oh, holy crap.*

Dropping her deli number, still clutching the grapes, she raced outside in time to see her cheerfully bright Fiesta peel onto the road. Had she left her keys inside? Patting her pockets, she found the car keys. Had she forgotten to lock it? Damnit. Thank the lord, she now had a cellphone and she pulled it out.

Ron was in his car, following Thomlin's SUV, when Cara called. "A magenta Ford Fiesta? What color is magenta?"

"A bright purplish red, like fuchsia, but deeper! My car conked out this morning and I rented it." She took a deep breath. "And no, I don't know the license number. It's on the paperwork in the car."

"I'll tell Thomlin. I think Frank Barnetti slipped out of the clinic a few minutes ago. I've gotta go."

"Cara doesn't drive a Ford," Thomlin said peering through the windshield. He'd already lost Barnetti. The snow was light and dry and slippery as snot on ice.

"The Ford's a rental. She said it's a reddish purple. She'd stopped at Fleming's market and when she was inside, someone must have hot-wired her car. She still has her keys." Ron grabbled a couple of sheets of paper towels he'd stashed under his seat and tried to mop up coffee he'd just spilled on his lap. "It might have been Frank."

Cara's anxiety-prone stomach was churning when she stepped back inside Fleming's. The number at the deli was now fourteen. Shit. She pulled the next number, seventeen, and got in line.

After she picked up the cheese and paid for everything, she walked outside and looked around. No Ron. Cara called him again, but his cellphone told her to leave a message. After another fifteen minutes she called Lucy and reached Ethel.

Chapter 36

Goldspring

Frank drove the Fiesta through a small side road and had almost reached the highway when he saw the troopers' SUV. Startled, he twirled the steering wheel and skidded on the black ice and ran into a tree.

Panicking, Frank struggled to dislodge himself from the banged-up Fiesta. Across the road he saw a couple of log cabins and a church. Otherwise, the neighborhood was quiet. He both ran and hobbled toward the back yard of the nearest cabin. There he saw something that just might save his ass.

"You see anything?" Thomlin asked. He was crouched behind a cluster of low bushes.

Next to him, Bill shook his head. "He crossed the road, I think he…." Just then a snow mobile roared past, drowning Bill's voice in a flurry of snow.

"Was that Barnetti?" Thomlin scrambled to his feet and started running back to his vehicle.

Chapter 37

Goldspring

Wednesday - Thursday

Ethel pulled up in front of Lucy's house and Cara and Lucy climbed out, their legs stiff from bracing themselves in the swerving car. Ethel was doing her weekly baking that night for Goldspring's homeless population and she drove home. "I hope she gets home alright," Lucy said, watching the Honda disappear. Ethel's haphazard driving skills left her passengers jittery.

Cara followed Lucy into her kitchen and dropped her overnight bag on the floor. She was surprised to find herself shaking. "You're pale as tissue paper." Lucy said, frowning

"I think I'm jinxed." Cara sat at the table, knotting her fingers together. "All my troubles with cars and…"

"You weren't driving that car so it's not your fault." Lucy interrupted.

"I wasn't talking about that. It's the Ravenstone. Frank and Brian are penny-ante, so who hired them?" Fury choked Cara. For a moment she couldn't speak. "And I wanted to talk to Sam again." She unzipped her parka and let it fall back on her chair.

Lucy regarded her with an odd expression. She filled the kettle with water and put it on the stove. "Earl Gray or English Breakfast?"

"Earl Gray," Cara paused. "I'm thinking about going to Anchorage…I want to see Clyne's Alaska Art shop and visit Julie at the Providence Hospital."

Lucy stared at her for a moment. "If you go, I'm going with

142

you." No way would she let Cara do this by herself. "Now we just have to get to Fairbanks, by train I guess, then to Anchorage."

"I'll call Ian and see if he can get us a car we can drive to Anchorage." Cara glanced at her watch. The next train to Fairbanks was in two hours.

"You'll be back by Monday?" Ian had said, grinning as he gave her his extra set of keys. Her car luck hadn't been good lately, but she nodded.

"You won't believe how careful I'll be," she replied drily.

The morning was sunshine beautiful in Fairbanks with a temperature of twenty-eight above. As Cara backed Ian's Suburban out of her small driveway, Lucy said, "I heard something interesting the other day. It was about the woman who's married to the man who owns that garage in Anchorage, the one where Wade Brown works. Do you know the one I mean?"

"Wade Brown? You mean Jimmy's stepfather?" Lucy nodded.

"When Lena and Lily stayed with me after they saw Sam, they said Wade's boss's wife—this Valerie – and Wade were, umm, hot and heavy is how they put it." Cara already knew this and smiled at Lucy's choice of words.

"Anyway," Lucy went on, "I heard that the police found her body in a room at the Captain Cook."

"Don't you think it's odd that Wade loses his trailer and their son, Jimmy? Then his wife leaves him and now his mistress is dead?" She stared at Cara. "Anyway, it strikes me as, well, overkill." Cara grinned.

"You just said all that so you could use *overkill*." She loved to tease her aunt who often borrowed words from People Magazine and television shows.

"I wonder if the police have arrested Wade or Valerie's husband?" Cara couldn't remember the husband's name, but spouses were usually the first suspects.

"They haven't said anything beyond finding her body," Lucy said. "I don't know if she was in the room with anyone, but why would you go to a hotel like the Captain Cook if not to be with someone? And isn't the Captain Cook near this Alaskan Art place?" Not waiting for an answer, Lucy said, "That's what made me think of this murder."

Oh indeed, Cara thought, and all this from her aunt!

After they made a stop at a bakery for a dozen homemade cookies for Lily Patrick's family, they headed for the Parks Highway and almost immediately got stuck in a growing line of traffic waiting for the road to clear after a multi-car accident.

By the time they reached downtown Anchorage they had been on the road for nine and a half hours. Caught on a one-way street, Cara steered around the Captain Cook Hotel before back tracking to the Marriott a block behind it. "It's pricey," Cara said, referring to the Marriott, "but the rooms are nice and we'll have two queen beds." She had stayed there when she was on the Doyon Shareholders Board and they held meetings in Anchorage.

Lucy nodded. She didn't care about the beds right now. She just wanted to find a bathroom.

"Oh, my, this is beautiful!" Lucy said, later, drying her hands on a towel as she walked into the large bedroom and looked through the windows. Their room was on the 21st floor.

"Tomorrow you'll be able to see more." Cara glanced at her watch. "I'll call Julie in the morning," It was almost ten o'clock and her back and shoulders were looking forward to a long hot bath.

The next morning, they walked one block over to Alaska Art and Antiques and peered through the window. It was gray and chilly and there were few others on the sidewalk. A "closed" sign on the door stopped them. As they turned away Lucy grabbed Cara's arm. "Wait a minute," she said. "I saw someone move back there."

She put her hand on the window, shielding the glare and stared into the glass. Cara moved next to her and looked inside. "Are you sure?" After several moments, Lucy dropped her hand and stood back, shaking her head. "Maybe it was the light, it can play tricks," Cara said.

Inside the shop, Frank saw the outline of two women through the window and ducked behind the counter. He cursed himself for being so careless. One of the women looked familiar, but no, it couldn't be. He was in Anchorage, not at Shem's in Fairbanks. Still, hungry as he was, he couldn't risk being on the streets in broad daylight.

Cara and Lucy drove to the hospital and were told that Julie had been discharged to a relative named Jane Patric. "Well at least we know who she's with and she couldn't be safer than with Aunt Jane, but when I talked to Julie before breakfast, she didn't say she was checking out." Cara was puzzled.

Before leaving the hospital, with Lucy reading the phone number from her small address book, Cara called Jane. No answer. She left a message then looked at her aunt. "Let's go get an early lunch and think about what to do next."

After they ate, Cara tried Jane Patric's number again. Still no answer. She decided to call Elsie. "No, I don't know where Jane is, but I'll tell her you called. I've got to run, I'm late for work."

"Well this was a wasted trip," Lucy said in exasperation.

"And an expensive one," Cara added, thinking of the hotel bill and the gas Ian's Explorer was eating up.

It was four in the afternoon and Cara and Lucy decided to have an early supper in their room. It was extravagant, but as Cara said, "This is our last night then it's back to the drawing board, so how about it?"

In the deepening twilight, they enjoyed crab and prawn salads, while gazing across the dark silver of Cook Inlet. The sun was slowly lowering behind Sleeping Lady and Cara thought of her flying lessons over the region. Her instructor was a furloughed Pan American Pilot with a short temper, which she admitted, she deserved. Below their window and circling the hotel, the lights of the city sparkled.

Earlier, they had been on the 3rd floor of a bank where Cara had a savings account and she was amazed at how much Anchorage had spread south and east in the foothills of the Chugach Range. "The city has really grown since I was last here," she murmured.

"Do you miss it?" Lucy said. Cara shrugged.

"Some days yes, most days no," she said. Lucy was the reason Cara had left Anchorage for Fairbanks. It was a move recommended by Lucy's doctor.

"Your aunt needs to be around family, especially if she has another stroke." he had said. And despite Lucy's many friends, Cara was the closest friend/relative Lucy had.

The next day Cara and Lucy wheeled their bags to the parking lot across from the hotel, and discovered Ian's Explorer had two flat tires. Suspicious, Cara bent down and looked under the SUV. An old screwdriver was lying in the dirty snow.

Lucy was horrified. "Who do you think did this?"

Cara leaned her suitcase against the bumper and circled the SUV looking for other signs of damage. "Anchorage has a bigger share of culprits than Fairbanks," she said, although vandalism was happening everywhere now.

"Chanh na hanh." Lucy swore, using her favorite word for dog shit.

They dragged their bags back to the hotel and reported the incident to the hotel manager who then called the police. By noon, Cara had two new tires and an added debt of $295. "Let's get out of here," she muttered to Lucy.

By the time they reached Palmer, Lucy was leaning back against the headrest and dozing. Minutes later they passed Wasilla where Elsie had her encounter with a murderer and Cara remembered Ian's warning. *This is police business, stay out of it.* All those who had been killed were somehow connected to the Ravenstone. Now her worry spread to Lucy.

Chapter 38

Goldspring

Sunday

By the time they had reached Fairbanks and after Cara put Lucy on the train to Goldspring, both women were exhausted. Arguing with Cara who wanted Lucy to stay in Fairbanks while Lucy protested she would always feel safer in her own home had taken Lucy's starch out.

As she stepped off the train in Goldspring, she spotted Ron, walking toward her with a smile on his face. His youthful energy gave her a welcome lift.

"How'd you like the big city?" he said, reaching for her small bag. It was on wheels and she could handle it, but she appreciated his gesture and besides she was at the end of her tether.

"Did Cara tell you about our little adventure? I wish you'd been there. Could've used your help."

"No, she just told me to pick you up. What happened?"

As he put her bag in the back seat, she told him about the flattened tires in Ian's truck. "What does Cara think about it?" he said, reaching around her to open the passenger door.

"She thinks the crime rate in Anchorage is higher than what I'm used to." Lucy shrugged. "I think it's got something to do with this Ravenstone business." Ron grimaced. Lucy thought everything was about the Ravenstone.

"She's right about Anchorage," Ron said, changing the subject. He climbed in the driver's side and started the engine. "You know, Anchorage has about 250,000 residents and that doesn't include the nearby outlying areas." He looked at Lucy. "It is the biggest city in Alaska..."

"I know," Lucy said, "But even the hotel people were surprised. They said it had never happened before."

"Well, hotel people would say that. After all it's their business to protect their customers. But you know Ian's SUV looks like hundreds, of others. Maybe someone targeted his by mistake."

Ron hoped to high heaven that Carl wasn't behind this. He didn't think slashing tires was Clyne's MO, but who knew? Ron had called Clyne yesterday in Seattle. He didn't sound good; he kept coughing like he had a cold or the flu. His last words were, "find that Ravenstone!"

The SUV hit a pothole and Lucy grabbed the safety handle above the door. Ron pulled into Lucy's driveway and came around to pull open her door, which stuck unless you smacked it hard. While Ron got her bag from the back seat, she looked at her cleared driveway and smiled. Good, he thought. She'd seen his shoveled efforts. He felt a better.

"You said you saw someone in that Alaska Art shop?" he said.

"Uh huh. Then Cara saw someone on TV and said it was Frank."

Ron was nervous. No way did he want Frank near Aunt Lucy

"I don't know what he looks like, but Cara does." Lucy said. "She saw him in Fairbanks at Shem's and said he was the one who had shot Ian. Anyway, Frank was on the news and he may have been who I saw lurking around in that shop."

Holding onto Ron's arm, Lucy climbed the steps to her front door and got out her house key. It was cold inside and she went to the thermostat to turn up the heat. "Just put that in the bedroom," she said when Ron entered with her overnight bag. Shedding her coat, she went into the kitchen and filled the kettle with water for tea.

Ron carried the bag to her bedroom and set it on foot of her bed. As he turned around he noticed the rack of Lucy's collection of hats. They were felt and fur and crocheted and knitted. For as long as he had known Lucy, she had been making hats and scarves and knitting gloves for friends and relatives. Like that beautiful fur hat she had made for Herb. He remembered looking for it at Herb's house and thinking he'd ask Lucy about it, but with so much happening, he'd forgotten.

Back in the kitchen Lucy was getting out plates and the muffins she'd bought in Anchorage. "Who were we talking about?"

"Julie," Ron said with a belabored sigh. Lucy smiled. She liked to tease Ron. She poured their tea. It was strong, the way he liked it and Ron reached for a muffin.

As they ate, she brought him up to date with their attempts to see Julie. "What a mistake it was to drive to Anchorage without talking to Jane and Elsie first!"

Lucy picked up a muffin and peeled the paper from the base. "Of course, if we hadn't gone we wouldn't have seen Frank, even if it was on the news. Did you see that newscast here?"

He shook his head, no and reached for his tea. "Do you know what happened to the fur hat that belonged to Herb? You made it out of muskrat?

"I assume the troopers have it…" Lucy began. A bit of muffin caught in her throat and she got up to get a glass of water. Her eyes were watering when she turned around. "I swallowed too fast,"

"That fur hat you made …" he began. Just then the phone rang.

It was Cara and she was full of apologies. "Aunt Lucy, I'm sorry about today. I didn't mean to push you into moving to Fairbanks, but we just don't know where these guys are and your house is in the middle of what's happening."

Lucy glanced at Ron who was buttering his third muffin. She turned back to the phone. "You're right, I'll call Ethel this afternoon, she can stay with me for a few days. Ron is here. We're having tea. I was telling him about our flattened tires at the hotel."

Cara had forgotten about Ron. She lowered her voice, even though Ron couldn't hear her. "We'll talk later."

Chapter 38

Fairbanks

Monday

"Hey Ian," Ron said, untwisting the telephone cord from the back of his chair, "have you heard anything about Frank? I heard he's in Anchorage." He could hear Ian munching something. Sounded like an apple. Ron had forgotten lunch and was so hungry he could almost smell the apple.

"No word, although the Anchorage PD has him under surveillance." Ian swallowed and cleared his throat. "The Feds are keeping an eye on the gallery owner, Carl Clyne in Seattle ..." Ron's stomach lurched.

"What do you think Frank's doing for money?"

"Funny you should ask. We got a call from the Wasilla PD. A man at a service station reported his wallet was lifted. He had about $250 and thinks it happened when he was getting gas. His description of the guy sounds like Frank—tall, skinny, pockmarked skin. He was gone before the Wasilla police arrived."

Ron chewed the inside of his cheek. "Is Brian still in Fairbanks Memorial?"

"Brian? Yeah, Thomlin has been talking to him. Why're you asking?"

Ron let out a sigh. "I wanted to tell Lucy something positive."

Using a credit card from his heisted wallet for the second time, Frank opened the back door and reentered Clyne's shop.

He'd gone to a burger joint on East Fourth Avenue and brought his half-eaten burger back to the shop.

Trying not to trip against paintings leaning against display cases and a collection of drums and masks and other carvings too large for the walls, he checked the desk. In the back of a drawer he found a spare key to the back door with another to a lock-box. To his amused surprise, he also found panties and a bra stuffed in the file drawer. Good ole Carl. Such carelessness about the key, though. But all he saw when he opened the lock-box were invoices and lease agreements. Finding no cash or jewelry, he shoved them back inside.

He found another safe on the wall behind an oil painting of a Siberian husky. But it had a combination lock. Combination locks weren't his strength; in the dim light, he couldn't see the numbers anyway.

Frank curled up on the ancient leather lounge in Carl's office and pulled a Tlingit blanket he'd found up to his chin. It was heavy and scratchy and the loveseat was lumpy and cracked, but after eating his firsts meal in what felt like days, he was too tired to care.

The night wore on and he drifted in and out of sleep. In the dark room, the masks and artwork seemed eerie. Through the windows, he could see streetlights through the dark haze of nightfall. He dozed again and woke up to loud cawing. Ravens he thought, drifting off again. He didn't think ravens were night birds.

At six o'clock the next morning, he woke up, his stomach growling. He'd scored some coke over on Third Avenue yesterday, but it turned out to be mainly baby powder. He peered through one of the back windows and saw no activity.

He pulled out his stolen wallet and recounted the cash. After stopping at the burger joint and later mistakenly giving a homeless guy a couple of twenties (which he'd thought were tens) to deflate the tires of Cara's SUV and then paying an inflated price for the overly cut coke, he had $90.00.

The owner of the driver's license was beefy and had black hair. Not even close to skinny pockmarked Frank. He stripped the billfold of the driver's license and credit cards. He'd drop them in trash bins on the east end of Fourth Avenue. Even after the '64 Quake, that section of downtown was still the heart of Anchorage's sleazier bars and saloons.

Frank was pleased with his progress. After he'd hitched a ride with a trucker on his way to the Matanuska Valley, then caught another lift from what he now considered his good luck gas station in Wasilla, his luck had improved. He smiled, remembering how easy it had been to be suddenly $250 richer.

The police had been watching Clyne's shop since Val's death. They had even installed an additional surveillance camera in the area. Which is when they spotted a strange figure entering the back door to the shop. They sent the photos, one of which was surprisingly clear of Frank, to the FBI, the state Troopers, and the Fairbanks and Anchorage police departments.

"Frank Barnetti has been in and out of Carl Clyne's shop across from the Captain Cook. He must have a key." Ian was looking at the surveillance photos he'd received and had called Ron in Goldspring. What the Troopers and Police now had on Frank and Carl was confirmed by Glori and the FBI.

In Goldspring, Ron chewed a hangnail on his index finger. The connection between the killers and Clyne – and Clyne and Ron – was tightening. He pulled the cuticle with his teeth and a bit of blood appeared.

He shoved his hand under his thigh. "Do you think Frank slashed your tires in Anchorage? He was close to the Marriott and could have seen Cara and Lucy."

Ian paused. "Maybe. Anchorage has a tail on him and that should lead to something." Ian took a deep breath as he stared at the emailed photos. "We are still collecting evidence of Clyne's association with Barnetti and this Ravenstone theft. As for Clyne, he's in Seattle."

Ron's shoulders slumped. Carl Clyne again. "Does Cara know?"

"She's teaching. I left a message on her home phone. I'll talk to her later."

Ron put down the phone and sat back. He was done for. He'd have to give himself up and that meant he'd lose his job and go to prison and there'd be no technical center for Goldspring or the surrounding villages. There'd be no place for villagers to set up computer networks or tune up cars or rebuild snow machines let alone repair or fly airplanes. Damn it all.

In Seattle, Carl Clyne's ulcer was acting up again. Resting on the hotel's ample bed, he chewed a couple of antacids. He couldn't find the prescription refill he'd picked up at the drugstore. Must be in the bag with the deli sandwich he'd left in the car.

He'd known for some time now that he was making mistakes. The cancer was eating at him, slowing his brain and erasing his appetite. He wasn't thinking right. The doc had warned him this would happen.

Worse, he wasn't on top of his game when it came to the amulet. There were too many loose ends: Brian was in custody and Clyne knew Frank soon would be caught. He didn't trust either of them to keep quiet.

Plus, Frank had just called from his shop in Anchorage and nearly scared the poop out of him. Didn't the idiot know that phone was most likely bugged?

Then there was Ron, another mistake Carl would never have made in his younger days, hiring someone whose day job was in law enforcement. That was beyond stupid. At first, he'd thought this arrangement could be on the up and up. He had planned for Ron to introduce him to Sam, after which Carl would see about making him an offer for the Ravenstone.

But before anything could happen, the old guy gave the Ravenstone to his nephew, Herb Ashenberg. That's when Carl really screwed up. Instead of waiting or even giving the whole idea a pass, (although, even in the old days, Carl doubted he'd do that), he hired Brian Pat and Frank—three bar musicians!—to approach Herb. He snorted. Some approach. The numb nuts had killed and dismembered Herb and they still didn't have the Ravenstone. The murder trail, with its big muddy prints, led straight to Clyne. This was like a bad movie. Taking a deep breath, he leaned back and rested his aching head against the bed's headboard.

That evening Clyne walked over to the Circle Ship, a new restaurant near his condo on Second Avenue. He took a seat at the bar and ordered a three-olive martini with Belvedere vodka. He knew he shouldn't but what the hell. Around him, the hum of relaxed conversations was calming.

As he stirred his martini, he wondered what would happen if he hired a lawyer in case the law called him. He could plead innocent, but innocent of what, Val's murder?

Later, his stomach aching again, Carl went home and got ready for bed, thinking about all the deaths involved in this fiasco. There was Herb Ashenberg and Sam Tallwell. Neither death had been with his approval. As for Valerie, Carl wondered who had done it and why? Was it her husband or maybe an old lover? Someone following her or maybe following him?

His pain grew sharper and he got out a small envelope of Hawaii Gold. He folded the paper into a wrinkled cigarette. Holding it gingerly between his thumb and index finger, he began taking small puffs. He was tempted to just eat it.

After a while and calmer, his thoughts drifted. Who else had Val known? She was a sexy woman and there had to be other men. Gradually, and with no effort at all, his thoughts wandered to Wade.

Well, of course. Why not let the police handle Wade and get rid of the guy for him? Carl leaned his head against the bed's pseudo-suede headboard and smiled. Was this a solution or what? Maybe he wasn't so out of it after all. He closed his eyes and thought about how to set it up, how to let the cops know without implicating himself.

His fingers slowly relaxed around the remains of his joint. He didn't notice his hand drop over the edge of the bed, nor did he hear the faint hiss or see the quick orange flame light the edge of the newspaper left on the floor.

Chapter 38

Anchorage

Monday

Elsie gave her sister a long look. "Wade was fooling around with Valerie you know." Kena glanced up in time to see her mother's flash of interest. Elsie reached for a Life magazine on the end table. "Did you ever meet Mack and Val McMillian?" A photograph of Bill Clinton was on the cover of Life.

Jane shook her head. "No, but I've seen them in town." She broke off the end of the thread with her teeth. Then she worked the material with her fingers as she stitched the hem, loosening the fabric around the thread so it wouldn't look like a hick job.

Elsie lowered her voice, "Mack let her get away with a lot."

"You mean men?" Jane's eyebrows rose. She and Paul had heard the rumors. Even Kena, with ears like a pitcher or whatever, had heard about Valerie being loose, not that she knew what that meant either.

Elsie nodded, "One or two drinks and if Val saw a fresh pair of pants in the garage, or anywhere else for that matter..." She sighed and looked out the window as if she might see some pants in the yard. "Mack couldn't control her, but I guess fooling around with Wade was too close to home."

"I would guess so!" Jane's mouth turned down on one side. It was one of her disgusted looks that Kena had been practicing without success in front of the mirror.

"Why did Mack stay with her?" Finished with the hem, Jane shook the dress out over the iron board.

155

This was more than Kena usually heard. Almost hypnotically, she poked the needle into the thick corduroy, leaving the stitches loose. From the silence that usually followed *spending time*, Kena knew it was a grownup thing, probably something to do with sex, about which she also knew nothing.

"Well, Valerie McMillian had the purse strings." Elsie said as if her sister should have known. "She was a Royton."

Jane's dark eyebrows shot up and Elsie looked pleased. "Didn't you know? Her uncle owns First Alaska Bank…she inherited a lot of money when her parents died in that boat accident." Elsie frowned. "When was that, seven or eight years ago? Anyway, it's her money that bought that garage and that big fancy house."

Jane looked bewildered. "If she's got all that money, why did she marry Mack? Women married for love, security and money. If not the first two and the third wasn't unnecessary, why bother?"

Elsie shrugged. "Mack's on the City Council. Clyde says he's got political ambitions. I think that's what Valerie wanted, status."

"Ah." Jane understood ambition, having fought hard to get where she was. Elsie took a deep breath and exhaled as if happy to get something off her chest.

"Do you think she wanted him to leave Judy?"

Elsie shook her head. Her black hair, like Jane's, reflected reddish highlights the sisters attributed to their Irish grandfather. "I doubt if Val cared that much. She liked men, not just *a man*. Wade really loved Jimmy even though he wasn't Jimmy's father."

Elsie paused. "Wade went on a real bender after the fire, remember? Sure, he takes jobs as a bartender, but he's no drinker."

Jane nodded. Still thinking, she draped a freshly-laundered dress over the iron board. It was a shirtwaist she had bought four years ago at Welch's Dress Shop on Fourth Avenue. The dark brown cotton had tiny raised flocked dots that had flattened over the years. Now, as she slammed the iron over the wrinkled cotton, the iron board wobbled. Everyone else was getting sex, not her, dammit.

"Wade told us he tried to break it off with Val," Elsie continued, fiddling with her gloves, picking them up and putting them down again.

"Uh huh," Jane's voice was heavy with skepticism. "She was a good-looking dame."

"Hmmm." Elsie shrugged. "Wade said she threatened to tell her husband that Wade was making passes at her if he stopped seeing her."

"Oh for goodness sakes!" Jane stopped ironing and looked at her sister. "Do you think she had anything to do with the trailer fire?"

Elsie blinked. "No…no. She plays with men and I don't think she'd leave Mac. Besides, how could she have arranged it? You'd think she'd want Judy gone more than little Jimmy." Elsie looked out the window, her expression sad, as if Jimmy's death had resettled inside her.

"Son of a glit," Jane muttered. Kena decided *glit* was a nun-approved swearword from her mother's days at Chemawa Indian School in Oregon. She was always talking about nuns.

Jane leaned over and unplugged the iron. "Are the police and fire chief certain it was an accident?" Jimmy was gone and his mother, Judy had returned to Fairbanks.

"As far as I know." Elsie dug in her purse and took out a handkerchief embroidered with tiny blue fleur de lyses. "You know how easy these trailer fires are." She dabbed at her nose, not wanting to ruin the pristine handkerchief with a good blow.

"How about Wade's gambling debts?" Ironing had made Jane sweat again. "Paul thinks the fire is something those gambling guys might have done."

Elsie looked doubtful. "It'd be a strange way to get their money, and Wade did owe several hundred dollars." She frowned. "Unless it was to set an example."

Caught up in what she was hearing, Jena had sewn the circular hem twice. She shook out the skirt. Bits of corduroy fuzz floated up and she sneezed.

Elsie jerked and stared at Kena as if she had just fallen from the sky. "Uh well." She glanced at her watch. "I'd better get going." She got to her feet and pulled on her coat. Tying a scarf around her head, she called "Tla, tla" as cold air rushed inside.

Overhead, ravens flew, cawing and Kena looked out the window watching them. "We don't have to say anything about this to your father," Jane said with a quick look at Kena as she folded the iron board and unplugged the Singer.

"This is just talk anyway." Jane put away the Singer she hadn't even used. Her sister seemed to hear things almost before they happened. She was better than the evening news.

Later that night, after Kena had gone to bed and Paul was snoring, Jane realized she hadn't felt blue all day. She had even forgotten her worries over whether she was still a woman now thanks to her surgery, she was missing crucial parts.

Chapter 39

Fairbanks

Monday Morning

Cara felt around her chair and her seat cushion. Her father had given her the gold Cross pen and pencil set when she graduated from high school. "To help you with your first novel," he'd said, smiling. Yeah right. Well it had to be here somewhere, she thought looking under her desk. She had already searched through her pockets and her tote bag. God, this was frustrating. But not as frustrating as her accidental meeting with Thomlin in the CoOp.

She had been looking for an empty seat at the CoOp's counter and hadn't noticed the man on her right as she slid onto the stool. "Hey," he said. "Are you stalking me?"

Startled, Cara looked at him then grinned. "Should I get in line?" Thomlin smiled as the waitress set a plate of eggs over easy, hash browns, and Canadian bacon in front of him. She handed a menu to Cara who nodded at the coffee pot in the waitress's hand.

After Cara had ordered. he said, "Do you know the Wright family in Anchorage?"

"The family who owned the property where Jimmy Brown died?"

He nodded. "I was in Anchorage last week and went over to talk to them and their daughter. The girl was at cheerleading practice."

Looking at Thomlin was distracting and Cara focused on the Coke machine across the counter from where she sat. "Another woman was with her," he added.

Cara frowned and shook her head. "Who was it?"

"That's why I thought I'd ask you," he said, smiling. Cara glanced at him involuntarily and noticed his teeth. They were white and straight and beautiful. Good golly.

"Hmmm, you'd have to talk to Jane Patric or Elsie Rapid," she said, clearing her throat. "They are both my aunts and live there and know the family,"

Cara forced herself to think. "I heard the daughter is boy-crazy. When I called Aunt Jane a few days ago, she said the girl's parents were crossing their fingers, hoping she graduates."

"How old is she?" he said, admiring her profile.

"Sixteen going on thirty-five. Are you wondering why she went home before the trailer caught fire?"

Cara's order came and she concentrated on spearing the sausage with her fork.

"The Anchorage police said she had gone home to get a tampon."

Cara burst into laughter. "Well there's an excuse you can't argue with. But wasn't the fire an accident?"

Thomlin lifted his cup and motioned to the waitress for a refill. "Yes, is was, officially."

Cara finished her eggs and ate the last of her sausage. A woman to her left asked for the salt and Cara handed it to her. Then she thought of Julie's laptop. "Did you ever find Julie's laptop and her printer?"

Thomlin was pouring cream in his coffee. "A laptop and a printer? I didn't see them on the list of missing items."

Breakfast had relaxed Cara as food usually did and she turned to face at him. He's like any other guy, she reassured herself. "Aunt Lucy gave Julie a Macintosh laptop and a printer just over a year ago. Both were used, but refurbished or whatever. I didn't see them when Ron and I were at the Ashenberg's looking for the Ravenstone. He said he'd ask you or Ian about it."

Thomlin nodded. "I'll put the word out on them." He paused. "I've been meaning to ask you about Ron."

"Ron?" This was so out of the blue, she turned and fully faced him.

"How has he seemed since Ashenberg's death?"

Cara shook her head at waitress's offer of a refill. "This is the first time I've seen him involved in anything like this," she said. "I don't know how he'd act if someone else in Goldspring was killed, but he and Herb were pretty close." She hesitated, "He seems quieter now, but isn't that normal when a killer has just rampaged your town? Also, there've been no murders in Goldspring for decades so it's not like he's trained to deal with them."

Thomlin shifted gears. "So, what do you know about the Ravenstone?" He changed the subject as quickly as Lucy, she thought.

"Not much, just what Aunt Lucy and Sam might have said in passing." She moved her empty plate toward the waitress. "Why?"

"It seems to be the link to everything that's happening." He looked at her and smiled. He was enjoying this. It had been awhile since he'd felt like flirting. Cara felt her cheeks get hot.

"Well, sure," she said, turning back to the coke machine. "You think the Anchorage fire is connected to it?"

"The same players may have been involved in that fire and the murders in Goldspring. I think both may tie in with the bigger picture and that could mean the Ravenstone."

Thomlin got to his feet and pulled out his wallet. He shoved a bill across the counter, gesturing to the waitress to include Cara's breakfast.

"This is on me," Thomlin said, cutting off her protest. "By the way, according to Sam's autopsy, he had a heart attack." He stood as close to her as he could without climbing on top of her. "Thanks for telling me about Jane and Elsie. We'll check the local pawnshops for Julie's computer."

After he left, Cara sat for a moment concentrating on her breathing. Whew. She looked up and saw a woman's reflection in the mirror behind the counter. She was looking at Cara and smiling. Oh boy, Cara thought, sliding off the counter's stool and gathering her coat and tote bag. There was no privacy even at the CoOP.

Chapter 40

Fairbanks

Thomlin ran into Ian at the entrance of the Alaska State Troopers' building. "Whatcha got?" He said as Ian followed him inside.

"Was hoping you'd tell me," Ian said. "I just got a call from Ron. He asked about Frank and what he's doing for money. He also wanted to know about Brian. It got me thinking. Ron was one of the first to find Ashenberg. I'm wondering if he knows more about the Ravenstone than he's letting on."

Thomlin pointed to a coffee cup and Ian shook his head, no. "You think he found the Ravenstone before I got there?" Thomlin poured himself some coffee and added creamer.

"He could have." Ian shrugged. "Of course, Cara and Aunt Lucy were there even earlier. They may even have it." He gave Thomlin a look. He sensed the trooper's interest in Cara and enjoyed teasing him.

Thomlin smiled. "Have you asked them?

Ian laughed. "Nope, thought I'd leave that to you. But I've seen Cara since then and she seems as puzzled as we are. And Lucy, well she can be cagey. If she's got it, or knows where it is, she's being damned quiet about it."

Thomlin had settled his chair and twirled around to look out the window. "Or she's motivated. But what would keep her quiet about the artifact? I doubt it's money."

Ian yawned. "But aren't you kind of scraping the bottom of the barrel here with Cara and Lucy? She's gotta be well over seventy and Cara?" He shook his head. "I don't buy it."

"Oh, the Anchorage Police found Clyne's fingerprints all over the hotel room where they'd found the dead woman. What's her name, Valerie McMillian? And they found a piece of her lingerie in his office across the street from the Captain Cook."

"Interesting," Thomlin said. "Have they notified Seattle?"

"Yep and Clyne is in the hospital there. They have a guard on him." Thomlin frowned.

"What's wrong with him?"

"They say he's got prostate cancer." Ian said.

Thomlin nodded. "Poor bastard." He twirled his chair back toward his desk. "By the way, I ran into your cousin this morning at the CoOP."

"Really?" Ian smiled. Interesting

"Yeah." Thomlin's expression said *enough*. He didn't want to get distracted and Ian was in a teasing mood. "She asked about the Ashenberg girl's laptop and printer."

Ian frowned and shook his head. "I forgot about Julie's laptop. But that could explain the computer mouse in the Ford that Frank rented. It must have fallen out of a backpack or pocket."

"Why would she need a mouse for a laptop?"

"It's easier to manipulate."

Matt raised his eyebrows. "Huh, well, let's see if we can find her laptop and that printer. "Cara said the laptop is a MacIntosh. I don't know about the printer."

After Ian left, Thomlin called Lucy who had the serial numbers of the computer and laptop in her address book. After she gave them to him, Thomlin passed that information on to Bill and told him to check the local pawnshops, newspaper ads, Craig's List and garage sales and anything else he could think of for both Anchorage and Fairbanks.

As he shuffled through the papers on his desk, his thoughts kept wandering. Sam had said Goldspring was Red Shirt's birthplace and he wanted to keep the Ravenstone there. If Herb had hidden the Ravenstone, it must still be somewhere in the village, maybe still on the Ashenberg property.

Thomlin shook his head. Herb's body had already been stripped and his clothing searched by the coroner. They'd found nothing. He threw a pencil across the room in frustration. Dammit, the FBI had Brian, which left Thomlin with Ron, Lucy and Connie, Sam's daughter. He decided to start with Connie.

Chapter 41

Goldspring

Trooper Thomlin Interviewing Connie, Lucy and Ron

"I spoke to Herb's daughter, Julie by phone and she thinks he might have hidden this artifact in a tree behind their house," Thomlin said. "We've searched the trees in the area twice, but found nothing. Did Sam or Herb say anything about where it could be kept?"

"Like a safe deposit box, you mean?" Connie tried to smile and shook her head. "No, I never heard him talk about it, but after Julie and Herb left he seemed *bengetdee'o*. Seeing Tomlin's blank face, she added, "Uneasy."

"Dad told Herb to take it someplace safe. Herb didn't want to do what my *tek 'aal*, asked." Connie sighed. "My father," she clarified. There, she thought with relief, she had managed to tell this white man what she knew in English.

Thomlin drove down the hill to Lucy Montalk's house on the other side of Goldspring. Her friend Ethel was at the table having coffee when Lucy ushered him into the kitchen. "I just made a fresh pot if you'd like some. That's a long drive from Fairbanks."

Ethel gave him a look of relief as she got to her feet. It must be tiring to be at someone else's beck and call, Thomlin thought, even with a close friend.

"We didn't know about the Ravenstone until after we found Herb. Ron told us," Lucy said, pushing a plate of blueberry muffins toward the trooper.

Thomlin nodded and sipped his coffee. From where he sat, he could see much of her small house. He liked her kitchen. This was the first time he'd been here without standing the entire time. But this was also his first time alone with Lucy. She offered a refill and he pushed his mug toward her. He'd seen the coffee bag on the counter. Polar Bear Express. Good stuff.

"I think the Ravenstone is the reason behind both deaths," he said. "Anyone who knows anything about it might be in danger."

"Hmmm" Lucy said, her round face calm.

"When we find it, what would you like to see done with it?" He sipped his coffee. Excellent.

"Donate it to the University I suppose," Lucy said, straightening her back. "Don't they have the mask it belongs to?"

"That's what I understand, but I haven't seen it." Thomlin thought he ought to get to the museum and take a look.

Lucy's brow furrowed. "I heard one of the killers got away?" News of that culprit's escape had spread through Goldspring like a brush fire.

"We know he's in Anchorage. The APD and the troopers have him under surveillance." Thomlin polished off his muffin and got to his feet.

"Thanks, Lucy, the coffee and your muffins hit the spot."

As he got into his vehicle, Thomlin recalled Ian describing Lucy as crafty. Boy, that's the truth, he thought. He also said her husband had been a VPSO. So, she wasn't unfamiliar with Alaska's criminal underbelly. But he didn't have the feeling she knew where the Ravenstone was.

As he drove to Ron's place in the center of Goldspring he suspected Connie and/or Lucy had already told Ron he was coming. He snorted. They'd probably sent a raven ahead to spread the word.

"You think Lucy or Cara has the Ravenstone?" Ron was both incredulous and relieved that Thomlin hadn't shown up to arrest him.

"Not necessarily." Thomlin was looking at a drawing on the wall. It was an architectural rendering of a building. "What's this?"

"Ah, well, so far that's just a dream, "It's a plan for a learning center for Goldspring." Ron said, his shoulders relaxing. "Where people who live here and in nearby villages can get hands-on training with aircraft and automobile maintenance and paramedic and nursing skills." He took a breath and looked at the trooper. Thomlin seemed interested.

Encouraged, Ron continued. "It could also offer cosmetology and hair cutting classes, anything to help people get jobs without having to move to Fairbanks or Anchorage."

Thomlin was impressed. "This sounds worthwhile, but where will you get the money?"

"I'm talking to the Native corporations, Doyon, Baan O Yeel Kon and CIRI…Along with the building and construction costs, I've worked out the annual cost of maintenance and salaries for the instructors. I've got a prospectus, it's around here somewhere." Ron looked around his living room/kitchen, which was cluttered with paperwork, books, CDs, and DVDs.

"Any private money?" Thomlin asked, thinking about the Ravenstone and how the sale of the artifact could boost a startup fund. Ron shook his head.

"I haven't gotten that far," he said. "I imagine private donors might want a guy with a proven track record."

Thomlin nodded. "Where did you learn all this?"

"I have a bachelor's degree in business from UAF. We had to do projects like this." He looked at the rendering he had tacked to the wall. "I hired an architecture student to draw that. There's a smaller version in the prospectus."

Thomlin took another look at what he knew would be a costly project. "I wish you well with it."

Cara's phone rang. It was Lucy. "Trooper Thomlin was just here … he thinks the Ravenstone is at the center of everything that's happened."

"The center of everything?" Cara was surprised. "I have tomorrow off so why don't I come up?"

What had set him off, she wondered, putting down the phone.

Was it something she said when she saw him at the CoOP? The troopers had Frank under surveillance in Anchorage. As for Brian, wasn't he in jail? There was also that gallery owner Clyne, who had hired them, but she'd heard he was in Seattle

Cara slid off the kitchen stool and went upstairs to change into her jeans. Thank the Lord she'd gotten her Toyota back. Ian had driven her back to Fairbanks and said he doubted she'd be liable for the damage to the Fiesta since the Troopers were holding it as evidence. She hoped he was right.

Chapter 42

Frank leaves Anchorage

When Frank saw a Chanel Two News van and cop cars surrounding Anchorage's Captain Cook Hotel, he turned on the small television Clyne kept in the back of his shop. Keeping the sound off, he was stunned to see his acne pitted face on the screen. He turned it up just enough to hear the reporter announce that Frank Barnetti was wanted for theft and murder! *Shit-shit*!

Panicking, he looked around Clyne's shop for something to put on over his battered jacket. Behind a tall rack displaying a Haida blanket, he saw a door. He pushed it open and found a large closet filled with janitorial supplies. Beyond the opposite wall he heard voices and remembered a gift store was in the same building.

The closet held a six-foot wooden ladder, paint brushes, a couple of paint rollers, and three unused paint trays.

Behind two unopened buckets of sheetrock mud lay a pair of painter's overalls and a cap. The pants were too long, but he pulled them on and rolled up the legs.

The voices from the next room had stopped. Had they heard the news and seen Clyne's shop on the screen? His heart pounding, he grabbed the cap and, moved the Haida blanket back in front of the door.

"Where you headed?" the truck driver said when Frank climbed into the passenger seat. He had turned his old parka, which was reversible, inside out. It was now a vivid blue. Worn over the white overalls and with the painters' cap perched on his head he felt quite different.

"Palmer," Frank said, situating his skinny rear end on the torn vinyl seat crammed with manuals. The driver checked the traffic on his left then pulled onto the Glenn Highway.

"I'm headed for Fairbanks," the driver said, looking into his rear-view mirror as he changed lanes. "I can drop you in Wasilla." Wasilla was next door to Palmer and that was good enough for Frank.

"Sounds good," he said, adjusting his cap and remembering his lucky gas station. The driver gave him a second look.

Thirty minutes later, he pulled into a filling station. "I need oil," he said, looking at his gage.

"Wha, what?" Frank had dozed off and jerked awake as the driver climbed out and headed inside the station.

Inside. the driver pulled out a faded blue handkerchief and dabbed his face. Nerves made him sweat. "You gotta a phone I can use?"

"Back there. Local calls only," The cashier pointed to a wall mounted telephone.

The overweight driver lumbered back to the phone and noticed the grimy handle on the receiver. He pulled out his equally soiled handkerchief and wiped the mouthpiece then dialed. "He's in my truck," he almost hissed into the phone.

"What, who is in your truck?"

That guy on TV" the driver said, glancing out the window. The passenger side door to his truck was open and the truck looked empty.

"Well, crap, he *was* in my truck."

"Think there's a reward?" Franks hands and feet were tied and he found himself on the floor and jammed against the back seat of a car. It was moving. The pain racing through his body was fierce. He felt like a Ritz cracker, broken, chewed and spit out.

"I'm sure this is the guy on TV," another voice said. The car rocked as a big rig roared by, blowing snow laden wind.

"Man, I haven't seen skin that bad since school. Don't touch him, you might catch something."

"Hey, watch out!" a woman's voice yelled from front.

Frank, blinded by the rag around his head, felt a hard jolt as the car slammed into another vehicle. With a screech of metal, it spun off the road and began rolling down a steep embankment. Frank's head banged again on the floor and then on the back of the seat ahead of him.

After what felt like days, the car stopped, tilted nose first, its rear tires spinning uselessly. Frank heard voices, then a bolt of searing pain ripped through him. Then he heard nothing.

Chapter 43

Fairbanks and Goldspring

Lucy was digging through her closet for her hat when she saw something that looked familiar. She pulled the nylon scarf free from the jumble of scarves and hats. She sat down on the bed as she remembered finding the hat beneath the brush near Herb's body. A light snow was falling and she'd stuffed it in the bag with the food she and Cara had brought to the Ashenbergs. Tears slid down her face as she remembered that day. But how had Herb's muskrat hat gotten into her closet?

She looked across the bed into her dresser mirror and saw her image with the hat. Thinking back, she remembered Ethel coming to her house and insisting they eat. Then Ethel had put everything away including the bags of food Lucy and Cara had brought back from Herb's house. Ethel must have thought the hat was Lucy's. Well, what did it matter now, she thought, stroking the soft fur.

"Are you ready?" Cara stood in the doorway watching Lucy.

Lucy looked up. "Look at this," she said, turning the hat in her hand.

"Isn't that Herb's hat? The one you made him?" Cara moved closer to get a better look

Lucy frowned. Turning the hat slightly, she felt something hard. Turning it inside out, she noticed the threads that held the lining to the fur were torn.

Beginning to sweat, Cara pulled off her parka and sat beside her. "What is it?" she said. Lucy shook her head, then something fell out and hit the braided rug with a thud. *What in the world?*

Cara leaned over and picked up a chamois bag. Holding it over the quilt, she shook it and a flat black stone fell out. "Oh, my word," Lucy said. It was carved in the shape of a raven's head. A tuft of fur, maybe bear fur, poked through a hole in the beak. Two dark red garnets on either side marked the eyes.

Stunned. Cara leaned closer. The carved lines of the raven's head had worn down over the decades. "Is this the Ravenstone?"

"It must be," Lucy said. She knew it was.

"Does anyone else know you have Herb's hat?"

Lucy shook her head. "Just Ethel, I imagine. She must have put it in the closet the day we found Herb." She stopped and looked worried, "Do you think that's why those men came? They thought I had it?"

Cara shook her head. "No, I don't think they know you and I found Herb. In fact, I don't think they knew Herb put it in his hat. Or that he even had a hat."

She looked at Lucy whose face was reminiscent of wrinkled tissue paper. The reality of what Lucy had found was sinking in. They had the Ravenstone. *She and Lucy had the Ravenstone!* Cara's heart fluttered. *Holy cow.*

Lucy recovered first. "What do you think we should do with it?" She took the Ravenstone and slid it back into the chamois bag.

"Why don't you leave it in the hat for now? And keep it in your closet," Cara said, looking at Lucy's crowded closet. She doubted any man would willingly go through it.

Lucy slid the bag into the opening between the lining and fur. Trembling, she got up and went to her dresser for a needle and thread and began stitching the lining shut. Her stitches were tiny and precise. "Don't you think we should tell the troopers? Or Ian or Ron?" Lucy said, snipping the thread with her scissors.

Cara stared at the fur hat on her aunt's lap. "Yes, we should," she said slowly.

"But you don't want to? You don't think it should be returned to the mask?" Lucy looked at her.

Cara sighed. "Sam said it should stay with the Dena, the people in Goldspring" She took another breath. "Maybe by the time we have a potlatch for Sam, we'll know what to do."

Lucy gave Cara a thoughtful look. "I don't want to worry about it though. And it would be safer at the University. We could present it to them in a ceremonial potlatch."

Cara was surprised. She had thought for sure that Lucy would side with Sam's wishes. But Lucy was right. And with Herb's death, they had no way to find the next deeyninh.

Lucy rewrapped Herb's hat loosely in the scarf. Getting up, she moved to her closet and put it under a pile of scarves and hats, some fur, some knitted and some crocheted. Then she whispered, *"Edeghoyeneegheleedeneek."*

Cara zipped her parka. "What did you say?"

"To stay safe." *Among other things.* There was too much interest in this Ravenstone. Lucy would be glad to get it to someplace more protected.

Chapter 44

Goldspring

Tuesday

Ethel finished loading her car with shopping bags filled with clothing she was donating to Salvation Army. Then she went back inside for her purse and keys. Her next stop was Lucy's to pick up a couple of boxes of clothing and kitchen items. Her car was already loaded with her easel, paints, paper, and canvases for her painting class in a few hours. She hoped there was enough room.

It was warm outside and she took a deep breath of the fresh air before getting in Lucy's car. There was little traffic as she approached Lucy's house and she was surprised to find the Cougar gone.

Ethel turned off her car's engine and considered waiting, but who knew how long that would be? She looked at her watch. Oh heck, Lucy had shown her where she kept her spare key under the back step. She wouldn't mind if Ethel went inside and picked up her donations. With a sigh, Ethel climbed out of her car and walked around to the back entrance.

She carried the first box to her car, noting it held a coat Lucy hadn't worn in years. As she tucked the box into her trunk, she remembered Lucy's hats and scarves. She was always knitting or crocheting, but when she went out, she chose from the same two or three hats. Ethel smiled when she opened Lucy's closet and saw the lynx fur hat on top of the pile. That was Lucy's favorite and Ethel didn't touch it. As for the others, she was always telling Ethel to help herself. "I'm not wearing these and someone should."

Well, someone will now, Ethel thought as she picked out a few hats and scarves she had never seen Lucy wear. Then she remembered the fur hat Lucy had made for Herb. It was a beautiful muskrat and had earflaps. Ethel remembered putting it in Lucy's closet the day she and Cara had found Herb's body.

Wondering if Lucy still had it, Ethel dug through the pile until she saw something near the back. It was wrapped in a rose-colored silk scarf. She pulled it out. Seeing Herb's hat again brought back that miserable day. This should definitely go, she thought, sitting back on her heels and staring at the fur. Lucy didn't need reminders of Herb's grisly death. Besides, if Ethel left it here, it would surely be moth-eaten. No, it was better to pass it on to someone who could use it. Isn't that what Lucy always said?

Chapter 45

Fairbanks

Tuesday

"We had a call from a guy at a gas station south of Wasilla." Thomlin told Ian. "He recognized Frank when he picked him up in Anchorage. Unfortunately, wily old Frank took off when the driver was phoning the police from a gas station. Troopers searched the area, but this time his luck ran out. The troopers found his body at a crash site about ten miles this side of Wasilla."

The trooper settled back in his chair and flicked a pencil over his desk in irritation. "He was beaten and tied up. The car had rolled, and was almost flattened, but we've got his fingerprints and the ME has confirmed his identity."

"So he's dead?" Ian said.

"Oh yeah, very."

"Well, you've still got Brian, he should be willing to talk by now."

Thomlin nodded. "Let's hope so. Especially now with Clyne in a hospital in Seattle."

"I'll call Lucy and Cara and let them know," Ian said.

"Frank is dead?" Cara couldn't believe it. "My God, how?"

"He was in a car accident. He'd been beaten pretty badly. I understand his weight was down to about a hundred pounds. Main thing is, the Troopers and the Feds still have Brian and they should be able to get what they need from him."

"What do they need? Do they think he has the Ravenstone?" Cara's thoughts were swirling. She needed to call Lucy.

"The Feds are looking for more information about art thefts in Anchorage and Seattle."

After Cara had hung up, she called Lucy and was in for another shock.

"Oh Cara, it's gone, the bird thing is gone."

"What? What do you mean?"

"I've searched everywhere and can't find it. The hat isn't in my closet. It's GONE."

"Listen, I'll be there in about forty-five minutes. I'll help you look."

Hats, scarves, mittens, coats and jackets and other assorted clothing were spread across Lucy's bed. Cara sank down next to a box of gloves and stared at the closet, shaking her head.

"The last time I saw the Ravenstone, you were with me." Lucy said. "I should call Ethel. She and Ron are the only ones who know where I keep the spare key when I lock the house."

"But you don't always lock your door." Cara said.

Lucy shook her head. "No one's around and you know hardly anyone locks their doors in Goldspring, especially here in the country."

"Let's check and see if the key is still there." Cara pulled on her parka. Together they went through the kitchen to the stairs beneath the deck. But the key was frozen in place on a nail beneath the deck. Other than a few animal tracks, wind had drifted the snow covering everything else.

"Why don't you call Ron and Ethel. Maybe they've seen Herb's hat? Just don't mention the Ravenstone." Cara said as they trooped upstairs.

"Nope," Ron said. "I haven't seen Herb's hat. I asked you about it, remember?" His coffee had scalded on the stove and his nose twitched at the odor. He reached over to turn off the burner.

"Oh yes," Lucy said, flustered. "I remember you telling me."

She then called Ethel who wasn't home. Lucy decided to try her later. Then she remembered her boxes filled with clothing to donate.

"I set them aside for Ethel to pick up. She must have come by when we were at Flemings Market."

"You didn't put Herb's hat in one of those boxes, did you?" Cara hoped not.

"No, no." Lucy shook her head. "I worked too hard on that hat, I was planning to give it to someone special."

She looked exhausted and Cara steered her toward the sofa. Lucy's cat, Major was asleep on the afghan, his tail curled over his nose. "Try not to worry about it," Cara said, pushing the heavy cat to one side. "We'll figure out something."

"I wrapped Herb's hat in a scarf to protect it from moths," Lucy said, stroking Major. She'd had a short nap and was feeling more alert "Some of the other hats I made are gone too," she looked at Cara. "Ethel must have taken them."

Cara's eyebrows rose. "Ethel wouldn't steal from you."

"No, no, I told her to take them often enough."

"Try her again. She may have seen it when she came by to pick up your donations."

Lucy dialed Ethel again, but there was still no answer.

"Didn't she say something about seeing her son and his wife in North Pole?" Cara added, mentioning a town a few miles outside Fairbanks. Do you have his phone number?"

"Yes!" Lucy's face cleared and she pulled her address book from beneath the phone book. Finding the number, she began dialing. No one answered so Lucy left a message. "No one's home anywhere," she said in disgust.

"Why don't we check with Salvation Army in Goldspring. They'll know if Ethel brought in anything."

"But why would she take it?' Lucy said slamming down the address book in disgust. Never would I have given away Herb's fur hat!"

"Well maybe she didn't, but why don't we go over there and see if they remember her?"

Lucy maneuvered her thirty-year old Mercury Cougar down

Goldspring's narrow streets to the Goodwill store. She parked and they started up the steps just as Millie was unlocking the door.

"Sure," Millie said. "Ethel brought in a large donation a day or so ago. I don't think it's all been sorted out." Millie glanced at the back room where Lucy and Cara could see boxes and bags and stacks of clothing on a table through the partially opened door. "We're a bit short-handed and I'm the only one here. You say it was a hat?" She stepped into a back room.

"Yes, it was a muskrat hat. It was a man's and had earflaps. I'd wrapped it in a rose-colored scarf." Lucy looked around. Near the window she saw a rack of knit hats and baseball caps. Next to it, white rabbit earmuffs were wrapped around a brown wig on a Styrofoam head.

"Aunt Lucy, isn't this your old coat?" Cara had pulled out a coat from a rack and waved a sleeve at her aunt.

Lucy moved around a rack of blouses toward Cara. "It sure looks like it."

She called out, "Millie, we found my coat."

"I don't see a fur hat back here," Millie said, emerging from the back room. "But it may have been sent to our store in Fairbanks. They send us things when they are full, like jeans and jackets and we do the same. And we have lots of hats! Do you see any of your other hats here?" Lucy shook her head. "Well, I bet we sent it to Fairbanks. I'll ask Celia when she comes in tomorrow."

Cara and Lucy returned to her car and sat, thinking. "Let's call the Salvation Army store in Fairbanks first," Lucy said. "I should have asked Millie for their number.

"I'll get their business card on the counter. Wait here."

Outside, Lucy had just pulled a tube of Chapstick from her bag when she saw the baker at Fleming's drive by. She did a double take. What was that on his usually baldhead? If it hadn't been for his huge, brown-framed glasses, she wouldn't have recognized him. The store was just a block behind her and she got out of the car.

Panting when she reached the market, she pulled the heavy

glass door open and headed for the deli. There he was, tying on his white apron. "Hey Gordon, did I just see you drive by the Salvation Army store?" Before he could answer, Lucy said. "Were you wearing a fur hat? He beamed at her.

"Yeah, my daughter made it for me. You want to see it?" Before she could answer, he went into the back and returned with his hat. Up close, Lucy could see it wasn't Herb's. This fur was newer and lush with deeper shades of brown and black. Lucy tried to hide her disappointment. "She did a beautiful job, Gordon. Is she still making these?"

"Naw, she's gone back to the university, studying social welfare. It took her a long time to make this one!" He looked at her. "Why'd you ask, anyway? Don't you make fur hats?" Lucy forced a laugh.

"Well, I used to, but yours is so finely done..." She paused, wishing a customer would come up and order something. Finally, she said, "I made one for Herb Ashenberg and this one looks like it. Anyway, my eyesight isn't so good now and I'm looking for someone to make another one."

Lucy returned to the car, carrying a small bag of pasta, chicken salad and something new called gluten-free cupcakes. Cara was standing by the car, staring at Lucy's glum expression.

"What happened, I came back to the car and you were gone?"

"Phooey. It's a long story, I'll tell you later."

Chapter 46

"Mom was caught in that avalanche on the Steese," Ethel's nephew said. "There was a pile-up and she was hit by a van. Her car was smashed up pretty bad."

"Was she hurt?" Lucy waved Cara over so they both could listen.

"She's in the hospital," he said. "We're going to go see her. I'll tell her you called."

Stunned, Cara stepped back from Lucy and almost fell over a dining chair that had been left pulled out. "Well damn," she said, straightening herself. "There must be something on the news about it." Cara switched on the radio and began searching for the all-news station.

"Wait, hold it," Lucy said, hearing a bulletin: '*An avalanche on the Steese highway has injured at least five and has blocked the southbound lanes. We'll have more information as we get it. Please stay tuned.*'

"I'll call Ian," Lucy said. "Ethel's probably at Fairbanks Memorial."

But Ian was out and she left a message. Lucy gave a violent shiver and pulled her old blue cardigan from the back of the sofa. Then she flipped open the Yellow Pages looking for the hospital number. After twenty minutes, she hung up and joined Cara in the kitchen.

"No luck, huh?" Cara was heating some soup. Having missed lunch, they were both hungry.

"I finally reached the hospital; they said to call back later this afternoon. There was also an eight-car accident near the university so they're busy." She sighed.

She took a bag of caramelized cinnamon muffins from the refrigerator and set them on a plate. It amazed Cara that Lucy could eat as she did and not gain weight.

"You're not Bulimic are you?" she said, eying her aunt.

"Oh, it's habit. I thought we could use something sweet after our soup. What is it by the way?" Lucy looked inside the pot. "Ah, vegetable. Good."

Lucy sat down and shoved the plate of muffins across the table. She was too upset to eat.

The avalanche covered several hundred feet of the Steese Highway. The area was covered with troopers and backed up traffic on both ends while people waited for a lane to clear. Thomlin watched a tow truck driver attach a winch to a maroon-colored Subaru. The vehicle, although battered, looked familiar. Mud had covered part of the license plate and he wrote down what he could see as it was hauled away. Back in his vehicle, he ran the plate numbers before calling Ian.

"Hey Ian, what color was Lucy's friend's Subaru?"

"You mean Ethel? It's a deep red like a maroon. Why"

"You might call Lucy and see if Ethel is still in Goldspring. A red or maroon Subaru was just hauled out of the avalanche site. The ambulance has already gone."

Lucy's face was gray when she put down the phone. "Ian said Ethel's car was totaled in that avalanche and she's in Fairbanks Memorial in serious condition." She exhaled and sat for a moment.

"Holy moly," Cara said and sat down abruptly.

"I want to go with you to Fairbanks."

"Sure," Cara said. "I'll call Ian and tell him we're coming." She hugged her aunt who seemed even thinner and more fragile than she had been an hour ago.

Chapter 47

Goldspring

Ron took a final look at his letter before putting it in the copy machine. In it, he had written how he'd colluded with Carl Clyne to acquire the Ravenstone in exchange for funds to build a training center in Goldspring. He dropped the original letter in his letter file then folded three copies into envelopes, one addressed to Trooper Thomlin and the other to Ian. The last would go to Lucy and Cara.

That should do it, he thought, sliding the three envelopes under his desk calendar. He got up and walked to the window. He wished Cindy hadn't gone to Galena. She was goofy and made him laugh and that alone took his mind off these deaths and that damned Ravenstone.

He and Cindy had been buddies since before college. He felt her real problem was she had so little ambition. She had dropped out of UAF after one year and returned to Goldspring and her part time job at Flemings' deli. She once mentioned beauty school, but that seemed to have fallen by the wayside. Sometimes he wondered if she had anything in her head. He imagined shaking her and her head rattling like a broken toy.

He sank into a beanbag chair he'd gotten at a yard sale. Cindy was one of the reasons he wanted to build a trade school in Goldspring. So she could take classes and keep her job and still live at home where she could keep an eye on her mother who kept falling down thanks to periodic dizzy spells.

Chapter 48

Fairbanks

Ethel was propped up in bed when Cara and Lucy walked into the room. Lucy saw a chair and pulled it closer to her friend. "What're you doin here?" Ethel's head, nose and right shoulder were wrapped in white bandages. Her words were slurred

"That's what I should be asking you." Lucy tried to look disapproving, but Ethel's appearance alarmed her. The nurse told them she had a broken arm, three cracked ribs, a broken nose, and suffered a concussion.

While Cara waited for the candy striper to bring her a chair, she tried to breathe lightly of the hospital's antiseptic smells. The room was full of cords, electronics, and racks holding bags, some filled with fluids. To her left, another patient was concealed behind a curtain.

An hour later, Cara and Lucy headed for the parking lot. "Ethel said she remembered taking Herb's hat from my closet, but she doesn't remember leaving it at Salvation Army. She thought she was doing me a favor." Lucy stared at Cara in disbelief. "I was going to give it to someone I know—maybe someone like Ron. I NEVER would have just given it away!" She was so upset she had lost her appetite.

Cara sighed and squeezed her aunt's hand. "Take a deep breath," she said, as they got in her car. "If Ethel took it from your house and doesn't remember leaving it at Salvation Army, do you think it's still in her car?"

Lucy looked at her, startled. "Maybe."

They reached Wolfe Creek Inn and Cara parked the Toyota. "You're clicking right along, aren't you?" Lucy said as they were shown a table by the window. "I'm glad one of us is. Now, where do you think her car is?" The waitress came and took their orders. Cara ordered a glass of chardonnay.

"I don't know," she said, "but Ian should know."

"Ethel's car was totaled." Ian said, avoiding looking at Lucy's distraught face. She was so pale and upset, he hardly recognized her. "It should be at Fairbanks Auto Salvage."

"We'll go there now." Cara said, with a glance at Lucy.

"I'll call and let them know you're coming. They only keep vehicles for a few days before stripping them and selling the parts."

Cara nodded and steered Lucy toward the door. "You said it's on the road to Fox?"

Ian reached over and pulled a sheet of paper from his printer. "I drew a map for you."

Fairbanks Auto Salvage was a forlorn sight, an automobile graveyard filled with damaged cars, vans and pickups that had once been someone's pride and joy. When Cara and Lucy arrived, they saw several dozen vehicles in various conditions. They wouldn't have been able to find Ethel's Subaru without the help of Bruce, who wore a name tag.

"Oh Lordy," Lucy said, taking in the smashed doors of Ethel's Subaru. The top was flattened by about ten inches. "How did she survive? It looks like a boulder landed on it."

Bruce, a muscular kid of about eighteen, grunted as he pulled open the passenger door under the less-flattened part of the roof. Cara peered inside and saw Ethel's easel, which had broken into a dozen pieces, and a scattering of brushes and tubes of paint. "We should take these," she called. over her shoulder to Lucy. "Ethel will want them."

Cara reached around the splintered easel and picked up several matt boards and small sized stretched canvases. The glove compartment had dropped open and half a dozen cassettes had fallen out. Cara scooped them up from the floor and checked to see if there was another in the cassette player. She found a Linda Ronstadt tape and saw the small coin purse Ethel had kept filled with parking meter change. It was empty.

Hunched over, she backed out of the Subaru. "Can you open the trunk?" Bruce nodded and moved to the rear of the car. A huge dent had collapsed the trunk lid, but he managed to pry it open.

Lucy saw the cardboard box first. "There it is, that's my box," Her voice rose in excitement.

Cara tried to pull it out, but it was so tightly wedged the attendant had to do it. She stood back and Lucy opened the crushed top.

"Oh Cara, you were right," Lucy whispered, lifting out the muskrat hat. It was still wrapped in the rose-colored scarf.

"That's a nice hat," Bruce said, staring at the fur.

She pulled the scarf off and felt something hard under the fur. She beamed at him, then turned to Cara. "Thank you, thank you," she said, fighting tears.

"You did it," she said. "You found it."

The Ravenstone was again in Athabascan hands.

Chapter 49

Wednesday

Fairbanks

Cara pulled into a parking spot outside the Alaska State Troopers building. "Oh there's Ian," Lucy said. "Wonder what he's doing here?"

Lucy and Cara caught him as he was going in to see Matt Thomlin.

"You found it?" Ian's eyes widened as Lucy began to speak.

"We'll tell you both," Cara said, pushing open the door to Matt's office

"So, you want to donate it to UAF's museum with a stipulation that they build a training center in Goldspring and name it The Ravenstone Center, right?" Thomlin sat back, frowning.

"Something like that," Lucy said. She looked at Cara who nodded.

"What does the University say about that?"

Cara cleared her throat. "We haven't spoken to them yet. We thought you should know we had it before we did anything else." Thomlin stared at her.

"You didn't think you could tell us you had it before now?" *Calm the frick down*, he thought. Exhaling, he turned to Ian. "What do you think?"

"The university has been trying to acquire the Ravenstone for years," Ian said slowly. "They should be told the conditions under which Lucy and Cara will donate it to the University." He leaned forward in his chair, thinking.

"It would add to UAF's Athabascan collection," he continued. "With the media coverage, it could attract scholars, academics and researchers as well as tourists and those interested in Athabascan lore."

He looked at Cara and Lucy. "You might talk to Doyon and some of the other Native corporations. They could help you approach the university."

Cara nodded. "We could use some help with that," she admitted. Lucy, tense from watching the exchange between Cara and Thomlin, felt her shoulders relax.

Thomlin cleared his throat. "I was at Ron's place the other day and saw a rendering of the training center he'd like to see built. Is that what you're talking about?"

Cara shook her head, puzzled. "A rendering? I haven't seen it." She looked at Lucy.

Lucy shook her head. "I haven't seen it either, but he's talked about how Goldspring could use a training center. He's tired of picking up drunk and drugged out kids. He thinks they need something positive to do." Thomlin nodded, that made sense.

"I can understand that. Well, let me know what happens."

After Ian and the women left, Matt got up and stared out the window. Cara had known where the Ravenstone was for days and not said a word. He was still mad.

Chapter 50

Goldspring
Wednesday

Lucy and Cara walked up the narrow, slippery steps to Ron's cabin and knocked. The crisp winter air with a hint of burning fireplaces and exhaust fumes was mild enough to inhale without fear of frostbite.

"We found the Ravenstone," Lucy announced as soon as Ron opened the door. Cara smiled when she saw his slow comprehension.

"Well… wow. Where was it?"

Cara had thought her elderly aunt would add authenticity when they approached the big wigs at Doyon and the University, but Lucy needed practice. Ron was a good place to start.

"So where was it?" Ron repeated, glancing surreptitiously at the three envelopes under his desk calendar.

"It was in Herb's hat," Lucy said, watching where she stepped amid the boots and other debris that cluttered Ron's small house.

"In Herb's hat? That's why you asked me about his hat?"

Lucy looked puzzled. "Oh, you mean when I called you the other day."

"We didn't mean to keep it from you…" Cara cleared her throat, "but we were so surprised when Lucy found it, we didn't know what to do at first. So we didn't tell anyone. Not Ian, not the Troopers. No one."

"Okay," he muttered, trying to conceal his relief. They had found that blasted Ravenstone. He didn't need to confess anything. He could tear up his letters. He could keep his job. He was so relieved; he didn't care that he was just now finding out they'd had it.

Books and DVD's were scattered on Ron's worn sofa. Lucy shoved them aside and sat down. All the excitement had worn her out. Sweet-smelling wood crackled in Ron's black stove, spreading its welcome heat.

Cara sank down beside her. "Thomlin told us you have a drawing of a training center you'd like to see built in Goldspring. Do you still have it?" It would be a miracle if he did, she thought, looking at his cluttered kitchen and living room.

"Sure, it's here on the wall." Ron pointed to a space near a bookshelf. Cara's glasses had fogged up after entering Ron's house and she took them off and moved closer.

"I've also got a prospectus with descriptions of proposed classes," he said, as he kicked his boots out of the way. "And a financial breakdown of building and maintenance costs. Why do you want to know?"

So they told him.

Chapter 51

Goldspring to Fairbanks

Meeting at the University of Alaska

The following week Lucy and Ron drove to the University of Alaska in Fairbanks where they joined Cara and UAF's President William Birch and Doyon's President Jonas Bison. An Art and Historical Director and two lawyers were already in the newly built conference room, chatting about the unusual sunshine. "Kinda rare for winter," said one of the lawyers. As this day was rare, Cara thought.

Birch was a tall, slender man with thick white hair and excellent skin for a white man of his age. Lucy thought.

She and Cara had earlier purchased a length of deep red velvet and stapled it to a square piece of plywood. After the group had settled in the leather chairs that surrounded a long conference table, Lucy set the Ravenstone on the velvet tray and placed it in the middle of the table.

Sunlight had seeped through the windows and the Ravenstone no longer looked like a flat rock or a bit of whale Baylene. In the beam of winter sun, it somehow looked anciently powerful.

At the end of the table a large mask with a twenty-two-inch diameter of wood and raven feathers was mounted on an easel. Cara had earlier noted a guard at the door. Good, the university was taking this seriously, she thought.

"May I?" Kathryn Irving, the director of the University's museum, gestured to the Ravenstone. Lucy, her back straight and feeling rather regal in her best kuspuk, nodded.

Irving picked up the Ravenstone and connected it to the prongs concealed by feathers in the center of the mask. She stepped back and silence fell over the group.

The full effect of the Ravenstone and the mask was riveting. For the first time in decades, Cara realized the Ravenstone and mask would be seen together. It would be experienced by thousands. Thank you, Sam, she whispered.

"Magnificent," she heard President Birch murmur.

With a smile she had practiced in front of her bathroom mirror, Lucy placed a sheet of paper on the table. "This is a letter of agreement," she said, her English breaking. "In exchange for the Ravenstone, a training center, as described in the prospectus, will be built in Goldspring."

Ron, his hands shaking, began passing around copies of his prospectus to accompany the agreement. Signature lines began with UAF's President William J. Birch and Doyon's President Jonas.

Everyone had questions. Would the courses be accredited, or would this be a community college with a mix of credited and non-credited courses? Where would the funds come from? Donors, a bond measure, grants?

The group flipped through the pages of the prospectus and set a date for the next meeting and Cara felt herself relax for the first time in weeks.

President Birch extended his hand to Lucy. "I want to thank you for your generous offer. We'll make a special announcement and have a presentation. I'll let you know the date." He gave Cara a long look. He knew how the budget cuts affected her classes.

"We are working on raising funds to expand the liberal arts department." He sighed. "It depends on how we structure the bond."

Lucy nodded. "We want to have a potlatch for Sam, our *deeyninh*." She looked at President Birch. "He died suddenly," she added, "*notleeghet'onh*, and with dignity."

President Birch had read about Sam Tallwell's death. He also knew Sam had held on to the Ravenstone for over fifty years. It was a major feat for the university to finally receive this valuable artifact.

"I am proud to have met you, Mrs. Montalk," he said. Then he grinned. "And it looks like the sun came out for us." He gestured toward the bright sky through the window. "Or maybe you brought it with you?"

Cara and her Aunt smiled. "I think maybe Sam did," Cara said.

Giddy with relief, they walked to the campus parking lot. "When they were signing the agreement, I felt like Thomas Jefferson with the Declaration of Independence," Lucy said

"That was amazing!" Ron said, happy for a lot of reasons, but also feeling guilty. Giving them a wave, he veered toward his car. He was returning to Goldspring, while Lucy and Cara would drive to Fairbanks Memorial and provide Ethel with an update.

Ethel looked even better after Lucy recounted their success with DOYON and the University. The nurse had told them Ethel would be released in a week or so. "We need to make sure she understands the limits of her legs. Her son came by and said he'd take her back to Goldspring once she can handle her wheelchair and crutches. And we have a nurse there to check on her daily."

"I can take care of her," Lucy said, glancing dubiously at the wheelchair.

"It takes strength helping her with the wheelchair and crutches," the nurse said. "Her insurance should cover someone to help her for at least a week, maybe more."

Cara and Lucy had a quick lunch at the CoOp then went to the railroad station where Lucy would catch the train for Goldspring. Frost covered the windows of the stationhouse and they sat inside.

Cara's thoughts were wandering when she caught Lucy staring at her. "What?" Cara realized Lucy had said something.

"What does Doyon get out of this?"

Cara forced herself to think. "Well, as a Native corporation, it's to their benefit to support the center." She shrugged. "The added income to the town would benefit the residents. Eventually, it could grow large enough to need a dormitory and food service…"

"How long will it take to get the school started?" Lucy liked to think she had a hand in promoting Goldspring's future and she was impatient for the details.

"It could take a few months to get started," Cara said. "I'd think they'd start in stages. First they need to get building permits, maybe start by renting that vacant paint store across from Fleming's. But even that involves getting approvals."

"Why need building approvals if renting is only temporary?"

"Yes, but they can't have classes sponsored by the university in a building that could be contaminated with asbestos."

"Oh," Lucy's shoulders sank. "Those kinds of inspections."

Cara nodded. "All kinds. And they have to hire faculty so they can begin to offer classes while they build the center. The thing is, it would eventually have to be self-sustaining. No university can afford to offer free or nearly-free classes indefinitely."

Lucy nodded. Everything took so damned long, but at least the Ravenstone Center—technical, learning, center whatever— was starting.

When the train was minutes from arriving, they went outside and began walking along the platform. After their meeting in the stuffy boardroom, the cool air felt wonderful, Cara thought as she pulled Lucy's overnight bag.

"Looks like you'll see ghost frost going home." Cara liked these names: ghost frost and ice fog.

"You're thinking of Portage," Lucy said, bringing Cara back to earth. Portage was the small village outside Anchorage on Turnagain Arm. The community was abandoned after the '64 Quake sank it ten feet and salt water killed the trees.

The train pulled to a stop and Cara helped her aunt climb aboard and settle into a window seat. As Lucy smoothed her kuspuk across her lap, she looked at Cara. "We did the right thing giving the Ravenstone to the University. I know that is where it is supposed to be."

Cara looked at her aunt and nodded. She knew Lucy was right

Chapter 52

Fairbanks

"I just got home," Cara said, propping the phone on her shoulder and anchoring it with her cheek. "And, nope, I'm job hunting."

"You've quite teaching?" Thomlin was so surprised he'd forgotten he was upset.

"No," she said with a sigh. "The university eliminated one of my classes – cost cutting time – and my hours next semester will be reduced."

"What are you looking for, what type of work?" He settled himself in his recliner and sipped his coffee, now cold.

"Last summer I got a job as an insurance investigator. I'm hoping to get back into it, part time."

It was three o'clock. The sky was dark and large flakes of snow were melting on the sidewalk outside.

"Well, before you get back to your job hunt, how about dinner tomorrow night at the Midnight Lounge?" Surprised, Cara looked down at Mister who was rubbing her leg and meowing, non-stop, Siamese fashion.

"You mean with you?" She smiled.

"That's the general idea, unless you've got a better one."

She shook her head even though he couldn't see her. "None I can think of."

"I'll pick you up tomorrow around 7:30," he said, his voice shifting lower.

At seven thirty, Cara heard a knock on the door and saw Matt Thomlin through the glass window. The falling snow was visible behind him as he knocked the ice from his boots.

"Hey," she said opening the door and stepping back. Matt looked at her, his expression going from pleased to stunned. Gloating inwardly, Cara took his down-filled parka. Beneath it he wore a light gray blazer and dark gray wool slacks. The blazer had a fine red stripe and looked expensive

"We outta be in pictures…" she said, trying to remember which film she was misquoting.

"You certainly should be," he said taking in her sleek one shoulder blue-black dress. Her upswept hair revealed a lovely neck he had never seen before.

Cara had heard about the upscale Midnight Lounge and was thankful for the Armani dress she had found at a consignment shop last winter. She usually wore so many layers, Matt had no idea she was so slender. Or curvy. "What time is our reservation?"

"Eight o'clock, why?"

"I had a call from my uncle, David Patric. You met him at Wolf Creek Inn." She took a deep breath. "He was in Seattle and our phone connection kept breaking up. He said he'd arrive at seven."

Thomlin grew still, his eyes were on her face.

"Tonight?"

Cara nodded. "Right. I left a message that I wouldn't be here. He would have called when he landed."

"You're sure he'd call?"

"I'm sure." Then, without thinking, she put her arms around him and buried her head against his tie. His jacket was soft. She had a feeling it was cashmere. She inhaled his faint scent, a lovely aroma. Oh my, he felt good.

Matt couldn't move for what he later calculated was about two minutes.

Their lobster appetizer was followed by prime rib and ended with a brandied crème caramel, which they shared. Cara sat back, looking at Matt, who had just fed her and earlier made remarkable love to her, but now she couldn't help thinking about her uncle. Where was he?

"It might have already been airborne and then doubled back. Or your friend may have taken another airline," Matt said, picking up her thoughts as they walked to the car. "In weather this cold, flights get cancelled all the time."

Finding no new information online, Thomlin heaved a sigh and set his laptop on the coffee table. Looking at Cara, he put his arm around her and pulled her to his lap. She sat back to look at him. He gave her a gentle squeeze. "Want to go upstairs?"

"Oh, why not," she said, smiling.

Chapter 53

Fairbanks

Brian still wasn't sure how he'd done it with the guards all around, but he had managed to slip out of the Fairbanks Correctional Facility and was now wearing a parka he'd lifted from a coat rack at a nearby food joint. Honestly, he thought, it was almost as if the cops were helping him leave.

As hungry as he was, he didn't want to hang around where he could be seen by the parka's owner. Plus, his wallet with all of ten bucks was still at the jail. He shoved his hands in the pockets and found a headband and a wrinkled mass of dollar bills and a few coins. At least he wasn't flat broke, he thought, pulling the headband over his naked ears. Outside, he pulled the parka hood over his head and tried to jog, but the freezing air was too cold to breathe and he slowed back down to a fast walk.

A Saving and Loan sign across the street read minus thirty-five degrees. The ice fog softened the glare of the sign, which now gave the current interest rate. The evening reminded him of a photograph he'd seen in an Edgar Allen Poe book, but the cold was biting and he didn't linger as he headed for the bus stop sign.

When the city center bus came, his fingers were so stiff he had trouble getting the money out of his pocket. The driver waved him to a seat and Brian continued to fish the change from his stolen parka. The ride was bumpy over the black ice and Brian kept dropping coins on the dark floor. After lurching back to the fare box and dropping in quarters, he fell onto a seat and caught his breath.

He thought about trying to reach Glori, but the police could be watching her after that fiasco at Sam's Saloon. She was most likely in Juneau anyway and he was stuck in Fairbanks. As for Frank, Brian had no idea where he was.

His thoughts shifted to his mother's sister. She had remarried for the third time and was living somewhere in Fairbanks. What was her last name? Feldenkraus? Floeberg? Fielding? That wasn't his aunt's name. but Fielding hit a nerve. That Athabascan woman they'd shot at near Shem's Saloon, wasn't her name Fielding? Brian was pretty sure he'd read that in the newspaper. She was with the cop Brian tried to call when he was in the hospital.

He got off the bus at the station on Two Street as the locals called Second Street. The building was empty, ice cold and drafty, but he found a phone and, lo and behold, a phone book. Some of the pages were ripped out, but the F's were there. Running his finger down the page, he saw nothing that looked like his aunt's new last name. Then he saw Fielding, Cara. He couldn't remember if her first name was Cara, but it was the only Fielding listed. Her address was on Noble Street. He looked at a map of Fairbanks on the wall of the station. He saw Noble Street and the red circle around the bus station. How far was Noble, a mile or two away, maybe less? His stomach growled again and he was about to leave when he spied a newspaper in a trashcan.

The front section of a day-old *Fairbanks Goldstar* was wrapped around a fast-food box containing the remains of French fries. He bit into one. It tasted awful and he dropped it back in the box.

Sneezing, he wiped his nose with a discarded napkin then picked up the newspaper again. A headline half way down caught his attention. His heart nearly stopping, Brian took the paper to a bench and sat down. It was about an Athabascan amulet called the Ravenstone. He was half way through the article when he saw a name, Cara Fielding. She was related to the guy he, Pat, and Frank had killed. Well, damn.

He read on. From Clyne's urgency about it ASAP, he suspected the Ravenstone was worth a lot, hundreds, maybe thousands of dollars. Cara Fielding, Lucy Montalk, and Ron somebody—from what he could see through a greasy smudge on the page—must have raked in big bucks.

The article continued, but he only had the front page. Frustrated, he returned to the trashcan and dug through empty boxes of fast food, soda cans, used napkins, and tissue, but found no more newspapers.

Sighing, he reread the article. Below an oil stain, he saw two lines about a training center in Goldspring. Hell, who cared about a training center. He folded the newspaper into a small square and stuffed it his pocket. Through the window, he looked across Second Street to The Bank of Alaska's sign. The temperature had dropped to forty below. A few doors to the right of the Bank, was Ginni's Burgers. It was open. He took the cash out of his pocket and counted seven dollars and eighty-five cents. Not enough for a room, but he should be able to get a burger.

Pushing the door open, he headed across the street toward Ginni's. The icy air stung his face and he wiped his nose with his sleeve hoping to God he could thaw out inside the burger joint..

A trooper in an unmarked car reached for the phone. "He's just gone into Ginni's."

"Stay on him until he checks into the Hospitality House," Thomlin said. "If he goes anywhere else, call me. Bill is inside. If this goes as planned, he'll take it from there."

Thomlin settled back and stared at the report from Quantico. None of the hair and fiber evidence from the Ashenberg house was a match for Brian. It was, however, a match for Frank and his brother, Pat.

Brian finished his burger and sat for a moment warming his still-chilled hands around a third cup of coffee. Then with a sigh he walked over to a wall phone at the back of Ginni's and flipped open the phone book. He dialed and when there was no answer, he left a message.

Brian was exhausted when he remembered Hospitality House. Hospitality House was a large one-story building that had once been a house of ill repute. It was now a shelter for those who lived on the streets. He had stayed there once on an earlier trip and thought it was just a couple of blocks away.

When he finally stumbled up the steps to the entrance, he didn't care what it had been, at least it was warm.

He entered a room filled with a serenade of snores and hacking coughs and found the attendant who pointed him to a cot against a far wall.

One night only, he promised, feeling eyes on him as he pulled his ear band down around his neck. He pulled his hood back over his head in an attempt to drown out the noise. It didn't work.

One night only, he thought. Tomorrow he'd have some money and would be out of here.

Chapter 54

Fairbanks to Goldspring

Mister's persistent meowing woke Cara. With a sigh, she glanced at the clock and saw that she had overslept. Damn. She shook her head as she grabbed her robe and slipped on her moccasins. She went downstairs and got Mister's canned food from the refrigerator. As she filled his dish, she noticed her phone's message light was blinking. She pressed play and poured Mister's dry food into a separate dish.

"You don't know me," a male voice said. "But you have something of mine and we need to talk."

Cara put down the cat food and stared at her phone. She pressed the play button and listened again. Mister was purring so loudly she had to turn up the volume. What did she have that belonged to anyone else? She took out the cassette and dug through the drawer for a fresh cassette to replace it. She didn't want to run scared, but the guy's voice alarmed her. She wanted Ian or Matt to hear this.

That afternoon, Cara returned home from the university and Safeway, loaded with groceries. After yesterday she decided she needed something in the refrigerator besides moldy cheese, brown lettuce, and two-year old freezer-burned fish. Especially after Matt opened her cupboard and found only a bag of coffee and two cans of soup.

Now, with her groceries, briefcase and shoulder bag, she reached her back door. It swung open before she could get her key in the lock.

Surprised, she stood a moment. Then she pulled out her cellphone and called Ian. "I just got home and my door is open," she whispered.

"Open? You mean it wasn't locked, but just standing open?"

"You know I always lock my door. Always."

"I'll be right over. Where are you?"

"I'm in back, near the kitchen. I'll wait for you in my car. Oh," she said, remembering the earlier phone call. "Some guy called this morning, I have it on tape. He said I have something of his and we needed to talk. No name. His voice was threatening."

"Do you have the tape?"

"In my bag," Cara said.

"I'll be there in five minutes."

Upstairs, Brian overheard Cara. Grabbing a sheet of paper from her desk, he scribbled a note. Leaving it on her bed, he crept downstairs and paused before opening the front door. There was only silence in the kitchen. Pulling up his hood, he casually walked outside then over to Ninth. He was on Cushman Street a block away before he let himself breathe.

"Did you check to see if anything is missing," Ian's eyes narrowed as he looked around her kitchen and living room. "Where is your cat, by the way?"

"He's behind the canisters in the kitchen," Cara said. She shivered. Heat had escaped through the open kitchen door and she turned up the furnace. "I don't think anything is missing, but I haven't been upstairs."

"Let's go up," Ian said. He looked at the carpet in the living room. "Looks like someone came through here with wet feet." There were two more footprints on the carpet inside the front door. "Don't touch anything," Ian said. "We'll fingerprint the doorknob and the stair rail."

Chewing her lip, Cara nodded and followed him upstairs. Just beyond her bedroom was a second, smaller room she used as an office. Always neat, it was now a mess. Desk drawers were pulled out and left upended on the floor. Her out-of-season clothing, previously hanging in the small closet, was on the floor along with photograph albums, shoeboxes, tote bags, and two suitcases.

"Cara, come look at this." Ian was in her bedroom, looking at a sheet of notepaper. It was face down on her bed and he flipped it over with his pen.

She read it aloud, 'I know you got a lot of money for the Ravenstone. I want $50,000 or Lucy Montalk is history.' The spelling was slap-dash and the writing looked like it was done with the non-writing hand.

"Well, wow," Cara murmured, staring at the note.

"I'm calling Matt," Ian said. Just then, they heard vehicles pull up outside. The FPD technicians had arrived.

Ian showed the fingerprint technicians the layout of the house and the note, now in cellophane. "Do you have anywhere you can go for a couple of hours?"

"If I can get some things together, I'll drive up to Goldspring and check on Aunt Lucy." Cara shivered and shoved her hands in her pockets.

Ian had coaxed Mister out from behind the canisters and was petting him. "You shouldn't be driving after the shock you've had."

"I'll be more of a mess if I stay here worrying about Aunt Lucy." A few minutes later Matt Thomlin came through the back door. His presence filled the kitchen.

"I'm trying to talk Cara out of driving to Goldspring," Ian said, frowning.

Cara cleared her throat. "The note we found upstairs threatened Aunt Lucy. I want to check on her." She pulled a kitchen chair from the table and managed to somehow fall into it.

"I've called Ron," Ian said. "He'll make sure someone is with her."

Thomlin nodded and watched Cara for a moment. "We spotted Brian a few blocks from here and were about to intercept him when we got your call.

I'll have a trooper drive you to Goldspring," he added, looking at Cara. "He'll stay with you and Lucy until we get Brian in custody."

"Why was he released?" Cara felt her anger flare. Matt shook his head.

"The FBI was trailing him. I don't know how he got to your house without being spotted."

Chapter 55

Fairbanks to Goldspring

Glori saw Brian on the sidewalk and pulled over. Leaning across the passenger seat, she opened the door. "Hey, Brian," she said. "Get in." Startled, Brian bent down to look at her.

"What are you doing here?"

"Come on." She glanced at her rearview mirror. "I think you're being followed." With a quick glance behind him, he got in and slid down in the seat.

"I saw in the newspaper about the Ravenstone…" he began.

"Those two woman and the VPSO guy in Goldspring sold it to the University," Glori said, turning on Johannesburg and heading for the Steese Highway.

"Yeah, I read that. They musta gotten big bucks for it." Brian slumped in his seat.

"And you want some of it?" She smiled.

"Sure, wouldn't you?" He looked out the window at the rapidly-passing scenery. "Where are we going by the way?"

"Goldspring," she said. "I want to see where Lucy lives." She didn't really, but she needed to get Brian to the village.

Brian shrugged. "I left Cara a note, I told her she had something of mine and we needed to talk about it or her aunt was history." Brian wasn't big on planning and he put his head back and stared up at the upholstery. He twitched his nose. Now that he was warming up, he could smell the interior of the car. Air freshener, cigar, and maybe a hotdog, something with mustard. It was a rental, what do you expect?

"So, what happened?

"I was upstairs when she got home. I couldn't get her back door to stay shut and I guess that spooked her. I heard her call the cops, so I split."

Chapter 56

Goldspring

"Yes, I'm pretty sure I saw her at Fleming's Market," Lucy said, gripping the phone. Her gray hair, normally neat, was frowsy and she had chewed off her lipstick. Her faded apron worn over baggy jeans and an old blue sweater, sleeves pushed up, was spattered with flour. She had just finished baking muffins.

"You know Valery McMillan was killed a few weeks ago in Anchorage?" Cara didn't mean to sound patronizing, but she was tired. The SUV hit a pothole and she jerked the steering wheel.

"I *know* she's dead." Lucy said, "But this woman had red hair and looked just like her."

"Okay, I'll be there in half an hour. Call Ron, he's there, but keep your doors locked." She hung up and glanced at Bill, who at Ian's orders was driving Cara to Goldspring.

He pulled into the left lane. "Not too many redheads around," he said, having overheard her conversation. "There's a woman we've seen with Frank and Brian. She has red hair, but I think she's back in Juneau." Cara looked at him quizzically. He shrugged. He knew Glori worked with the FBI, but would leave it to Tomlin to tell Cara. "You'll have to ask Ian or Matt about her."

Lucy's house was lit up as he turned in and pulled to a stop. "I'll be at Beth & Barney's," Bill said referring to Goldspring's bed and breakfast. "Call me if you see anything suspicious."

"What do you think?" Lucy said after Cara dropped her tote

bag by the sofa. "Are we in danger?" Cara shook her head and sank down on the sofa. She looked at her aunt.

"I don't know, but we've got to be careful. So, tell me, where and when did you see this woman, the one who looked like Valerie?"

"A few days ago at Fleming's. Why?"

"Was anyone with her?"

Lucy chewed her lip as she thought. "There were others ordering, but I didn't see her talk to anyone."

"Well, she isn't Valerie. There was a redhead at Shem's Saloon where Frank and his brother and Brian shot at us."

"Was she pretty?" Lucy asked. Cara raised her eyebrows, surprised

"From what I could see, she wouldn't scare anyone. Especially for a place like Shem's."

Lucy nodded. "When I saw her at Fleming's, she was wearing a black scarf, but it didn't cover her hair in back. It was red. I just caught a glimpse of her face. She was *neege*."

As a child, Cara had been called neege, meaning pretty or beautiful. Back then, whenever someone called her *neege* she felt like a movie star.

Chapter 57

Goldspring

"This is it? This is where Lucy Montalk lives? This is where I got knocked out. It's where the troopers nabbed me." Brian's voice rose.

Glori pulled over and stopped the car beyond an overgrowth of scrawny spruce that concealed them from Lucy's house. The afternoon sky had grown darker and snow fell in small flakes that forecast a heavy snowfall.

Brian took a deep breath and let his head drop back against the headrest. "Frank and me, we were heading for the Ashenberg's. We had this SUV. It conked out and our cell phone didn't work. So I knocked on the door to see if I could use the phone. No answer so I walked around back 'cause I had to pee. That's when I slipped and hit my head."

That bear trap, Glori thought, remembering what her handler had told her. "Where was Frank?"

"He went to the Ashenberg's to look for the Ravenstone." Brian shook his head. "I don't know if he got there."

"Let's drive by the Ashenberg house. Then unless I get a better idea, we'll go get something to eat." Glori had done everything she had been told to soften up Brian and find out who he wanted to see. Food and drink were next on her list.

After Trooper Bill showed up at Lucy's house with Cara, Ron went home for a shower and a change of clothes. Despite Cara's protests, the trooper said he'd stay with the women until Ron returned. A few hours later, when all was quiet, Cara and Lucy decided to drive to Fleming's deli.

Lucy had just backed her Cougar out of the driveway when it stalled. She tried to shift but the gearshift was stuck in reverse. "Oh, heckter," she swore.

She and Cara climbed out and stared at the Cougar. It was sitting crosswise in the road where it blocked oncoming traffic.

"It's too heavy to push back onto your driveway," Cara said, looking in both directions.

"I'll call Mike's Auto Service," Lucy said. Mike used a heavy-duty pickup and didn't officially run a tow service.

Cara looked at the road's shoulder. It was too narrow for anything wider than a wheelbarrow. Then she thought of Trooper Bill. "Lucy, let's call Bill. He can push us back up your driveway and he might even be able to get the gears to shift."

Chapter 58

Goldspring

Glori stopped when she reached Herb Ashenberg's driveway and pulled to the side of the road. Yellow tape and a "do not enter" sign hung across the door. Vehicle and foot tracks were faint. Beneath the falling snow, a sense of depression hung over the sad house.

"I suppose you want to get out and look around?" Brian's parka hood blocked his vision and he pushed it back.

Glori stared at the little house. She'd had no instructions about entering the place. "Nope," she said. "Let's get out of here. I'm ready for something to eat." Relieved, Brian put his head back and shut his eyes.

Moments later, Glori pulled up in front of Lucy's house. "Well damn," she muttered. Up ahead, an Alaska State Trooper's vehicle and a vintage Mercury were blocking the road.

She put the car in reverse, then jerked to a stop when an SUV behind her honked. Brian sat up.

"What's going on?"

"No idea," she said, but she had an idea. This was Trooper territory and she was out of her jurisdiction. Brian stared ahead at the trooper's vehicle. When he saw Lucy and Cara next to the Mercury he pulled his hood up and covered his head.

Trooper Bill walked over to them, his breath a white cloud. Leaning down, he peered at them through the driver's window. "I'm trying to get this woman's car back in her driveway. If you can help, we can clear the road faster."

"Sure," Glori said, flashing Bill a white-toothed smile. He looked at Brian a moment longer. With a faint nod he returned to Cara and Lucy.

"I gotta call Thomlin," he said, his voice low. "Brian and Glori just showed up."

Cara glanced quickly at the car then turned her attention toward the house. Lucy ducked her head and moved behind the Mercury.

The driver behind Glori climbed out of his oversized SUV and walked toward the trooper, his boots crunching in the gravel-covered snow. "I'm Hank Peterson. I live just up the road. Anything I can do to help?" He looked at the aging Mercury. "I had one of those back in college. This is a '67, isn't it? How many miles on her?" He looked at Cara who turned to Lucy.

"About 50,000 miles," Lucy tried to smile. "I don't drive it much. We bought it in Anchorage."

Cara glanced back at Glori's car but didn't see Brian. Where had he gone?

Bill slapped his gloved hands together and turned toward the SUV driver. "The Mercury's gear is stuck in reverse," he said. Turning toward Lucy, he said, "Lucy, why don't you get in and steer and Mr. Peterson and I will see about getting it turned around and back on your driveway."

While Lucy, Bill and Mike discussed their strategy, Cara trotted up the steps to Lucy's front door. The cold had gotten to her, and she needed to use the bathroom. Sighing, Cara trudged to the back of the house and dashed to the bathroom. The small bathroom smelled of bath powder and the Coty scent Lucy always wore.

As Cara flushed the toilet and zipped up her jeans, she heard the sound of glass breaking. Opening the door, she looked across the hall to see a man climbing over the window ledge in Lucy's office. For a moment Cara couldn't move, then she ran into the room and grabbed his leg.

"Hey!" Brian kicked back, his boot hitting Cara in the chest. She reached for a better grip and her fingernails ripped through the weatherproof fabric of his parka.

Enraged, he swung around, hitting her face with his arm and knocking her glasses to the floor. He swung again, knocking her across Lucy's desk where she fell, amid pens, a desk calendar, loose papers, and a Theo H. Davies paperweight.

He made another run for the window but Cara, still on the floor managed to yank the lamp cord that stretched across his path. She heard cursing as he knocked his head on a large carved stone bear by the bookcase.

Lurching to his feet, Brian tried again to kick her, but Cara swung her legs around and knocked his feet from under him.

With blood dripping from his face, Brian scrambled to his feet and grabbed a pair of scissors that had fallen to the floor. He tried to stab her through her parka. Failing that, he kicked her again, then dashed to the window.

Blood covered her face, smearing her vision. When she looked up again she glimpsed Brian's feet disappearing over the window ledge.

• • •

Matt dropped his phone and stomped on the gas. Minutes later, he slid to a stop at Lucy's driveway. "Where is she?" he yelled, nearly falling out of the truck.

"She's inside!" Bill's voice, normally controlled, was raised. "I called Fairbanks Memorial. They're sending an ambulance."

Lucy was kneeling by Cara. Her face was bloody and her left eye was swollen shut. Broken glass and books, papers from Lucy's desk covered the floor. By the window a potted plant had toppled, spilling dirt on the rug. A large carved bear lay nearby, spattered with blood.

Lucy had pulled Cara's parka away from her neck and was holding another washcloth, now bloody, over the wound. "It's very close to her carotid artery. I don't want to move her," she said.

A cloud of icy air rolled off Tomlin's parka as he kneeled over Cara. "An ambulance is coming," he said, giving her hand a light squeeze. He turned to Bill. "I'm going after this asshole."

Chapter 59

Goldspring

The flashlight's beam was weak, but Matt could make out a faint pattern of blood spatter and boot tracks. Wading through the almost hip-deep snow, he followed them from Lucy's back window to the road. There they disappeared. Aiming his flashlight along the snow-covered shoulder of the road he saw larger dark splotches. Blood. Good, he thought, Cara had gotten the bastard, although with what he didn't know.

In the distance, he saw a small house with smoke rising from the chimney. Pulling out his phone, he called Bill. "I'm following some tracks to a house across the road. It's darker than hades out here and my battery's about dead so bring a couple of flashlights."

"Got it," Bill said, looking through the window. The Goldspring ambulance had pulled up and Cara was being loaded inside.

Brian was crouched near the side of the cabin. His face and jaw hurt like hell and he could feel a couple of broken teeth with his tongue.

He heard voices and was startled to see two figures with flash lights lurching through the snow toward him. Gripping a shovel he had found in the shed, Brian scooted under the cover of the trees and deeper into the woods.

"See that?" Matt said, his voice low as he pointed to the left of the shed. "Looks like fresh tracks."

"Brian," Thomlin yelled. "Alaska State Troopers. Come out with your hands up!"

With the beam of their flashlights cutting through the darkness, they moved beyond the shed. "Why don't …" Bill stopped.

Thomlin, who was to Bill's left, turned. "Bill?"

The trooper was face down, spread in the snow. Matt dropped to his knees and pulled off his glove and tried to feel Bill's throat. There was a faint pulse. Then he heard a rasping sound, like someone trying to breathe. Then nothing.

Chapter 60

Goldspring

Cara had a concussion, three cracked ribs, a broken nose, and a neck wound, She moved in with Lucy for a few days, bringing Mister, her cat. After initial displays of getting acquainted with Major, Lucy's orange tom, both felines behaved surprisingly well.

"Well, Mister knows who feeds him," Cara said. Lucy smiled, eyeing her big tom lying on the table.

Lucy sighed. "Did Matt recognize you?" His memory loss had bothered her.

"Oh yes," Cara laughed, remembering her visit with Matt in the hospital. "He definitely knows who I am. By the way, he told me the Anchorage Police picked up two guys for a robbery and they started admitting to other offenses, including setting the fire that killed Jimmy."

Lucy was startled. She had adored the little boy Wade and his wife had adopted. "Do they know who hired them?"

Cara nodded. "Would you believe Carl Clyne? He told them he wanted to get rid of the trailer's owner. The troopers are working with the Seattle police and have found ties between Cline and the west coast mob."

Anyway, Clyne told them where the trailer was and to be there incase Brian and Frank didn't arrive by a certain time." Cara shook her head and continued. "Frank and Brian were late, so these two burned down the trailer themselves."

"Two sets of arsonists seem like overkill, don't you think?" Lucy said.

Cara smiled. "Well, Carl Clyne, was behind it. But who was he working with to find the Ravenstone? Someone local must have been helping him."

That Ravenstone again, Lucy thought as she got up to refill their tea. "Did I ever tell you the story of how Sam helped your Uncle Hamilton and me?" Cara shook her head. "This was just after your parents died and you moved in with us." Lucy paused, looking out the window. The accident had killed both Cara's parents and her younger sister, Eileen. The tragedy had shaken everyone in Goldspring.

"Well Hamilton was having health problems," she continued. "So I went to see Sam and he did a ceremony ... he had the Ravenstone and he said I might not remember what happened and I don't, not really..." She took a breath and pushed Cara's cup toward her.

"Did you tell Ham about it?" Cara had called her uncle Ham since she was twelve. She picked up her cup and swirled the sweet-smelling tea.

"Wasn't much to tell," Lucy said. He knew I'd gone to see Sam, but didn't ask when I didn't talk about it." She let a moment pass as she thought back. "Talking to Sam felt sacred to me. I thought talking about it could weaken it in some way. Like a secret can lose its power when talked about too much.

Anyway, over the next few days Ham seemed to relax." She looked at Cara and smiled. "A week later, the doctor called and told us Ham's tumor was benign." She took a deep breath. "Two weeks after that we sold three acres from our homestead and that helped us get out of our financial hole."

"I never knew this." Cara was surprised.

"Oh no, you were only about twelve and we didn't want to burden you. You had enough to deal with—your parents' dying and moving in with us old folks who knew nothing about kids." Lucy shook her head.

"It was our problem, but at that time Sam and the Ravenstone were part of the solution."

"Did you recognize it when it fell out of Herb's hat? I mean you'd seen the Ravenstone before?" Lucy nodded.

"Sam didn't wave it around, but I remember seeing something dark in his hand when he held it up…and I could see the dark red eyes and the fur or hair in its beak. I didn't recognize it at first, but later when I remembered… It gave me chills."

Chapter 62

Fairbanks

Ian left the captain's office and called Ralph, his second in command, into his office. "We've uncovered some evidence connecting Phil Emerson with Sam Tallwell, so get a car and meet me at the front entrance. Oh, and wear your vest." Ralph nodded and headed back to the locker room where he kept his gear.

Phil's apartment was off Geist Road. When Ian and Ralph knocked, there was no answer. Ian held up his hand to cut the glare off the window and peered inside. "Looks empty."

Ralph walked down to the carports, each assigned to an apartment. "If he left, it wasn't long ago." A spot of fresh oil reflecting rainbow colors marked where Phil would have parked.

"Put out a BOLO on his Honda, I'll talk to the manager and take a look inside. Then let's head to the anthropology department. Maybe he left a calendar or notes on his computer."

Sitting a block away, Phil watched the two cops climb the stairs to his apartment. Good. That should take care of them for fifteen or twenty minutes, he thought. From there, they'd probably go the University's campus and the anthropology department. That should give him at least another half hour. He adjusted the rearview mirror of the four-year old Buick he had retrieved from the campus parking lot and pulled onto the road. He knew the car's owner had checked out a University van and gone to Circle Hot Springs on a field trip. He also knew where his colleague kept a spare car key in his desk.

That would give him at least a few days before the car was missed and he'd be on his way to London by the time the cops were on to him.

A stiff breeze blew across the George Parks highway and patches of snow dotted the pavement. The sky was gray and as he drove, the wind pushed the car sideways. Phil slowed down and turned up the car's heater, keeping an eye out for swerving traffic and wandering moose who preferred walking on pavement to plowing through snow.

The previous August he had applied for a teaching position at Exeter, a research university in Cornwall, England. The university had finally responded and asked to meet with him in January. His degree from Dartmouth was a Bachelor of Science in Anthropology. He felt it should give him some leeway in teaching either science or sociology. He had also used the name Rey Gilly on his application. It was the name Phil used for his new passport, his new driver's license and his airline reservations.

In Fairbanks, Ian and Ralph parked in the UAF visitors' lot and crunched their way through the snow to the Bunnell building. Professor Skarfeld, head of the anthropology department was out, but he had told his secretary to assist the police when they showed up.

"A laptop was issued to Phil from the department, but it isn't here so he must have it." The petite woman turned to her computer and brought up Phil's teaching files. "He's required to log his teaching plan in weekly," she leaned over and peered at the screen, "I'm not seeing anything here out of the ordinary." She stood back and Ian and Ralph stepped forward to take a look.

"Mind if we look through his desk?" Ian glanced to his left at the small room to the left of her space.

"No, not at all." She looked worried. "Did he do something wrong?"

Ian shook his head. "We just need to talk to him." Her phone rang and with a sigh she left them to it.

Ralph rifled through Phil's desk drawers, finding pens, erasers, pads of paper, and a stick of clover chewing gum. Ian saw a notepad by the phone and squinted as he made out the indentation made by an earlier note. He picked up a pencil and gently shaded the area. It appeared to be Alaska Airlines and a time: 7:45 PM. The trashcan held three Protein bar wrappers. Holding them by the edges, he put them inside a plastic bag to check fingerprints.

After they left the Bunnell Building, Ian called the station. "Do you have anything on that Honda."

"Not so far."

Twenty minutes later, the dispatcher called. The university police had located Phil's Honda parked on the other side of the campus. This was not even close to where he usually parked. They were now questioning a student who had seen Mr. Emerson driving a silver-colored vehicle about an hour earlier. "Do you want to talk to the student?" the dispatcher said.

"Yes, I do," Ian said, motioning for Ralph to turn around.

"Ho boy," Ralph muttered. "Wonder whose car he lifted."

"Could belong to another faculty member. Let's get a list of all the vehicles with campus parking permits. Should have done this earlier, dammit."

Chapter 63

Fairbanks to Anchorage

There was little traffic when Phil stopped for gas near the Denali Park entrance. A moaning wind broke the snow filled silence when he got out of the Buick. He pulled up the hood of his parka and filled the tank. He wondered how long it would take for the police to know what he was driving. Should he change vehicles? He looked around and saw an SUV full of kids. A man climbed out and hustled to the rest room to the side of the gas station.

Phil wondered if he ought to use the facilities as well. Nope, he decided, stick with the plan. Surely, he could reach the Anchorage's International Airport by 7 PM. He'd brought a different jacket in his bag. It was dark blue plaid and he had a baseball cap. It wouldn't hide his face, but that, plus his computer glasses, would alter his appearance.

The sky was gray and low. It was also freezing cold and as soon as he filled up the gas tank he was back on the road. He had an uneasy feeling that not using the bathroom would be a problem.

Concentrate, he thought. Think about London. Think about Exeter and getting to Cornwall. By train, he knew that much. Or he could fly, but he wanted to see the country. And Bath was on the way to Exeter. A friend had once told him Bath was beautiful. He tried not to think about Sam, who kept popping into his thoughts.

As he passed Wasilla, heading for Anchorage. his thoughts were still on England. He didn't see the Alaska State Trooper vehicle pull in two lengths behind him.

Chapter 64

Fairbanks and Anchorage

In Fairbanks, Ian called Matt Thomlin, who was now out of the hospital and back in his office. "Apparently Emerson took another car from the university. A student there said he saw Phil driving a silver or gray car. We put a BOLO on it. He could be heading for Anchorage, possibly to the airport. We just don't yet know which vehicle he took, other than that it's an American make."

"I'll alert Anchorage PD and the Troopers, but let's not give up on him staying in Fairbanks, or even in Goldspring. Although I can't imagine him wanting to go back there."

That evening, Matt got a call from Anchorage and he immediately called Ian. "You were right. Emerson was spotted in Anchorage, downtown. They've got him on camera, but he slipped away before they could pick him up."

"He may be heading for the airport," Ian said. "Unless he changed his flight, it should be at 7:45 on Alaska Airlines."

"I've called Alaska Airlines," Matt said. "They don't have an Emerson on the passenger list for any of their flights to Seattle or anywhere else this evening. He's most likely using another name and I sent his photo to the airport and Alaska and United Airlines. I told them he's wanted in connection with a homicide."

"We don't know for sure that Phil killed Sam."

"No, but someone did and he's our chief suspect. When I was at Sam's house, what struck me were Sam's crossed legs. Connie said Sam never sat like that. His joints were too stiff. And the traces of blood where Sam had been hit. Lot of little things didn't add up."

Phil pulled into Anchorage's Marriott Hotel parking lot. From three o'clock on, Alaska's winter skies were dark as coal. After checking the car thoroughly, he wiped the keys clean and slipped them under the floor mat. Then he pulled his bag down the street to the Sheraton where he waved down a cab. "The Comfort Inn near the airport."

In the warmth of the cab's heater he slipped out of his parka and baseball cap and unpacked his wool jacket. Making sure he couldn't be seen by the cab driver, he transferred his passport, credit cards and about three thousand dollars into the large pocket he'd sewn into the back of blazer. He had another two thousand dollars concealed in the false bottom of his carry-on. With a sigh he sank back on his seat and tried to relax as he watched the lights of the buildings in Spenard flash by.

A mile up ahead he saw the Comfort Inn and a mile beyond it, the bright lights of the airport. He took out a twenty-dollar bill as the cab pulled into the Comfort Inn's lot. "Going to Juneau tomorrow. An early flight," he told the driver, smiling as he waved off his change. He believed a medium sized tip would make him less memorable than a big one or none at all.

He pulled his knit cap lower over his forehead and headed to the glass doors of the hotel. All he had to do now was get a room, make an online reservation for Seattle under the name Rey Gilly and, most importantly, turn himself into an old man.

The next morning an aging gentleman, pulling a roll-on bag, approached the front desk. He walked with a limp and was somewhat hunched over the way many eighty-year-old people are. His hair beneath his hat, which today had ear flaps, was gray. His skin was wrinkled and his complexion was pallid. His eyes appeared red rimmed behind his glasses. At first the woman at the counter thought he looked familiar. But no, he was just wearing a jacket so common on men of a certain age.

"How much?" he said, clearing his throat. His voice was raspy like that of a smoker.

"Seventy-five dollars," she replied and he got out his wallet. He pulled out the money, all small bills and pushed it toward her. She tapped a few keys to print out his receipt, but he was already walking out the door. His limp and slow gait reminded her of her grandfather.

"We lost him after he arrived at the Comfort Inn. We had Troopers, airport police and cops at all the entrances and exits. No one saw him. We'll keep looking, but I think he's gone."

"And you checked the airport, all the airlines?" Matt said.

"Checked everything," Trooper Evans said. "We've even got people at Merrill Field." Merrill Field is a small airport, operated by the Anchorage Municipality. It is maintained for commercial service/public use, meaning bush planes and other small aircraft like Cessnas and Beavers.

Matt hung up the phone and stared at Ian. "Looks like he's changed his name and probably his appearance. Matt flung his ballpoint pen on his desk.

He pulled out a lower drawer in his desk and rested his feet on it. His recovery from Brian's attack was slow and he found himself sitting down whenever he saw a chair.

Ian nodded. "I found some hair in the trashcan in his apartment. There was no root or follicle, so I don't know how much help it will be, but I sent it to the lab to be analyzed. I also found a torn piece from what could be hair dye instructions. But no box, so if he did change his hair, I don't know which color."

Thomlin leaned forward. "Well since he has black hair, let's assume he went gray. That would be the easiest. And if he's going that route, he could age himself in other ways. It wouldn't be that hard to get him past security."

Bill had stepped into Matt's office and overheard the trooper. "He's gotta be running out of time and ideas."

"Yeah well, he's outsmarted us so far." Ian said.

The next day Matt called. "Any word on Phil?"

"Nope," Ian said. "They said it could take another week. Why?"

"I got a call from Anchorage. A man was found at the airport. He was hit by a car and is at the hospital in Spenard. He has about three thousand dollars in the lining of his jacket. Trooper Evans sent a photo. It's our guy."

"Ah, no kidding," Ian sat back surprised. "Is he talking?"

"His driver's license and wallet are gone. He also had a passport with the cash in the back of his jacket. It was under the name of Rey Gilly." Matt said.

"Rey with an e, like maybe Reynard? The fox?"

Matt paused. "Could be." He smiled. "What made you think of that?"

"A re-run on TV last week. *Day Of The Jackal*, have you seen it?"

"Some of us work for a living."

"Yeah well," Ian said, "How badly is he hurt?"

He is still unconscious. The nurses said his hair and eyebrows were dyed gray and he was wearing makeup. When they cleaned him up they said he looked forty years younger."

Chapter 65

Fairbanks

"How are you feeling?" Matt's voice was still scratchy after his battle with Brian and his on-going condition worried Cara. She heard a car honk in the background.

"It sounds like you're driving, where are you?"

"I'm headed your way. Thought I'd bring you and Lucy up to date. I should be there in about half an hour."

Cara smiled. "I'll tell Lucy. She's making cinnamon buns."

Lucy was squirming with impatience by the time Matt had polished off one of her award-winning cinnamon rolls. "So tell us," she said, "what happened to Sam, because I can't believe he committed suicide."

Matt wiped his mouth as Cara refilled his coffee cup. "Do you remember that redhead you saw in Goldspring, the one who reminded you of Valerie McMillian, the woman who was killed in Anchorage?"

"Yes!" Lucy had been wondering about her. In the mostly Native village of Goldspring, natural redheads were rare.

"Her name is Glori and she's with the FBI."

"She was undercover?" Lucy loved using words she'd picked up from television. Pulling her chair closer to the table she turned her good ear toward Matt. Her other ear hadn't been pulling its weight for a few months.

Matt nodded. "The FBI was trying to find out if Brian was working with anyone besides Clyne."

Lucy eyebrows went up. "Was he?" Matt shook his head.

"No, Brian didn't seem to be working with anyone else in that racket. He also denies knowing Phil Emerson, Sam's son."

Cara lifted an eyebrow. "And they believe him?"

Matt stretched his back and shoulders, still stiff and nodded. "They're pretty sure. As for Phil, he used the Ravenstone to try to get closer to Sam. The amulet also fit into Emerson's field of study at the University, so his curiosity could be legitimate."

Cara was puzzled. "Phil didn't care about the Ravestone's value?"

"Apparently not," Matt said. "At least that wasn't why he attacked Sam."

Lucy raised her eyebrows. "So, this was a revenge killing?"

Matt nodded. "More likely it was rage…He couldn't believe Sam hadn't recognized him, or not until Phil said his mother's name, Eliza. That triggered Sam."

"Ruby must have known about Eliza," Lucy murmured. Ruby had been around for so long she knew everything, including who might have gotten pregnant and fled Goldspring.

"The FBI talked to Eliza in Juneau," Matt continued. "She told them Phil had always been curious about his father. When he learned Sam had once been part of the anthropology department in Fairbanks, he transferred to UAF."

Lucy chewed her lip thinking. "I thought I saw a resemblance between them when I was visiting Connie and Phil showed up."

"Phil was mugged before he could board a flight in Anchorage," Matt said glancing at Cara.

"Where was he headed?"

"England. He was in line for a position with a University near London."

Cara shook her head. "Well, he dreamed big even if he didn't get far."

There was silence as the two women mulled it over. Matt helped himself to coffee and continued. "Phil is in the Spenard hospital being questioned by the FBI. I understand he didn't know Clyne."

"Didn't he die last week in Seattle?" Lucy said. "I read that somewhere."

"Clyne had cancer like Sam." Cara shifted in her chair. Her back still ached after her battle with Brian. The cast on her arm and shoulder wasn't helping.

Lucy got up to pour more tea. "What about Valery McMillan? Who do you think killed her in the hotel? An old lover?"

"Her husband, Mack, is under suspicion. According to his lawyer, Valerie refused to finance Mac's run for election and he was pretty upset about that. Also, he wasn't out of town as he'd said. The guy who provided Mac's alibi was nabbed for stealing tires and gave him up."

"Tires! It's always the details that trip up people," Cara said. "One of my students wrote about it. The thief sells the tires online to garages, to anyone who'd look the other way. It's quite a racket."

"So let's back up," Lucy said. "Herb was murdered for the Ravenstone by those guys from Juneau, Pat, Frank, and Brian, right?" She looked at Matt and Cara. They nodded.

"And Pat froze to death near Shem's Saloon in Fairbanks?" More nods. Lucy arranged herself more comfortably in her chair, before proceeding. "And Sam was killed by his son, Phil Emerson as you said. Then Frank, who killed Herb and scared Julie, died in the car crash on the Parks Highway?"

"Frank was beaten up before the crash," Matt said, "But yes, Frank and three others died in that crash"

Lucy took a deep breath. "What about our VPSO, Ron Whitfield? And my sister, Elsie Rapid, who took the train here to see Sam and get a healing? Oh! And Brian? What will happen to him?" Matt's stomach growled and he reached for another cinnamon roll.

"I'll start with Brian," Matt said, picking up a napkin. "He's wanted in Fairbanks for murder but The FBI in Seattle has him and I doubt we'll see him again. They're using his testimony in charges against the now-deceased Carl Clyne and other art thefts over the past four years. From there Brian should go to prison."

"Should being the operative word," Cara said, not pleased that Brian was in FBI custody. She wanted to see him punished, without being fed slippery dialogue about his helping the FBI

Matt, still aching from his battle with Brian, felt the same, but plowed on. "You remember Ed Stuart, the fellow in Wasilla?" Cara and Lucy nodded.

"We questioned Elsie who had given him a ride home and then we talked to Ed Stuart's wife." Matt said. "She told us her husband had murdered her two sons and a neighbor woman who lived nearby. The cops didn't believe her at first, not until they found over half a dozen bodies in the shed behind their house.

"Brian said that last year Clyne had him take a farmer to Ed Stuart's house. in Wasilla. The guy was terrified according to Brian and that's the last he saw of the guy. When Brian asked Clyne why he wanted to get rid of the guy so far outside Anchorage, Clyne said he didn't like to leave messes close to home."

Cara shook her head and sighed. "Okay, what about Ron, our VPSO? He must have known something?

"Ah, Ron," Matt said, shaking his head. "His crime was concealing evidence from the get-go. We found letters in his trash that admitted he was working with Clyne. The letters and his efforts to build the Ravenstone Technical Center should work in his favor."

"I can't imagine anyone who would testify against his character." Lucy muttered.

Matt smiled. "Doyon hired a lawyer for him. And their Board will make some of their own tribal decisions."

Tribal Board decisions were sometimes lenient, but he'd been wrong before.

"Doyan has deep pockets," Cara murmured, smiling.

Lucy nodded and tapped the wooden table top for good luck.

After Matt left, Lucy and Cara sat for a while thinking. "I'm worried about Connie," Lucy said. "How do you think she's taking it? Her half-brother murdering her father?" She shuddered.

"Connie should be okay," Cara said, with a slow smile. "She's already got a steady friend. Did you know that she and Ron's older brother are well, shall we say, in a relationship?"

"Connie? Our Connie?" Lucy was dumbfounded.

Cara grinned. "Sweet overweight Connie, hair growing out of a frizzled perm and with two kids, has guys panting over her."

Lucy took another sip of her coffee and set the mug on the table

"Well, I'm stupefied, she said. "But, you know, Connie always did have charisma."

Chapter 66

Goldspring

"You still don't feel good, do you?" Cara said, frowning. She had heard Matt groaning after they had gone to bed and had gotten up to check his temperature.

"Doc Snodgrass wants me to go to Anchorage, to a specialist, for more tests." Matt tried to raise his head then let it drop back on the pillow. His skin was grey and covered with sweat.

"Why didn't you tell me? What kind of tests?"

"He wants me to see a specialist there. Someone who deals with head injuries. At least I think that's what he said."

Suddenly Matt lurched half across the bed and vomited on the floor and his slippers.

"I'm taking you to the hospital, now!"

The next day Cara stepped into Matt's room and was surprised to see him sitting up. "Hey there," he said, smiling. His speech was a bit slurred but his eyes were bright. He patted the bed. "Come here." He reached toward her."

"You're looking…" she paused, fighting sudden tears, "better than last night when I brought you here." He pulled her closer and his touch was electrifying. "So, what did the doctor say?" she managed, catching her breath.

"It's an after effect of the concussion. Not common," Matt said, "But it isn't fatal, and I need to stay calm and watch what I eat for a few days. Nothing that could upset my stomach." He grinned

"Like cinnamon rolls," Cara said, smiling. Matt nodded.

"Just don't tell Lucy, I don't want her to stop baking."

He paused. "There's something I'd like you to do. Get my jacket from the closet." Puzzled Cara got up and went to the closet, but there was no jacket.

"Are you sure you wore it here. I remember your parka but that isn't here either." She looked at Matt again. "I'll ask the nurse about it."

"I know I had it on, maybe it was my parka. Damn it all," he muttered and struggled to sit all the way up. "I wanted to propose to you and the ring was in the inside pocket'" He hadn't meant to say it, but the words just fell out of his mouth.

Cara stared at him, stunned. "You wanted to propose? Well, my goodness, we have to find it now." Matt's gave her a feeble smile. "So, I guess that's a yes?"

"Yes, sure, absolutely," she whispered "Of course, you bet." She sat back and stared at him. "Did I leave anything out? I don't want there to be any confusion about my response."

He grinned. "I just want to make sure you're certain, that this isn't an answer given out of mercy."

Cara reared back, exaggerating her response. "Mercy! Of course not."

They heard a tap on the glass door and a nurse stepped into the room.

"Excuse me, this was left in the recovery room by mistake." She held Matt's parka, still covered with patches of blood. "I think it belongs to…" she stopped and looked at a slip of paper, "Matthew Thomlin?"

"I'll take it," Cara said. She reached for the jacket and nearly fell off the bed handing it to Matt. He began digging through its pockets and finally pulled out a small, square box.

With a deep sigh of relief, he looked at her. "Now, let's do this right."

About the Author

Over the years, Jan Harper Haines has collected the often shamanic stories of her Athabascan ancestors. In 1935 her mother was the first Alaska Native woman to graduate from the University of Alaska and a building was named for her. Jan has written for numerous publications, including articles about her great uncle Walter Harper, who in 1913 was the first man to summit Denali. A former secondary education teacher, Jan also has a twenty-year career in advertising. She is a graduate of the University of Alaska and lives in northern California with her husband, Lawrence Haines, an architect.